Love 'N' Stuff

Short Fiction, Poetry, Essay and Memoir

by

L.L. Morton

Third Millennium Publishing
A Cooperative of Writers and Resources
On the INTERNET
http://3mpub.com

ISBN 1-934805-49-1
 978-1-934805-49-7

362 pages

Copyright © 2011 by L.L. Morton
Cover Design by L. L. Morton

All rights reserved under International and Pan-American Copyright Conventions. Published in the United States of America by Third Millennium Publishing, located on the INTERNET at http://3mpub.com/morton.

L. L. Morton
PO Box 3203
Ashland, OR 97520-1422
Email: LL.Morton1@gmail.com

Third Millennium Publishing
PO Box 14026
Tempe, AZ 85284-0068
mccollum@3mpub.com

For my loving son,

"Thatcher"

Table of Contents

LOVE TALK
MEMOIR
pg. 1

DOORSTOP DIPLOMACY
MEMOIR
pg. 9

THE LION AND THE MASSEUSE
FICTION
pg. 13

UNAWARE
FICTION
pg. 27

THE SECOND SAIL
FICTION
pg. 35

TOO MUCH IS NEVER ENOUGH
ALLEGORY
pg. 181

THE WHITE MARBLE DOORKNOB
FICTION
pg. 185

A CHILD'S WISDOM
MEMOIR
pg. 193

VACATION INTO HEAVEN
FICTION
pg. 197

WHY?
MEMOIR
pg. 211

THE SEVEN
FICTION
pg. 217

GET OVER IT!
ESSAY
pg. 225

OLD SOLDIERS NEVER DIE...
ESSAY
pg. 229

DOREEN
FICTION
pg. 235

OLLIE THE ELEPHANT
ALLEGORY
pg. 243

PRIMARY LOVE
FICTION
pg. 247

THE CULTURAL DILEMMA
ESSAY
pg. 253

HEART SONGS
POETRY
pg. 271

A FUZZY TALE
FICTION
pg. 287

A NICE WAY TO LOOK AT THINGS
FICTION
pg. 297

A HABIT SHE HAD
FICTION
pg. 303

KISSIN' COUSINS
FICTION
pg. 309

OTHER PATHWAYS
MEMOIR
pg. 313

THERE COMES A TIME
FICTION
pg. 329

FAREWELL TO MAKE-BELIEVE
MEMOIR
pg. 339

THE IMAGE
MEMOIR
pg. 349

BIOGRAPHY
pg. 353

LOVE TALK

MEMOIR

It was one of those Monday mornings when I wished I hadn't signed up for this volunteer work, assisting the visiting three-year-olds, each from emotionally needy homes, to somehow communicate with the elderly residents in this huge nursing home. The sight always filled me with such aching; I would never get used to it, the large hallway sprinkled with occupants in wheelchairs and one strolling with the aid of a walker. We counselors had discussed at length, during our orientation, the usefulness of these institutional places for such in need of constant care, but I still had enormous reservations seeing many who were apparently well enough to be at home with their families. The loneliness. Not enough touching to go around. But I was only in my forties, I told myself. Lots of time yet before *I'll* have to worry.

"We're so glad you made it," said Annie, the initiator and director of the program, cheerily reinforcing my presence as I took off my coat.

"My. Where are all our friends?" I asked, in comment to the full attendance of the small group of three-year-olds, but only one visitor from the rooms adjoining.

"I don't know, but would you like to run upstairs and see who you can round up?" asked Annie, "and take Sherri here with you, why don't you?" she suggested, and I agreed, grabbing the out-stretched hand of the smiling child still clutching a small doll she had extracted from the pile of toys provided for the children's two-hour stay.

"What is your baby's name?" I asked the child, as we walked through the wide halls to the elevator.

"She doesn't *have* a name," answered the pert Sherri.

"Well," I said, just as pertly back, but softening my words with a slight giggle, a habit I noticed I had when I talked to my little granddaughter the same age. "She should have a name. All mommies give their babies a name when they are born," I said. "I never heard of a baby without a name!"

"It's just a baby-doll," she said with impatience, ready to be off the subject.

"Why don't you *give* her a name, Sherri?" I asked gently.

Sherri looked down at the shiny, clean floor and rigorously shook her head.

The elevator was empty and we rode in silence to the top floor. The hallways were filled with occupants and nurses going every which way but the sight of little curly headed Sherri, clutching her doll, drew comments from all.

"My, what is your sweet baby's name," the nurses began asking, and Sherri turned away from them and hid her face in my skirt, grasping my hand even tighter. The enthusiastic group finally tired of no response.

Of the head nurse, I asked, "Where is Sally White today?"

"Oh, she's been moved over to the next wing," came the reply.

Knowing a move anywhere meant a change in mobility, I asked in slight alarm, "Is she ill?"

"She broke her hip..." the nurse said in a matter-of-fact tone, "... so she had to be moved."

I took an extra deep breath to hide my anxiety, as I realized my new found friend, Sally White, ninety-two and a spittin' image of my own grandmother (also in a nursing home back home) was no doubt beginning the gradual decline in levels, each level geared to specific limitations according to ability. And Sally had been so active. The sadness hit me, but quickly I dismissed the feeling and proceeded to round up several ambulatory people.

"Arnold, this is Sherri... Sherri do you want to say hello to Mr. Arnold?" I asked, touching the slender old gent in the grey business suit. His white dress shirt was buttoned all the way up to the top — minus a collar and tie.

Sherri's shyness overcame her again as she stuck her face into my skirt.

Arnold looked down at her and said, "Aw, see there, she taint a bit interested in me... and you can't blame her," he added under his breath.

At that moment an aide brought Edith, a frizzy headed robust looking woman, over to us suggesting she go along with us. "Edith is a bit deaf," the aide said. "You have to talk into her ear quite loudly like this," yelling into the woman's ear. "You go with them downstairs for awhile and see the kids," she said, "You'll like that." The aide patted Edith on the shoulder as she helped us all into the elevator.

Edith's eyes lit up into a bright smile as she noticed Sherri. "Oh, Pete would love to go along. Pete's my husband. He *loves* children."

"He can come, too," I assured her brightly just as the aide caught my eye.

Motioning with her hand to leave that subject alone, the aide whispered, "No. No. He's not here; but she still *thinks* he is. That's one of her problems."

As the elevator moved, we all hung onto each other — Sherri still clutching her new found doll-baby.

On the lower floor, we walked down the hall towards the game room: Arnold and Edith, arm in arm — he to steady her; and she, it seemed, for sheer pleasure. Arnold took Edith to the table near the children doing their games.

She sat and stared and smiled, repeating again, "Pete just *loves* kids. They love him to. They call him *Pete-t*," she said, accenting the t.

Sherri had gone off on her own to find a familiar lap.

Arnold was left standing in the center of the room. He surveyed the busy group. I had introduced them all to each other and Arnold was saying to no one in particular how his children were strewn all over the country. And then he turned and walked out, shaking his head and mumbling. "I can't take it' I can't take it," he was saying as I followed him into the hallway.

Touching seemed to be what I did best, so I rubbed Arnold on his shoulder as I spoke, walking with him. I touched all of them as often as possible and they soaked it up like a dry plant took water. I had little touching in my own life just then; it fulfilled a need in me too, as well. I asked Arnold kindly, "Do you miss your children?"

He was still shaking his head, and seemed totally oblivious to my being there. He did not answer me. Instead he kept walking on down the hall...

Back in the game room, Edith was sitting at the end of the table, alone, just looking. I wondered about the feeling of isolation she must have had in her silent world, remembering one of my caretakers as a child, who was deaf. Trisha was coming around the back of Edith on a small plastic trike donated by a toy store. I caught the child's eye. "Come here, Trish; I want you to meet Edith." I said, getting down on my knees to her level as I spoke. "Edith is deaf, Trish. You know what deaf is, don't you?" As I spoke, I was rubbing Edith's back. Edith was absorbed in all the activity going on at the other end of the long table.

Trisha looked up at the woman with her big brown

eyes, questioning.

"Deaf is like when you put cotton in your ears and you can't hear too good," I continued, "so when you talk to Edith you must touch her so that she knows you are speaking to her."

Trisha got off her tricycle then and came around the chair to the front of the woman. I waited. At that moment I decided to step back away from them and watch, a new experience for me. I had a habit of being an expert director. But love needs no direction, I was learning.

Trisha was peering up into the soft and time worn face of this new quiet visitor who as yet, with so much to look at, had not noticed the child at her lap. Trisha touched the woman gently on the knee. Edith turned her head, and as her eyes rested on the child, Trisha lifted her small hand above her own head to Edith's eye level, and bending her tiny fingers up and down very slowly, she gave a little wave, her eyes dancing in a grin from ear to ear.

Edith lit into a big smile and reached down and put her arm around her new little friend, giving her a big squeeze. Then she touched her own cheek with her pointer finger, ever so lightly.

Trisha, without a word, stood on her tiptoes and reached up with her tiny face, puckered her lips, and placed a kiss on Edith's cheek.

"I love you," mouthed Edith silently, still holding Trisha by the shoulders.

At this, Trisha responded all on her own by reaching up with her face and putting another kiss on the same wrinkled spot.

As I watched, emotion swelled up inside of me and I knew then for what this inter-generational program was designed — to bring about just such interchanges. And that no matter how it ached for me to be here for two hours every week, that this one moment had made it worth it, and I was suddenly ashamed that I had given my time begrudgingly earlier in the morning.

On my way to Sally White's new wing, a stop I would have to make on my way home, I wondered as I went... *Was Sherri's refusal to name the baby-doll the three-year-old's way of being able to leave it behind?*

~ ~

DOORSTOP DIPLOMACY

MEMOIR

After an overnite at an Embassy Suites Hotel where breakfast buffet is complimentary, I was in line behind a small, dark complected man who I noticed was not speaking English. He had a head full of bushy hair, heavy eyebrows, and a thick, black moustache that almost swallowed him. He carried a heavily laden food tray and was walking behind his tiny dark-headed wife, who also carried a similar food tray. She was, at the same time, unobtrusively maneuvering their three bushy-headed children as they chattered and darted every-which-way towards the outdoor café. As we reached the doorway, the young man stepped ahead and since both hands were full, cleverly engaged his rump to hold the dining room door open for them.

As his family was passing through, totally oblivious to his doorstop maneuvering, I noticed the door begin to slip slowly from his narrow hips. My hands were full also: handbag; folded newspaper; a piece of fruit; and a cup of coffee held rather precariously. Quickly and carefully I turned and caught the slipping door with my own rump.

As the weight of the door shifted between us, the young man turned to look at me, recognition of our silent conspiracy registering in his eyes.

I grinned in response.

Wrinkling his little speck of a nose that showed above that giant fuzzy moustache, tickled laughter emanated from his voice as he said, "T'ank you. T'ank you. T'ank you."

Chuckling a "You're welcome," I let the door swing shut behind me as we went our separate ways.

~ ~

THE LION AND THE MASSEUSE

FICTION

It was such a beautiful day, too, as Laura eased up to the stop light, the radio so loud that the curly headed guy in the low white car to her left turned and looked at her. Embarrassed, she looked the other way and sneakily slid a finger up her cheek to catch the tear that was beginning to slide past her sunglasses. Who *was* that singing?... *Younger than spring time are you...* And why couldn't she keep the tears back all of a sudden? How long had it been since she felt like this, filled up and running over with feelings? Need-feelings. Want-to or Wish-I-Could feelings. That song! Boy. What *had* happened to spring, anyway, the spring of her life?

The light turned green and she stepped on the accelerator easy like. She hated getting into a "pissing contest with the gas pedal," Bud would've said. The guy in the low, sleek car next to her was driving just as slow as she was. Smart ass, she thought, looking down at him. One of these days she was going to have to exert her independence and get a smaller car. Bud loved Cadillacs. It was their generation's mark of success, before the foreign trade had burst upon the scene. The filling station man told her she looked too young to be driving that "old fuddy duddy car. You should be in a little hot shot convertible, like a Maserati, or a Porsche." Her face had turned scarlet from the embarrassment. She tried to avoid men who spoke to her as though she was a whole woman.

Caught between her sexuality and her conscience, she grew angry, believing she had settled this once and for all a long time ago. It just had to be borne. But when she took the vow of celibacy in that Army hospital in Munich, she was barely thirty and her womanhood had not really dawned on her yet. '50's women didn't know their clitoris from their anus anyway; it was their daughters who had educated them. And Laura, without any daughters, was an habitually slow learner. It helped none to see the man she adored, had waited for through the peace marches and sleepless nights, open his eyes and smile at her. That look had sent spasms of fresh need through her entire body.

On the car radio, Sammy Davis was singing *Little Bo Jangles*. I have to get that album, she thought. It was so strange, hearing that voice as though he were still alive. Life had become so illusionary, confusing. You didn't know who was alive or dead anymore. She was hitting the steering wheel to the beat of the music with the silver ring she wore on her right index finger. Bud had gotten it for her that time in Tucson. After she'd spent a bundle on the earrings and necklace, she'd spied the ring as she was walking out of the store. "Oh. Look, Bud. It matches."

"Buy it," he'd said, like always. He never seemed to care about anything she spent. "What are you saving it for?" he would ask when she'd say it was too much money. "Who you gonna leave it to?"

That always hurt, but she'd go ahead, somehow believing that rings and things would fill up the gap. And they had, for a while. But now she needed help, serious help.

Something had happened to her just recently, since the last therapist had confronted her with her sexuality. "Laura. Listen to me. You can't run from it any longer. You are a woman with physical needs. And if you don't stop denying them you are going to have one stupid illness after the other, rashes, colitis, you name it. Unfulfilled needs scream out in a myriad of ways. Yours have just begun."

Her first reaction was to run. And run she did. She told Bud that she had to get away for a while. Her job had gotten too hectic, and he'd agreed she did look tired. Summer off-season in the desert was really cheap and quiet. Not too many people to have to deal with. That's what she needed. A place where she could be with herself, alone, without her wedding band, to fight it out between her yes-yes and her no-no's.

The neon light was flashing over the word "French." Next to the word "Café" was a bright yellow outline of a pie slice. *Frenchies* was known for their quiche. She swung the car into the drive, only to see the low, white car follow her. Something in her middle moved. She grabbed her stomach. "Oh, for crying-out-loud. It's lunch time," she told herself. *Everybody eats lunch.*

She pulled into one of the last parking spaces. There was room for a small compact between her and the Palm waving in the breeze. She turned her head the other way when she caught the white of the car ease past in her rear view mirror. She cracked her windows. It would get to 100 degrees before mid-afternoon. She was shocked when she first learned of the high temperatures. It just didn't seem to feel that hot. She pulled the sun visor down and looked into the mirror. Her hair was just dirty enough to lay neatly. She tucked it behind her ears and straightened the bangs. Sometimes, when she looked through them, into the mirror, she saw that young woman of yesterday, eager for love. Little did she know then what price she would be asked to pay for it.

She absent-mindedly locked her car. It was a habit Bud had instilled in her. He was so paranoid he locked it in the garage. After the cold air-conditioning in the car, the warmth of the sun felt good. She could feel her breasts with each step she took. Too sensitive, she thought. Too conscious of every speck of her body. And it was getting worse. She had to have some release, some honest to goodness sex, she thought, and immediately reprimanded herself with the flash-back of Munich, that first shock of what her future held. At first when the doctors had given her the real scoop on Bud's condition, her denial is all that kept her going. She realized how important her acceptance of his *their* loss might mean. The difference between his living or dying. It was the least she could do for this beautiful man. Laughter would sustain her. And it had, for an eternity. But those damnable hormones. No one really prepared her for such an onslaught. God. If she could just turn them off. Music was her downfall. She had to stop up her ears, submerge herself into emotional nothingness. "Of course, you'll need counseling, therapy," the doctors had said. And the Army had provided plenty of that. Hours, yea weeks, to get to the "real me" only to find out the "real me" was the true enemy. Things would have been much better if she had just stayed locked up. The more emotional doors that got pried open, the more her sexual desires grew. And then there were all the stupid illnesses. And never anything verifiable. Just nuisance stuff. At first, Bud begged her to leave, go somewhere and start over. But what kind of a wife would do that, after what he'd been through? How could she face having with another what she so desperately wanted with the one man she had ever loved? So she'd stayed.

Now she was being advised to find a support group. Just the thought of it upset her. Of having to come right out and *say* it. What good could possibly come of it? What could anyone else possibly do to ease her condition?

Love 'N' Stuff

The hostess, a young girl, was trying to get her attention. "Oh, yes. Forgive me," said Laura. "I do wander off, sometimes."

They both laughed.

"Any preference in seating?" the younger one asked.

"Yes. A window seat, if you have one," she said. Laura liked to gaze out into the unlimited horizon, at the mountains, which reminded her of the permanence of things, and how long they took to get that way.

He looked so familiar. He had caught her watching him, so she had looked away. Had they met somewhere? She was racking her brain. His staring at her suddenly made her feel like a girl again. Like when people would ask her, "Do you know Sylvia so and so, or Sarah such and such? You look just like her!" She must have been asked things like that a million times. Then the questions had stopped, after she'd plunged into making herself over into Bud's proper wife, a robot of a woman.

Laura daydreamed constantly of a week like this, of meeting someone, anyone, who would make love to her around the clock, make love to her like he didn't even know her, a fantasy that had driven her, kept her sane, or was it really making her crazy? Flashing through her mind was Bud and his unpacking his war souvenirs: A machete knife, still stained with the blood of some Vietcong (her stomach still turned over at the thought); the giant, solid brass padlock in the form of a roaring lion. It was so heavy, she'd almost dropped it. "What on earth *is* this?" she'd asked.

"Oh, that's for your chastity belt. And I've got the only key!" he'd said with a grin. He had a way of telling her things without telling her things. The lion became a paperweight on his desk, in plain view...

Feeling justifiably chastised for her fantasies, she ate her quiche with the relish of a last supper. Toying with whether to get dessert or just a cup of coffee, the waitress interrupted her thoughts with a tall frosty pink squirrel. She was grinning and rolling her eyes, "You have an admirer," she said as she put the tall, pretty glass in front of her. "He said he thinks you look like you'd like this. If you don't, he said to order whatever you'd like, on him."

Laura turned to look in his direction, the guy from the sleek, white car who'd followed her. He did look *so* familiar. She had believed him to be in his thirties, but now she could see he was nearer her age. His natural curly hair lay in tight blonde ringlets, the color highlighted in white throughout his whole head. He was sitting in a booth, with his elbows on the table, resting his chin into his folded hands. He was looking at her and smiling. "How did you guess?" she said, mouthing the words just softly enough so that he got up and moved in her direction.

"Pardon?" he said.

She looked up into his friendly face.

"How did you guess?" she repeated. "This is the only thing I ever drink."

He was standing next to her table, waiting. The waitress had disappeared. "Do you mind if I sit?" he asked, reaching for the other chair.

"No. Not at all. I hate to eat alone."

"So do I," he said, and slid into the chair.

Suddenly her throat froze up. She got a mental flash of Bud and the roaring lion. Then she looked into those crystal clear, blue eyes. There were smile lines around them, cheeks tanned from the sun. She wondered what he'd think if he knew. Should she tell him, or just enjoy?

Love 'N' Stuff

"New in town?" he asked.

"Yes. Well no, not really. We've been coming here for years, on vacation. I needed a rest, to sort out my life. I just decided to come and stay for a while. I figured off-season would be a good time for that, not too hectic."

"Yeah. It is quiet all right. If you can stand this summer heat. Did I hear you say *we?*"

"No. Well, yes. We've always come together but not this time."

"Oh, Good. I mean, I hope it's *good*. I mean, I hope it's not *bad*. I mean, *Is* it good?" he finally blurted out.

She burst into relieved laughter and felt like she wanted to touch him; touch somebody so they'd touch her back. Instead, she said, "Yes. It is good. A little scary, but good."

They were laughing together. Finally she had to ask. "Have we met? You look so familiar to me."

"I work at the Marriott," he said, smiling.

"Oh. That's it then. That's where I'm staying. Where abouts do you work?"

"At the Spa. I'm a masseuse. I do massage. Have you used the Spa yet?"

"Yes. Well actually, No. I went there for the beauty shop. Nothing else."

"You haven't' had a massage yet?" he asked with a bit of surprise. "That is one of the pleasures of this hotel, you know."

"No. I haven't gotten up the nerve yet. I'm a little shy about taking my clothes off," she said with a pink flush reaching clear to her ears. "It sounds great, though. I sure could use some... some..."

"Touching?" he added with a gentleness that caught her off guard.

"Does it show?" she asked, and reached for the pink frosty glass in front of her.

"In a way. You look kind of lost. Are you?"

"Oh, god," she said, and burst into sudden tears, embarrassed. "I'm not very good at hiding things... That's why I've never had an affair..." she said, wishing she could disappear.

"I'm sorry. I didn't mean to create a problem for you." he said, looking at her with such a penetrating stare that she felt he could see right through her.

His looking, in fact everything about him, made her self-conscious. "No. It's not you at all. It's me. I just don't know what to do with myself anymore. You see, I'm married to this absolutely terrific guy who loves me more than life, I do believe. And I adore him, too. But he's like a brother... since the Vietnam War. He was injured... Anyway, I don't want to think about it anymore, I came here to forget... for just a little while. Do you mind?" His gentleness and understanding had opened her up like a drawer. "But the worst of it is, nobody really knows about it. Just me and my therapist. I haven't even told my best friend. Bud begged me not to. It's a thing with him. He says it's bad enough that it is so, without telling the whole world. My therapist thinks it's really Bud's way of keeping me. Because he's afraid if word got around, men would be all over me, whether or not I did anything to encourage them."

"Your therapist just might have something there," he said smiling. Then he slipped his hand into his shirt pocket and pulled out a card. "Here's how to reach me at the spa. I'd like to introduce you to massage therapy. It might meet some needs you are having right now in a safe environment."

"Boy, safe is the way, these days, huh?"

Love 'N' Stuff

They both laughed as she took the card.

Laura looked at it; it simply read, "Antonio," The Marriott Hotel Spa, address and phone number. "Latin, huh? I guess your profession comes pretty natural to you."

"Yes it does. I couldn't live without touching. It's part of me, it's how I breathe, relate to the world, through my hands."

"It's been so long, I wonder if my heart could stand it," she said, grinning.

"There is always a medic on duty. It's the policy of the hotel because of the heated baths and saunas," he said rather seriously as he leaned back in his chair.

She stirred the whipped cream in the bottom of the tall glass. "There's not very much to these things, are there? I guess that's why I like them. For the sugar. It's funny how I always want sweet things when I'm down."

"That makes you pretty normal, I'd say. Would you like another one?" he asked.

"Oh. Goodness no. This was quite enough, and thank you."

"The pleasure was all mine," he said, tipping his make-believe hat to her. "Can I walk you to your car?" he asked shoving back his chair.

"Yes. That would be nice," she said as she stood to leave.

Laura lay rigidly on the table, grasping the large sheet, pulling it up under her chin. She had chosen to leave her panties on. It was too scary to take them off. Antonio came into the room. He looked so much smaller today than yesterday, she thought. His arms and shoulders were a mass of solid muscle, his hands large and smooth skinned. "How are you today?" he asked as he reached for the knob on the loud speaker piping in canned music. He turned the speaker off and instead put on a small cassette player that filled the air with soft drum beats and intermittent twangs of Hawaiian guitar.

It was a restful sound as Laura awaited instructions.

"I usually start with the back," he said, taking hold of the sheet.

"Oh, don't take it off," she said, anxiously.

"Oh, I'm not. I'll just hold it so you can turn over on your stomach. Just rest your face into the split pad there."

Laura did as she was told. The air was warm that hit her shoulders as he lowered the sheet to her waistline. He began with a finger-tip massage of her neck, behind her ears, down into her shoulders. The touch of his hands laid to rest that moment of fear she expected to have, as she traced his touch over her entire body, one inch at a time. It was the kind of feeling that she had dreamed of for years lying next to Bud, wishing for some kind of interest in her body, even this, the firm movement reaffirming her personhood.

For the next week, Laura kept her daily appointments with Antonio, the Latin masseuse. He said little, but his hands spoke to her of gentleness and caring, a healing balm to her depleted spirit. He left her inner walls intact, as he smoothed and soothed away her rigid shell she'd built up to the outer world.

It was Friday, her last day before leaving for home. She had arrived in the Desert feeling helpless, powerless. She would be going home with a rejuvenated spirit. And all she had done was lie on a table for two hours every day and allow a man's hands to move over every inch of her body. He had been so sensitive to her shyness too, keeping a small towel carefully and strategically placed. She was lying on her back as he pulled her toes, sticking his fingers between each one. She wanted to say something to him, thank him for keeping her from acting out her anger at her lot in a self-destructive way. But he spoke first, "You look like a different person, you know. As though you just woke up from a hundred-year sleep."

"Oh, but I have," she said so happily. "My body has been asleep more years than not. But you've awakened me. I want to thank you for that."

"You don't have to live without touching, you know," he said, still in his intense demeanor. "There are all kinds of ways to get it, too. Try the geriatric wards of any hospital, or the children's terminal wards. Then you will both benefit — just like we have both benefitted this week," he said a slight dimple of a smile showing through his seriousness. "I wish you the best of luck, and don't wait so long...."

It was the best of things, the worst of things, that Laura carried with her from the Spa at the Marriott Hotel in the California desert. She'd found a way of counterbalancing the sexual void of the roaring lion she was returning to at home.

And she didn't even know Antonio's last name, or anything whatsoever about him, except — that he had marvelous hands.

~ ~

UNAWARE

FICTION

Once someone said she had the look of an angel. Her countenance glowed like light on a snow-covered mountain top. But it was not of herself that the light came, but rather when she looked at others, she would see in them the beauty of the stars and the firmament. What she saw was reflected in her face, for she could see, sense, understand as few others. She had this special gift of looking beneath the surface of things, of reaching beyond the roughness, the loud angry voice, the shriveled up skin of a crotchety old person. Beneath all the layers of rank and status some spent their lifetime acquiring, she could feel their pain, their sadness, their anxiety. It was as though she was some kind of conscience, a mirror of humanity so to speak. They looked at her and hated her, loved her, revered her, reviled her, adored her, despised her. She was an object, a symbol, a tool, a ladder to heaven, a road into hell. At times she seemed more than a woman, more than a wife, more than a mother. More than light, more than brave, more than wealth, more than life, she was the ray of light in a dark corner of a forgotten mind, the beacon of help to a lost ship sailing over the horizon into unchartered waters. She was the ragged truth in dressed up lies; she was warm to the frigid soul. She was all these things, but of her existence, the one special one she had chosen was *unaware.*

He hardly noticed that she spoke, that she moved in and out of the rooms as he sat on his couch and racked his mind for the right letters to the puzzle. What was that word: *face… grin?* He couldn't think; she was in the house.

He felt her and that was all he needed, to know she was there. But she was no more than a presence that floated in and out of his consciousness. When she spoke: *How was your day?* she was no longer there because *he* became the subject, the focus. She had a way of making him *feel,* which he hated. He wanted to forget all that, so he kept writing with his sharp black pencil, heavy and bold, so he could see it in the dark of his cluttered mind amidst the sounds of the TV, the kitchen faucet, the clock ticking, the cricket chirping, the refrigerator humming, the noises in his ears — the soft mellow sound of the workings of his blood sliding in and around his eardrums. These noises he believed to be the squealing of the turns his blood took in the vessels, the tiny constricted passageways of all his inner tunnels. He could just feel the oxygenated blood filled up with air from this movement like gas from a pump into the car, the renewed blood mixing with the corpuscles, helping them to slide all around his eardrums. Sometimes if he swallowed just right, he could pop the sounds into quietness; smack the little buggers out of the way so he couldn't hear them.

"What are your druthers?" she was asking.

"What do you mean? I told you I don't want anything," he said holding his pencil to his lips, a habit he had of sucking the very tip of the lead, making it wet so it would write darker, help it along. The lead had a taste of chalk. It felt solid, hard, dependable — all the things he wasn't.

"Aren't you going to eat *again?*" she asked.

"I'll get something," he said, putting the lead of the pencil to the paper. Maybe *mink* was the right word. The letters just fit. Or *seal*, or... Not many four-letter furs to choose from, *mink* was the most common. Could be *lamb*?

"Why don't you want to eat lately," she asked?

Her persistence pressed into his mind, right through

Love 'N' Stuff 31

the wall he had erected inside his head, around his brain, to protect it from an onslaught from someone just like her.

She ignored the barrier though, and went right on through it, forcing herself in. "I don't like it that you are not eating," she said.

First she says I am fat, then she wants me to eat. Can't this woman make up her mind? Nothing suits her. No matter what, she will find something wrong with it. So like my mother. "Your shoes, put on the feet right," she would say...

He had managed to get them on all by himself, and he was so proud. He had struggled and struggled with the shoe strings. The knot was in there sturdy. Looking down at his very proud accomplishment, he walked into the kitchen, and pointed, "Look, Mom."

But all she could say was, *"Your shoes on the wrong feet, they are. Wrong, you got them."* She laughed her laugh of derision, of cruelty.

It pierced to the heart this slight, but tall, bony child who was trying so hard. "But, Mom. I tied it good. See?"

She passed her eyes over his feet, but too quickly they were back to her frying pan. She said, *"Uh huh, that's nice. But on the wrong feet, they are! So what good does it make to tie them tight, when tying them all over, you must?"*

He hung his head, and turned to go back to his room where he would just lie down on his bed for a minute with the big brown, safe, comfortable bear and sniff back the tears. Into his mouth would go his big and fat filler-upper. It was crusted, sucked up into a blister and then a callous, and finally a hard bump that had become numb to all the biting and searching of his tongue for just the right place. The ear of the bear, now hairless, had grown smooth and shiny from being crushed by the little hand with the leftover three fingers that held it tightly while he sucked the air out of the skin, the knuckle hitting his bottom teeth. He curled up on top of the bedspread with the bear tucked into his tummy, his knees cupped up under the bear's fat legs which had no feet — just stubs to fit into his little body that held the aches of a tender heart which had again been bruised.

Reaching out for approval, he had been struck down one time too many. The hurt fell out through his tears like a pot running over, scalding, pouring. Down and out through his snotty nose the pain ran until his face was covered with ooze, with goo — first warm, then cool, then stiff — as his eyes closed, and his ears sang to cover the noises in the kitchen where she was moving, floating, fixing, making, doing. He was only aware that she was there, and he was here with his bear — sucking, sucking, and feeling nothing, finally hearing nothing, and seeing nothing but the stars in his red sky as his eyes shut in sleep, *his* stars that always came out and hovered over him, his special lights overhead — his angels.

As he slept, he was unaware that his out turned shoes were being pulled from their unmatched feet; unaware that a blanket was being gently laid over him to cover him and make him warm; unaware that the cruel mouth that had spoken cruel words reached down its lips and touched his tear-soaked and snotty wet cheek... *unaware*.

Unaware, because he was ascending up into the dark of the sky. With the lights, he floated — out, and over, and with. The stars were certain; he was confident in they're being and never to change. Safe in this knowing, the lights got dimmer and the sounds got quieter, and the tight clench of his cheeks loosened as his mouth let go of its charge — a fat, swollen, scarred and forlorn thumb that gave him safe and brought him warm, so always-there, and a lifetime of *unaware.*

~ ~

THE SECOND SAIL

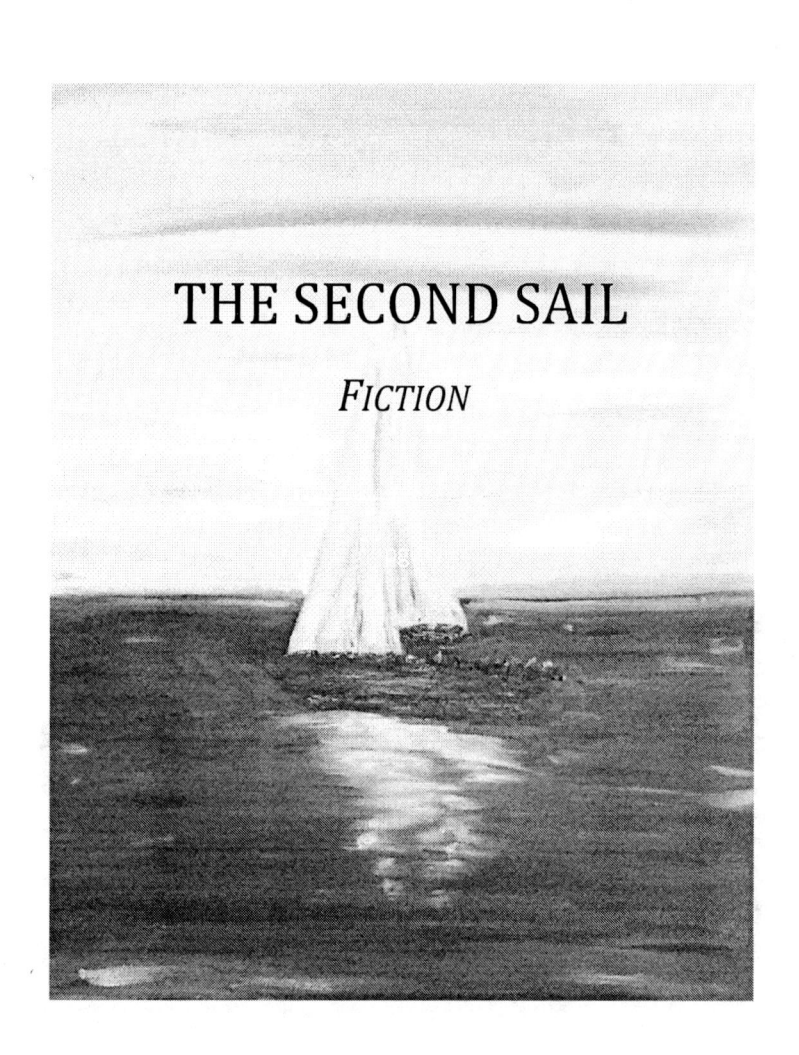

FICTION

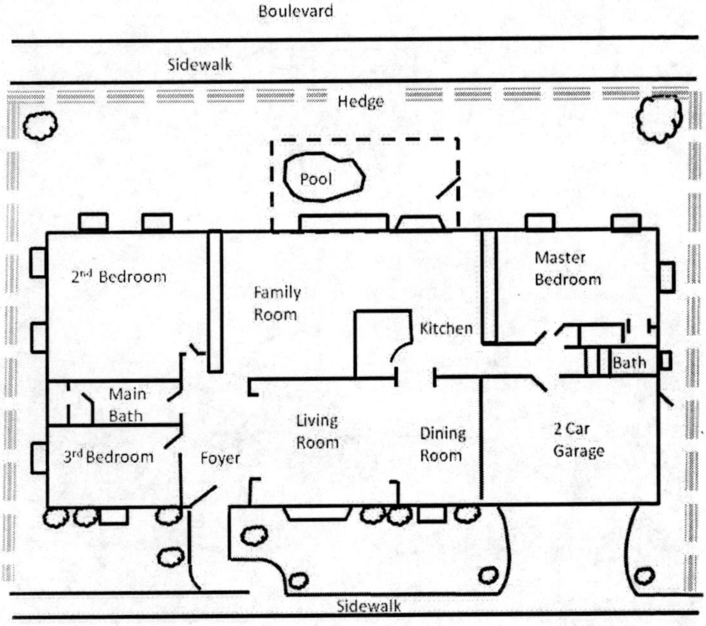
Boulevard
Sidewalk
Hedge
Pool
2nd Bedroom
Family Room
Kitchen
Master Bedroom
Bath
Main Bath
Living Room
Dining Room
2 Car Garage
3rd Bedroom
Foyer
Sidewalk

Until I'm sure where Herschel is, I better not get up and out from under this bed just yet. He must have brought the cop home in his own car and then drove him back to the station, or else he went to eat breakfast.

Too bad I'm disappeared under here, as it looks as if it's going to be one of them quiet, lazy Sundays. The kind where we just don't want to get up, out of bed. Sunday is our usual day to *do it*. I think it is because it is the only day we don't have an alarm clock ringing. Even on Saturday Herschel sets the clock so he don't oversleep for golf. It is really aggravating, to be honest. He gets up an hour earlier then, too. He is a kid going to the circus every day he can play. I wish I had something I liked to do like that. To get me up and at it with a feverish pitch to it.

Sundays just sort of evolved as *The Day*. He says it's because he always had to go to church. At his house, his ma said to them, "If you are going to set your feet under my table than you're going to my church on Sundays." Typical of one of them church-y mothers, I'm told. My ma, on the other hand, could've cared less about what I did. As long as I didn't bother her, make a mess, or ask her for money. When she wasn't cleaning, she usually had her nose in a book. That's why I hated books so much for so many years. A way to rebel, I guess, and tell her that what she likes, stinks. It's too bad, too. Because I think I might have been more confident in school if I had followed in her steps. In that way, at least. But Herschel's ma, she was something else. I think she was a little touched, between you and me.

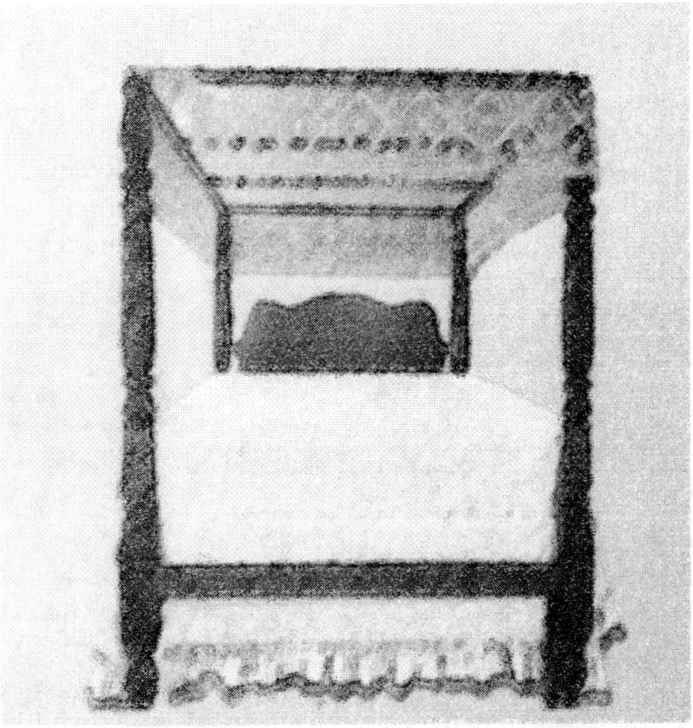

Love 'N' Stuff 39

He thinks so, anyhow, and I have to agree. When she brought their little baby sister home, she wheels the baby carriage — you know one of them brown straw jobbies back there in the '30's? — to the front door. The kids were staying across the street at their grandmom's house, and when they run out to see, the old lady pulls the covers back, and says, "Take a look at your new little sister."

They look down at this black china doll that gleams like freshly dug coal. Herschel says at first he really believed it, until he got closer. He was only eight or nine at the time.

Then when he sees it's a doll, his ma just looks at him, and giggles. "Did I fool ya?"

Herschel said he never will forget that as long as he lives, how she made him feel. It was the kind of thing she was good at, teaching him to scoff at anything different. Herschel never was very trusting towards her. She was always doing something to upset him. But the church part... Herschel says that's why he loves to stay in bed on Sundays and just screw the hell out of somebody. And of course, that somebody better be me, I tell him. Now, instead of having to get up and go to "f—ing church," he says in his ever-loving flowery way, we just stay in bed and... skip the church.

It is heading towards noon and I am hungry. I wiggle my upper torso to the end of the bed, the part that I've made into my kitchen, and reach for a can of fruit. It's sliced peaches. I always loved them as a kid. My grandma, from the South, always had some on the table at every meal I ever ate with her. She would have fried chicken, biscuits, navy beans cooked with fat-back — and a bowl of peaches. Not the hairy kind. The smooth. Every time I put one of them silky pieces of fruit into my mouth, I think of her.

This is stupid, I say to myself, to lie here all cuddled up

when I could be out, sitting up. I slide my head to the edge of the bed. I pull myself all the way out, and then reach for the can of peaches I haven't opened yet. The sun is out bright. I can see the backyard. I think maybe I should go look out the living room window so I can be sure Herschel's not out there. I take the can of peaches with me. For some reason, I feel like I should look, you know, I have this hunch. Sure enough his car is parked on the street curb but he's nowhere in sight. Did he go back to the station with the cop, I wonder? I decide to check out the other windows. Maybe he is around back, fooling with the pool, putting chemicals into it, or something. I still haven't opened the peaches.

Back in Toni's old room, I still don't see any sign of Herschel. I decide to open the peaches. I'm thinking, I better get rid of this sharp top; these pull-ups are dangerous. I go over to the trash can and it is clean. I'm good about keeping the trash emptied. Ever since that time a neighbor came with her baby and changed a diaper in the spare room. It was when those disposables first got popular. She must've thought I would come in behind her because she put the darn thing into the trash, poop and all. I kept smelling something awful. I don't go in the spare room too often when nobody is coming to visit. So it don't occur to me to follow the smell. Until it gets so bad, Herschel even mentions it. "Boy something in this house smells like shit," he keeps saying. We start walking around, to the other bathroom, on that end of the house, thinking maybe the toilet didn't flush right. But it is clean, blue water still in it. I flush it again to be sure. Then we walk on back to the spare room, and sure as shootin' right there in that trash can is this smelly old diaper. Had to have been in there over a week. Not just pee stink, but can you believe that woman never even dumped the poop into the toilet? I just can't believe some new mothers these days, I say to Herschel.

He is chuckling. Then he starts to really laugh.

I am carrying this bag of unmentionable, holding it out a ways from my body, like it might get into my skin somehow. "I'm glad you think this is so funny," I tell him.

He doubles over and says, "It's just that, someone got past your Mr. Clean suit. For once, you got had. And in your own house. I think that's a barrel of laughs."

Then I get mad. "Well let's see how funny you think this is if I was to shove this mess right into your puss," I say walking over to him. When I get to his smug, silly face, I want to do it so badly, but then I think: What the hell, it is only me that's got to clean it up. He'd sit there in pig heaven forever just to make me have to smell it. So I just run it past his nose a good whiff on the way to the garbage can, all the way outdoors. After that I always check the trash cans in every room. You never know. Somebody could come in while you're gone, a robber, or anyone, and drop in something rotten. This is why I think better of putting the lid to the peaches in that can. Besides, he would know it wasn't supposed to be there.

On the way back to the kitchen, I'm walking to the trash compactor, and I hear a noise in the garage. I can't take the chance of walking past the garage door — in case he opens it — so I step into the dining room.

We have this beautiful antique set I refinished right after we was married. I keep a pad and a scalloped lace cloth on the table, a big one, to fit when the table opens up with two more sections. When the pieces aren't in, the lace hangs around its claw feet, like a bridal gown.

I hear the noise again. Ducking in there seems the only place to go, under the table. Before I can get behind the other end to pull the chair out, I hear the doorknob turn. I haven't got time, so I quick duck behind the end of the big buffet china cabinet. The bottom drawers were once a "high-boy," until I cut the big, round, knobby legs off at the first joint, all eight of them. Now the china cabinet just sets on its top, in the middle, to make one huge piece. Big. Big enough to hide little ol' me. Herschel says I'm not big enough to swat.

Herschel never comes into the living room unless we've got company. And since Toni... Since nobody plays the piano anymore, we and this house is really just a museum of what we used to be — when we was happy, always laughing...

Footsteps sound in the hall. He stomps his feet. I know it's Herschel; it's his stomp. By now I'm sitting down with my knees up under my chin. There is no way anyone could see me unless they fell over me. The table and cloth and chairs all hide me. Sitting in this position feels good. Just what my back needs. The sip of my peaches' juice goes down smooth.

Herschel must be doing something back in the bedroom. Maybe going to the john? I wait. The TV comes on. Oh, shoot, now he's going to be in *there* and I am in *here*. What kind of stuff is this? I wanna be in there, where I can be close, hear him, smell him. Close enough to touch him; it *is* Sunday. Wonder if he's feeling the same way?

I am almost ready to stretch my legs out, when I hear him come into the kitchen. The refrigerator door slaps shut as he pops his diet Coke. I want to peek around the corner of the buffet, but I always heard that when you watch someone, they can feel it and will turn around eventually, if you keep it up. So I think better of peeking. He's over at the table, grabs the paper he was reading, before he went and got the cop, and takes it back into the bedroom.

The rest of my juice goes down fine as I reach into the can for a slippery thin slice of shiny peach. God, it's good. I could eat a big can of these babies any day of the week. I am on the last slice, licking my fingers, when the front doorbell rings.

The way the house is, the traffic pattern going round in a circle, I am just exactly straight across the living room from the foyer, with the baby grand between us. If someone was looking in this corner, they might see me. What do I do? Sit still, or try to get over behind the tall, round vase of artificial flowers I have in front of the window, to my left? But that is risky, because if he decides not to walk through the dining room, but goes around through the family room, I am smack dab in front of the kitchen door. So I gotta think. He's already into the family room and I have to move fast. I can't take the chance of being seen. Staying disappeared until he goes on a trip will tell the tale. Whether he sees *her* or not, I gotta find out; it's just making me crazy.

Up on my knees, sitting on my feet and leaning back against the window ledge, I hear Herschel open the door, and he says, "She ain't here.... I don't know.... No, I don't. Are you the guy that called for the homeless stuff?... You're not? What do you want then? What? Oh, a receipt. Thanks. She gave you all this stuff?... Well, yeah, I guess, if she said so. She takes care of all that, the taxes. Just what did she give you? This here says she gave you some clothes. Just what was it she gave you?... You weren't? Well, who could tell me that?... No. No, I don't care that she gave them to you. It's just that... Hey, do you want to come in a minute?" The front door closes. Herschel is saying, "The air-conditioning don't work too good in this Florida heat when the doors are open."

I know what you mean," the young kid says.

"See, my wife seems to be missing," says Herschel. "And if we can, the police, I should say, if they can find out what she was thinking or doing just before she left, went disappeared, maybe they can figure out something. So you say you weren't the guy who picked it up? But you saw the stuff?"

"No. Not all."

"All? Just what part *did* you see?"

"There was a waffle iron."

"A waffle iron? I thought you said it was clothes."

"Well, it was mostly clothes. But my friend told me he was trying to find a waffle iron for this family. Their kids had never had a waffle, and I guess your wife decided no kid in the U. S. of A. should grow up without at least tasting a waffle. So she goes into her cupboard and gets this perfectly good waffle iron. My friend says she told him, *My husband loves waffles, and he wouldn't like it, but he don't need them.* So that's why I didn't mention it at first. Where do you think she is?"

"I haven't a clue, I tell you. Everybody has their own theory, it seems. But the cops, right now, are checking *me* out. I had to fill out a damn credit application. I tell them, *I ain't looking to buy a house, Mate.* They say it's just routine. But I don't buy it. I think they think I done her in. And you know what, it really *pisses* me off. Just what the hell is a guy supposed to do when he's worried sick over his wife being missing, and the cops are blaming *him* for it?"

"Gee, I'm sorry. Wish I could do something. Maybe if I

Love 'N' Stuff

tell my friend the circumstances..."

"He already called. I think. Didn't he call?"

"I don't know."

"Yeah, it was your friend. He hangs up on me the minute I ask his name. What is it, by the way?"

"All I know him by is Jay. That's all anyone calls him. And I'm not so sure it's his real name. See, he won't wear anything but blue. His lucky color, he says, and why I think they call him Jay. You know, for Blue Jay."

"What you're saying is you think this guy's a little touched?"

The kid laughs. "You might call it that. He just has some funny ideas sometimes. He works real hard for the homeless shelter. I think he lives there, too."

"Oh, one of *them*." says Herschel.

"But maybe if he understands that he won't get into trouble, he'll talk to you. I'll try to run him down."

The front door opens and Herschel says, "Hey, thanks a lot Bub, for taking the time."

"Oh, not at all. I just wish I could help. It must be awful, wondering."

"Yeah," says Herschel.

I want to think his voice is cracking from feeling, hoping he is really worried I'm strung up somewhere.

He says, "I try not to think about it. I'd go crazy, you know."

The door slams shut, and Herschel is coming through the living room. Oh god, it's a good thing I moved. I feel my heart pounding. I am not moving a muscle; I'm afraid to breathe. He walks past the table and turns left, into the kitchen. I duck down quick and slide over behind the hutch again. I think I made some noise. I sit still waiting for him to come back and look. But I guess the TV back in the bedroom covers the sound. Or maybe he didn't hear it at all. I am still holding this empty peach can and the curled lid that would make noise if I tried to push it back down inside the can. Under the hutch, I shove it out of sight. I worry that it is going to stink and draw ants, have to remember to wash it out. But there's no way to do it now. All these things I have to do when he leaves tomorrow, if I can just make it till then. At least it is cooler out here with the blue shears on the windows that barely show from under the heavy brocade draperies.

The lady who built this house was a native Floridian who loved antiques and colonial houses. She dressed this one up New England style. It struck my fancy too, when I first saw it, until I lived in it one summer. At least the colors were cool. But the fussy, dressy look makes you hot, it turns out. Guess the house wouldn't sell, why we got such a deal on it. We could redecorate, or at least take the wallpaper off. There is a different pattern in every room in the house. In fact, there's one spot in the kitchen you can stand and see five different patterns without moving your head. Even so, it was all so elegant I just couldn't bear to tear it apart. And who could afford five different patterns of wallpaper?

I'm sitting there thinking about what I'd do to the house if I had the money. When I suddenly realize — if I had the money, I wouldn't be sitting in this darn corner waiting to get back under the bed where I've taken up residence, trying to scare the bejesus out of my husband so he'd act like I'm alive again. Just think, I could be taking a cruise, or flying to Rome, or visiting the tower of Pizza, or what's that big church in Paris? The Notre Dame Cathedral? All those places I could be visiting, leaving him to wonder, am I having a good time? Am I meeting somebody new? All the things I think about *him* every time he gets a plane ticket.

Love 'N' Stuff

Money. That's all that stands in my way of being who I want to be. Money, and not having any is what started all this insanity.

When I crawled under the bed the first time, I decided this was better than living on the street. I'll show *him*. Disappearing was an idea I had played with in my mind for some time. I had to get out, to find a way to feel unstuck. But I didn't have any extra money. I really thought if I could disappear for a while, Herschel might come to his senses. It seemed as though he didn't even know I was alive. He'd walk into the house, grunt, "Ella, you here?" And when I'd answer from the other room, he'd head for the TV, turn it on, and then hit the couch. He'd be snoring within minutes with the TV guide in his hand. I'd wake him for dinner, and he'd eat in silence, mumbling answers to me like it was an effort to speak. I was alone all day, and then all night, too. I just couldn't stand it anymore. But I have this terrible sense of responsibility. It kept me from taking the little savings we had and just taking off. A desire to run and a desire to stay, both feelings so strong in me I had a fight going on in me all the time. But after the last trip when he came home without two pairs of his briefies that he left with, I decided things had gone on long enough. That's when I started thinking about disappearing.

At first I had been toying with living in the attic. There was a partial floor in it. The air conditioning pipes and equipment went right down the middle and were covered with silver paper, over the insulation. The part that was not floored had that fiberglass stuff sticking up and it was so itchy I knew I didn't want to have it near my skin. Herschel almost never went up there. It was full of my sewing stuff, so I was the one who usually climbed into the heat. In the summers I knew I couldn't stand it; the Florida mug was too much. Even at night with the attic vent fan going or the ceiling fan Herschel put in last summer to cut our electric bills, it was too hot.

When I ruled the attic out, I started thinking about living in the deep closet in the back hall. It had a rollaway standing in there and I could sit up very comfortably behind it, on Toni's little chair, and stay hid. There was a light in there that didn't even shine through, around the door. We burned out several light bulbs forgetting to turn it off. I could even sit and write, or sew; I knew my back would start to hurt lying flat on the floor with such little room under the Hollywood bed we had.

When I happened to find this big, high canopy bed, I knew I had to have it. I guess I had already made up my mind to disappear when I was writing the check to pay for it.

It was an island bed, like down in Jamaica, or some tropical paradise place, handmade out of natural raw cedar. It was decked out in a blue organdy canopy, with matching netting for mosquitoes, that hung down all around it. The spread was blue too, with lots of wear left in it. The man who built it said he'd seen a picture of one once and thought it was clever. It was built so high off the floor that a small step ladder went with it, just like on a kid's bunk-bed, should you need it. "Guess they built the beds high like that, to keep snakes and things from crawling in with you," the old man said. "Style is from a hundred years old. I made it a king size though, so it uses regulation sheets and bed linens. My wife, she loved it. Said she always felt like a queen sleeping in it. But she's gone now."

I guess the old man liked my enthusiasm over his talented carpenter skills, or else I might've reminded him of his dead wife, when she was alive, I hope. Whatever it was, he sold it to me for next to nothing.

There were four deep drawers built under the bed, two on each side. When you took them out, there was a space left under it nearly two feet high. From the looks of it, I could see that it gave enough clearance for Herschel to get under there and turn over. I could even bend my knees to relieve the backache I usually got from sleeping too long. The idea of disappearing into the attic wouldn't help me any if I wanted to hear what Herschel was up to. And that was the main reason I wanted to do it. I had to find out, and I couldn't afford a private detective. Under the bed just seemed natural. I figured if I was gone long enough, and he was really carrying on with a tootsie, I would find out a heck of a lot being hid like that, just like Candid Camera! Only you'd have to call it Snug-as-a-Bug-in-a-Rug, or something like that.

At first, when I bought the bed, Herschel had a fit. Of course, the sheer blue canopy was *not* a hit. But the bed got so much attention from people who saw it — I fixed up the canopy real pretty, so it would stay out of the way — he finally got used to the idea. The dark and light colors of the raw cedar is striking, too. It's nice having something so unique — a conversation piece when anyone comes to fix something. The plumber, the TV repairman...

The base of the bed, above the drawers, is made of wood and has grooved slots, which the drawers slide into. The mattress sets directly on the wood, above. How all beds were made, before box springs, they say. A thin foam mattress came with it, and since we already had a box springs and mattress set, the double thickness makes the bed higher, and very comfy.

The drawers are fourteen inches deep, and solid cedar,

a perfect place to keep woolens, year 'round. There is a narrow wooden rail that holds the drawer frame together and supports the front of the drawers. The bottom drawer slides into grooved slots. When they are removed, the space under the bed goes from an already generous area of fifteen inches high to close to thirty. I debated whether to put the drawers into the attic, since the islet bed-skirt I made would cover them. But it might be a place where Herschel might look automatically, and if the drawers were missing he'd know for sure, even if I didn't happen to be under there at the time.

While I was deciding all this, I had the one drawer out, and I realized that the way the drawer was made, with a rim on the bottom just like the top, I could turn it upside down, and it looked almost the same. Of course if he opened it, he would wonder, *What the hell is this?* But I was counting on Herschel's lack of imagination. He never saw past his nose. That was one of our problems. Well, I was going to make him think, just once, make him think about me. I just couldn't stand the loneliness any longer, and we were tied together forever by our love for Toni.

When Toni was little, in the first or second grade I think he was, I remember him coming home one day all upset at his friend's parents splitting up. He was in tears, "Please Mom, please, tell me you and Poppy will never, ever go away, or anywhere without me, please, promise," he begged, hanging on to me so pitifully.

I hugged him a big one and said, "I promise on my heart that's full of love for you that I will never leave you." *Who would've thought then... ?*

Herschel was in the room watching his sports on TV, but he just sat there shaking his head and didn't say anything. I could see he was upset, but he never answered

Toni. Even so, I knew Herschel loved his son. More than he loved me, probably.

Why did I have to marry such a cold fart? It was like I pined for my husband when he was right in the same room. How could two people live together and be so separate from one another? I just didn't know how it happened.

While Herschel was getting ready to turn in, or after he got up in the morning, I'd lie on top of the bed and imagine being under it and what it would be like, him missing me, looking for me, maybe thinking something happened to me and worrying about me. It made me so sad and happy all at once. Knowing I could hear every word he said to anybody, even on the phone, was just too exciting. After awhile, my living under the bed started to seem sort of natural. The amount of space was the only problem.

My small size is the only thing that made this undertaking possible. I am under five feet, and I weigh less than a hundred pounds. I fit fairly well in the space that was left after I had set up housekeeping under there.

The space was partitioned off into sections so that I could find things in the dark. The first thing I did when I started planning this, was to draw out what could be called a map of the areas, where everything would be. The first list I made looked something like this:

> Battery operated clock (with a lighted dial)
> Small bedpan - just in case!
> Pillow
> Sleeping bag with a zipper
> Large square batteries flashlight
> Books to read

Pencil and paper
Food (small pull-open cans)
Fruit
Baby food (meats & vegetables)
Peanut butter
Plastic eating utensils
Paper plates/napkins
Ziplock baggie, small and large
Juices in pull-open cartons
Quart jug of water (with a straw made into its
Screw-on lid so it wouldn't spill)

Most of what I might need were things I had, except the things Herschel might miss; things like the flashlight had to be bought extra. He kept one in the trunk of each car, so I had to buy another one. But I bought a yellow one, instead of red, like the others. Most of this stuff I found at garage sales so the whole operation didn't cost too much.

The space under the bed, I partitioned off into areas just as if they were rooms. The bathroom had the toothbrushes, Handiwipes, and the like, and, of course, the bedpan. It was a small pink plastic one I found at a hospital clearing house sale for ten cents, brand new. It still had the picture sticker on it showing you how to use it, lying down. It's a good thing, as I never used one in my life before.

In the bedroom section I put the extra clothes, shoes. A pillow, a sleeping bag with a zipper. The yellow flashlight with a large square 'D' battery, and a pile of books that I'd been intending to read for years. In the other corner I stuck the sleeping bag, crosswise, since I was so short I fit just perfectly.

Everything got tested out when Herschel was gone on one of his famous trips. The light from the flashlight was

Love 'N' Stuff

plain to see through the thin cotton bed-skirt, so I took apart an old, black window shade I found, cut it into four pieces and then tacked them to the underside of the bed-board to make one end completely light proof. As long as I kept the light facing the back end, on the wall, it didn't show, even at night. If I was really stuck for something to do, I could read all night and not worry. I was so pleased with all my cleverness, I couldn't believe myself. I should've been a fixer-upper for the Peace Corps, where people didn't have a whole lot of first class stuff.

Looking around under there, I expected that once I got into the routine of living this way, I would no doubt have little trouble keeping to a regular routine. I am a fool for schedules. If I get off one, I am the devil to live with. My body needs to receive its expectations. No surprises and no changes. The only thing I had yet to figure out was how to see Herschel's face when he walked into the house that first time and called my name — if I could just figure out how to rig up a camera. But even if I would be such a genius, and could afford it, I knew the cops would surely find it. And I was betting Herschel would call them mighty quick when I didn't come home. The question was, how long would it take him? One week? One night? One hour?

It was four o'clock. I'd been practicing this routine for several days. One day I'd crawled under to test it out and fell asleep. This really scared me, so I set up my little tape recorder to see if I made any noises while I slept. Herschel said I did sometimes, when I'd roll over on my back and start to snore. Finding a way to sleep on my side or my stomach was the tricky part. Finally, I decided I would have to sleep in the daytime when he was at work, and use the night time, after he was asleep, to do things.

As I planned all this, my enthusiasm perked and I

didn't feel as sad as I had been feeling. Just thinking about finding out all those things I'd been guessing about Herschel for over twenty-five years got me so excited. In fact, now my heart was pounding a mile a minute as I lay stretched out on my stomach, my head on my arms, with the pillow under my chest. I looked around at all the little things I had collected, duplicate things I would need if the cops might ask. Things like makeup, a hairbrush, some new clothes, so it would look as though I had just disappeared, as if someone had dropped into the house and snatched me. There was no one I was friendly with on this street since Carrie left, so I didn't expect nosey neighbors to be a problem.

I'm fairly comfortable as I lie there listening for Herschel's car. I'm thinking, let's see, I just went to the bathroom, but now I had to go again. *Well, you're going to have to just get used to it,* I said to myself right out loud. The sound of my own voice shocked me. Sometimes I would catch myself talking a mile a minute into the air to an imaginary person. But no sound ever came out before. Until now. *Am I losing it?* I took a deep breath and tried to still the pounding of my heart. The sound of the garage door going up, broke into my head's silence. *If Herschel ever finds out I'm doing this, he will surely have me committed!* He'd threatened to do it that last fight we had. A story to cover me, was my plan: I would tell him I had amnesia and was wondering around the mall over in Tampa. And then woke up one morning, remembering. He'd buy it; he wasn't all that swift. At least he seemed to believe just about everything else I told him.

I could hear his car's motor gunning. Then the sound stopped dead. I waited for quite a while to hear the car door open. What in the world is he doing so long out there?

Looking in the mirror? Checking his face to see if there was lipstick smears on it? His collar? His handkerchief to see if lipstick from some tootsie had gotten on it? Taking the rubbers out of his pocket and putting them into the glove compartment — where I never *used* to go? It seemed like an eternity until he opened that car door.

Then I hear the sound of something brushing up against the wall in the garage. Something hard hits the door. Must be a button or buckle on the raincoat he always carries, but never wears, says it's too hot. Then the sound of the doorknob turning is followed by a loud bang on the inside of the hall. I think it is his briefcase hitting the floor. He always sets it inside before he steps up into the house. Next I hear him close the door behind him. I can imagine his bent head in deep thought, when I hear him grunt, "Ella?"

I hold my breath. For some reason I feel like he can hear the air as it comes out of my mouth.

"Ella?" he says again. This time I hear the hangers rattle in the closet. He is only a few feet from me. Our bedroom door faces the outside door to the garage, the back hall separating them. Next I hear the hanger go click onto the rod. The briefcase makes a noise when he lets it fall to the floor of the closet. "Ella," he bellows this time.

Oh no! He must have something to tell me! Oh gosh! It is so seldom he finds something to talk about. Oh darn! I wish I was out there now. Oh, gee whiz! I'm feeling very upset all of a sudden, feeling guilty that I am not there now to listen when he finally decides to speak. But before I can get too upset, I hear his footsteps come into the room and I see their shadow at the corner of the bed, just a few feet inside the door.

"Ella?" he says again.

I hold my breath until I just can't anymore and finally

let it out very softly and slowly.

"What the hell," Herschel says softly to himself.

His feet, I can see now as plain as day as they continue on past the end of the bed, towards the bathroom. He steps one foot onto the thick carpet that continues on into the small room, and says, "Ella?" again and then turns around and walks back past the end of the bed. I can see the shadow of his footsteps as they move past me.

Herschel walks on out of the room, into the hall, and after only a couple steps, takes a right turn only a few feet, into the kitchen. It is hard to hear his footsteps, as the kitchen is carpeted with a thin, hard commercial carpeting you usually see in hotels. The lady that sold us the house told us she got tired of having her feet stick to the waxed floor, with the hot Florida mug. That's why Herschel's footsteps get softer as he leaves the kitchen and goes into the family-room, the central room of the house.

You can hear the sound of the sliding doors that lead out onto the screened-in porch. It is carpeted too, with outdoor gold carpeting. The cool-decking starts right next to the porch, not much yard left to speak of inside the white picket fence surrounding the swimming pool. "Ella?" he yells.

Then he goes out onto the porch, as I can hear the screen door open. I keep asking him to fix that squeak. But he keeps forgetting. "Ella?" he calls again.

He lets the door slam and I can hear the sliding door inside the family-room bounce against the door jam. It is such a heavy door, it is a job getting it closed tight enough to lock it. We just got in a habit of slamming it hard the first time.

"Ella," I hear, sort of muffled; he's way back in the back bedroom, Toni's bedroom it used to be. It is still just

Love 'N' Stuff 57

about the way he left it. Herschel is coming back through the house calling, "Ella, Ella, you here?"

Of course, I'm dying to see his face right now. Wonder, is it hurting his heart? Think he's scared? Wonder just what is he thinking this very minute? Probably is mad as he doesn't smell any dinner cooking. That seems the first thing he notices. "What's that funny smell?" he might ask if it was cabbage cooking, or turnips. He hates those two things. But I fix them sometimes when I get hungry for them. Usually when I have his favorite thing so he won't get too grumpy about the smell.

He's coming back into the bedroom. He walks around to his side of the bed and sits down in the wingback chair, next to the bedside table that has the phone on it. The drawer to the table, that has the phone book in it, slides open. The big heavy directory is a mess to get out of the drawer. I usually just call Information; it's easier. But Herschel hates to talk to anyone he doesn't have to, even the operator. So he usually will fight the drawer. I hear the noise of the book, the pages being flipped, and finally his punching the phone buttons. I can even hear the busy signal. *God, my ears are too good! I bet I could hear the talking from the other end if I didn't breathe!* The sound of the pages flipping makes me wonder what he's looking for. This time it must ring because he says, "Yes, did my wife, Ella, pick up my cleaning today? It's a blue... Oh, yes, it's *Goodlove*. Yes, two words in one. It's a blue suit. Dark blue."

Everything gets quiet, and then he starts whistling, *I can't give you anything but love... Baby..."* She didn't? That's funny. I told her I needed that suit for tomorrow. How much is it?... Maybe that's where she is now, on her way. Okay, thanks." The phone makes a clinking sound when he hangs it up.

Sounds like he is mad. Then he flips the pages again and dials another phone number. It must be ringing. He is waiting, tapping his right foot on the floor. I could reach out and grab his toe if I wanted to bend sideways. "Hey. How are you? No, I'm just looking for Ella. You seen her, or talked to her? No? Yeah, she usually leaves a note. The car is here. She must've walked, wherever... Well, she'll probably be right back. Thanks, anyhow. Then he waits a minute, and laughs. "Yeah, I should, shouldn't I. Not often I get such peace and quiet, you're right. All to myself, too, you're right. Thanks anyhow," he says and hangs up the phone.

Can't figure out who that was.

He is sitting very still, not making a sound. I'm waiting for him to get up and head for the couch, but he sits there instead. I wait, trying not to breathe. He finally stands up and walks to the end of the bed. He stops, turns around and is facing the bed. I wonder what he is doing? *Oh god, is something sticking out from under here? Did I forget something?* I go over all the last minute things I did, the bed-skirt has tiny holes in the islet. I imagine he can see the whites of my eyes peering up at him through the holes. I think he must be able to see something. I am forever forgetting something, I'm so scatterbrained. Herschel is always telling me how careless I am. I'm waiting for him to bend down and grab my hair, or something. Instead he just stands there. Must be looking out the window. Or maybe at the picture over the bed, of the ocean he loves. Of two sailing ships side by side. They are so close together they almost look like one. *Hersh and me?* I hear the loose change in his pockets rattle. I can just see him, his hands in them, staring, daydreaming. *About me? Does he really wonder where I am?* Pretty soon he turns around again and walks over to the other end of the bed, turns left, out the bedroom door. His walking stirs up some carpet dust; I can smell it; my smeller is just too good. *E-gads, what if I sneeze?* But the sensation passes and the footsteps disappear into the other end of the house.

The house is quiet, just like it usually is when Hersh is sleeping on the couch.

Waiting for Herschel to do something else makes me tired. It's too early to read; he might get up. I'm picturing him asleep on the couch. It is so quiet, I am almost asleep myself. Sleep comes easily to me when I get still. The clock on the dresser is ticking. It's an extra clock he keeps, just in case the power goes out and the alarm doesn't ring. I am so used to the ticking, I hardly hear it anymore. Until now. It's ticking very loudly. *Maybe I could count how many times it ticks in a minute?* No, it's ticking too fast. I just can't keep up with the ticks.

My throat is aching all of a sudden, and my ear is beginning to hurt. *What? Am I getting sick? Oh, Lord, I didn't think about that happening. Now what?* I swallow and the ache in my throat gets worse. *Awe, I must just be nervous.* That doctor told me I had a thing in my throat when I was nervous, when I wanted to say stuff, but the ache kept me from it. It was a mental lock on my voice box, a permanent lock, and when I thought about talking about certain things, it would ache, telling me to keep quiet. Suddenly, I'm back in the hospital room with my pop, waiting for him to wake up, out of the coma. The last time we talked, we had words over the way I treated Toni, said I was too protective. "He's a boy, for god's sake. Let him go, stop hovering." How could my own father not understand how I felt? Just wanting my son to be safe, and able to learn in school? Didn't he realize Toni wasn't like other kids? So many problems, coping and learning. "Why don't you just tie him to a chair?" were Poppy's last words, before I stormed out, angry and hurt.

Not more than a week later, Pop had a stroke and slipped into a coma. I was back there, sitting at his bedside, praying for him to wake up so I could apologize, ask him what he meant, tell me how to be different. With the one person in the world who I knew really loved me, I never had the chance to right things. *And Toni — I had let loose of him, finally. Yeah, finally.*

I swallow again. This time, my ears pop. Oy, I guess I'll have to get some lemons to suck on under here. But not now. He doesn't sleep that sound in the daytime. Only at night, when he is snoring good. Then I can get up.

I roll over and the light from the setting sun is coming through the bedroom window and shines under the bed. It is light enough to read. So I reach for the book on top of the stack, and open it to read. It's a book about birds. This guy is a bird watcher and he meets a girl who runs a sanctuary. I open the book to the book mark. It is not as light as I thought it was, so I slip over to the edge of the space to see a little better. I am reading and my eyes get so sleepy that I close the book and shut my eyes. The book falls out of my hand and makes a slight noise. My eyes fly open with a jolt. *I gotta watch that.* I put the book back on the stack and go back to dozing.

This waiting is going to be the death of me. But I have gone too far now to turn back. *Past the point of no return? Isn't that what they say on TV?.* What could I say? "I was under the bed hiding from you, Herschel?" *No, I'll stick it out.*

Love 'N' Stuff

The TV goes on in the other room. Some talk show, either Merv Griffin or Mike Douglas. Herschel hates talk shows, says they're boring. *If he's leaving it on, maybe he's wondering about me.* I get a good feeling just thinking about that. The news broadcaster breaks into the station. "The hostage negotiation with President Carter is at a standstill." Says something about that Khomeini guy, over in Iran, who thinks he's god of the world. I can't hear what he is saying exactly, but I recognize President Carter's voice. Then Herschel turns up the volume to hear the newscaster say, "There is some speculation that there may be some kind of end to this national crisis, but not on Carter's watch. Some believe that the Iranian's would be more willing to work with a new Republican president, more out of fear than of good will, if Ronald Reagan should win, as he has the reputation of being more of a hawk on international matters, and may not be as tolerant of this egregious act against U. S. citizens." *Can you believe both candidates for President are running on religion, when the pilgrims came here to get away from all that religious stuff in their government?*

The TV goes silent. That's funny. He never would turn off the news before. I just lie there and wait.

It must be a good half hour before I hear him in the kitchen; the refrigerator door opens. He mumbles, "Sonofabitch." Must be hungry and there's nothing to eat, I made sure of that. The way to a man's heart. "What the fuck?" he says very loudly as he slams the refrigerator door shut. I had let quite a few things run out, the mayonnaise, the mustard, catsup. Things that would take a lot to replace. I want him to see just how hard it is to keep things up. Maybe he'll appreciate what I do for a change. "Grocery shopping ain't no lark," I always tell him. The canned goods,

I let get sparse, too. As long as he has food on the table, he never even opens a cupboard. *What a change for you, huh, Hershey Baby!* I left a little spill of milk in the bottom of the carton, just like he likes to do to me, so he doesn't have to wash the carton out to keep it from souring and smelling up the trash compactor. There is about one little glass of fresh orange juice left. Just enough to keep from shocking the poor baby.

Wait until you get the bank statement. At first I was going to save his checks back, but then I decide that would give me away. So I deposit them, but I write checks for cash here and there. The bank balance is supposed to stay above a thousand to keep from paying any bank charges. Just to be safe, I always keep about three times that. I decide to fake a bunch of mistakes, so it looks as if there is a lot more money in it than there really is. That way it doesn't look *on purpose*. I had to have money just in case things turn funny on me — you never know what can happen when you disappear.

The water faucet in the kitchen goes on and I hear glass ping against something. The sound of the cupboard door banging shut lets me know he's getting steamed. *Good for you, Ella, old girl. Now you're cooking with gas!* Inside the bread box, there is one slice of bread and a crust, just so he won't go without, but he hates the crust. I usually save them up for toast in the mornings. The bread wrapper is rattling, so I figure he must be too hungry to wait around. The crinkling noise of the bread wrapper when he wads it up and throws it into the trash muffles his cursing. But I know the sound of all those four-letter jobbies too well to mistake them. The silverware drawer makes a heck of a noise when he pulls it open. Must be for a knife. The peanut butter jar has enough in it for one sandwich; I made sure of that. Knowing how lazy he is, I figured he'd eat that first, before he'd open a can of tuna or fry an egg. Those were his standbys that time I went into the hospital on emergency. I had a freezer full of stuff to cook, canned soups, too, but he was too lazy to open the cans, he said. The cupboard door slams and I have to giggle to myself until the sound of his footsteps hush me up.

He's suddenly at the end of the bed. I had rolled onto my back to rest it just a few minutes before, so I am stuck twisting my head around to see his feet. He is standing, facing the closet when I hear the folding closet door squeak open. He is rummaging around in there, in my clothes. My hand-tooled leather bag he brought me from a Texas trip, is sitting on the first shelf in plain sight. I hear my keys when he pulls them out of the bag. My purse falls on the floor and some change rolls out, across the room. "Oh shit," he says to the rolling penny that keeps coming, under the bed.

I catch it. My heart is in my throat. Oh, god, please don't let him find me already. It's too soon.

"Oh, shit," he says again.

I hold my breath waiting for him to pull the bed-skirt up and see me. I quick shove the penny right up close to the edge of the skirt and quietly pull my arm back. The bed-skirt suddenly swings inward, and his fingers reach for it. I hear it go clunk into his pocket with other change.

He is standing at the corner of the bed, facing it, and it sounds like he has the purse up on it while he is rummaging through it. I hear my keys rattle again. It sounds like he is examining them. Must be looking for my house key, to see if I am gone out. "Sonofabitch," he says all of a sudden, and then walks around the end of the bed to the telephone.

Uh huh. You're finally getting the picture, Sweet thing.

He is still standing there, facing the telephone that sets

on the night stand next to the bed. There is a window behind the table that has Venetian blinds always facing downward, so nobody could see up, into the bedroom, unless they were in the eucalyptus tree over in the corner of the yard. I never even bother to close them because the blue sheers shade the sunlight in the daytime. Sometimes when the full moon is out, Herschel complains about it being too light at night, and I have to get up and close it. But that only happens when he has indigestion, which doesn't happen too often, unless he goes out for Chinese, at lunch. He is standing there so long, I think he must be looking out the window. It is almost dusk; summer nights the sun sets soon after the nightly news is over.

    I think he must be planning to call someone, standing by the phone like that, and then he turns around and walks around the bed, over to my dresser. He starts pulling all the drawers open, one at a time. I can hear his knuckles hit the edge of the drawers inside. *Boy, what a mess he is making in them! Oh, well, you didn't think this was going to be a fancy walk in the park, now did you, Ella? Not with a messy fart like Herschel!* I'm wondering just what he thinks he is going to see in those drawers? He wouldn't know my stuff from that hotsy-totsy black gal just moved in on the corner. *What's he looking for?* He pushes all the drawers shut and just stands there. Maybe he's trying to figure out what I'm wearing? That's a laugh. He's color-blind in the first place, and clothes is something this guy doesn't have much appreciation for. "A shirt is a shirt is a shirt," he always says to me, when I complain he "don't have no pizzaz" to him. Of course, I buy him things on sale. To save a buck I'll give up pizzaz. It don't matter to him, so why should I care?

    He goes back to the closet. Opens the doors again, and this time pulls all the hangers back, one at time. He rummages around on the floor of the closet feeling for something. I can see the back of his shoes and his little tiny rear as he squats down rummaging through the closet. Finally, he stands up again, slams the closet door shut, and walks back into the kitchen.

It is now an hour since he came home and I'm not there. What'll he do next?

He goes to the garage door and opens it. Out in the garage I can tell by the squeaky hinges he is opening my car door. The sounds are muted so he must be inside of it. First, the glove compartment, next the trunk. He must be moving the boxes around I left in there. Empty boxes. *Never know when I'll need one.* The trunk closes with a bang.

Back in the house, the door slams behind him. He's talking to himself again. "Shit, Ella, where are you?" he says with an angry whine to his voice.

My throat tightens. Guess I'm in for it now, for sure. *I'll have to stay disappeared longer. Until he starts to* really *worry.* He comes around the side of the bed again and sits down by the phone. He's dialing the number. "Yes, how long does someone have to be missing before you can report it?... No, I don't know. I just can't find my wife." He has a silly little laugh. "Well, believe me, if it was that easy, I would've already.... No, actually I've only been home an hour."

There is such a long pause, I can't swallow, waiting.

"You don't understand. My wife never does anything unexpected. She is just not an *un-expecting* person.... No, that's the thing. Her purse is here with her wallet in it. Car keys. I can't tell anything is missing. As though she just went next door, except she don't know anyone next door. She doesn't go for neighbor types. She wouldn't... Well, that's true, she might've.... No, I'll wait and see if she comes back."

He slams the phone down, and says, "Ella, you really irritate the shit out of me, you know that?" I see his feet leave the floor, and I can almost feel the weight of his body on top of me through the bed — *and on top of the bedspread.* Never does he *dare* to do that; he got broke of that years ago. The springs over my head squeal as he rolls over. *Why you so-and-so; you've got a nerve. With your shoes on!*

Now all I can do is wait for his next move. The TV goes on in the middle of the weather. A severe storm warning in Tampa. I wonder how close it's going to come to us? Flipping channels. National news on all three networks is over; he flips to Channel 19 reruns. The clicker hits the bed just as *I Love Lucy* starts, followed by *Father Knows Best,* and *MASH* reruns.

Before long he is snoring with a sound so loud I can hardly hear myself think. I rummage around for something to stick into my ears. Kleenex is all I can find without making noise.

I'm just starting to doze when he wakes up. He clicks off the TV. He gets up and goes into the bathroom. Listening to him take a whiz is comforting. But I don't hear the seat go back down. *Oh, I hate that!* How many times I've gone in the night, to sit down right into the cold water. Screaming at him to be more considerate seems the story of my life. Living with a man is a pain, at least this one.

He goes to the closet in the hall, gets his briefcase and car keys, puts the brief case back, and takes what sounds like a jacket out. The garage door opens and the car starts up and leaves the garage with the door closing after.

The silence in the house is deafening. He is gone. Now what do I do? The time is exactly 8:40 p.m., Friday night,

Love 'N' Stuff

the first day of my being disappeared.

It is 9:20 when he returns. I can hear the ruffle of the paper bag, and the smell of french fries reach my nose. Such a good smeller, I got. It's a curse. Toni used to say I had a six-million dollar nose! I hear paper rustling in the kitchen. He must be sitting at the table with the newspaper, eating something from MacDonald's. *All the stuff I never let him have.* French fries, onion rings, quarter-pounder with cheese. And cherry pie turnovers. Probably has an extra-large shake too. Chocolate to be sure. He has the TV on in the family room, blasting. God, the neighbors must be able to hear it. He definitely has a hearing problem. Except he is mad, and when he is mad he does all the things he knows I hate. *He's probably even spilling catsup on his shirt.* I'm getting hungry. He isn't going to go to bed, it looks like. Does he think I'm out this late without my purse and car? He is such a dumkopf.

My left foot is getting a bad cramp in it. I pull it up and grab the middle toe. Usually I have to step on it to stop the grabbing pain. Trying to relax might help. The TV clicks off in the other room. He comes into the bedroom and opens the closet. Sounds like he's taking my purse out again. *Counting the money.* His feet turn to the bed and I hear the change dumping out over my head. He's so mad he's talking to himself. "What a bunch of shit," he says. I hear him moving the stuff all over the bed. I can just see all the stuff I so carefully put in it: keys, glasses, make-up case, checkbook. *That* ought to get his attention. His feet turn around and he sits down in the chair next to the bed. He is flipping pages of something, probably the check book. "Holy Jesus, I don't understand this. Nothing seems missing here. What the hell." He throws something over onto the bed and walks around it to the phone. The bedside table drawer opens and he pulls the telephone book out. He's punching in the numbers. "Yes, I think I should report that my wife appears to be missing.... Well, I know it's only the first night, but there are some things that are strange here.... Yes, I realize that, but not my wife. She's not that independent, she wouldn't.... No, everything is here that I can tell. Her purse, her checkbook, car keys, no clothes missing that I can tell. Of course, I wouldn't really know, I never pay attention. She wears pretty much the same things. No, not every day, but... I don't know... I'm just telling you, nothing's missing but *her*... Yes, I see. Where are you located? In that building? When would you do it? Why three days?... I'm telling you, she's not here. Alright. Alright, I'll be right over." The phone goes clunk. He slams the telephone book drawer shut and gets up.

He is standing still again, facing the bed. At this moment, I have trouble holding my breath. He takes a step closer to the bed. Next, I see his pants legs go up and he is reaching down, scratching his ankle. Then he stands up, turns around, and walks around the bed, and out into the garage. He pulls the door to behind him, and the garage door after that. It is 11:20, still Friday night, the first night of my being disappeared.

I'm all huddled up, waiting. He must be going to the police already. I want to crawl out, but I'm afraid he will come back. The police department is about twenty minutes from our house. I hear the clock ticking. He left the hall light on so I can see well enough to get around. My bladder is feeling like it'll burst. I scoot to the edge of the space and listen. Out from under the bed, I stretch my right arm and leg out, on the bathroom side of the bed. I'm hoisting my

Love 'N' Stuff

rear end up, over the throw rug, to get out from under the bed when the ringing of the phone scares the ever-lovin' bejesus out of me. It rings three times before I move another muscle. It is like I'm suspended in between life and death for those forever seconds. *What am I so scared of? Nobody can see through the stupid telephone.* It continues to ring, but finally I am able to ignore it and pull the rest of me out from within my dark cocoon.

Over on my tummy, I crawl on all fours to the bathroom, just in case someone might see me or my shadow through the curtains. The toilet seat is up. *What else is new?* It slips out of my hand with a crack. Remember to put it back up. *It's things like that what's going to trip you up.* The relief I feel is like being on a long trip and Herschel finally stops to let me go after I've begged, ending in tears. Angrily, he'll pull in somewhere, and tell me to *Hurry up. Don't take all day.* I'm so gratefully relieved that when I get back into the car, I give him a hug. As usual, he shoves me away. Just thinking about it makes me feel all the hurt all over again. *Such a cold fart.* Pulling the toilet paper out, I'm back to business as I notice the roll is getting past the middle. *I have to remember never to use too much. Should have hid an extra roll somewhere. Have to do that.*

Just as the flush of the toilet starts and I'm standing up and remembering to put the seat up, I hear the sound of the garage door. *He's back. Oh, my god.* My slacks are caught around my knees. The floor is the fastest way; I scoot mermaid-like towards the bed. Headfirst, I go under, when the bed-skirt catches on my zipper. *Damn.* The car door slams all too loudly. The toilet has just sang its last note, a squeal-like sound it makes at the end, and I pull at the bed-skirt, unhooking it just as the doorknob turns. I manage to get my feet in just as he steps into the hall, only ten feet away.

Lying flat on my stomach, my face is buried in my hands awaiting his next move; my heart is thumping in my ears. Into the hall closet, I hear him hang up his jacket, his keys getting pitched into his brief case, where he keeps them. Click goes the case. I listen as he walks into the kitchen. A paper bag rattles as he takes something out of it. The refrigerator closes and I recognize the sound of the bag being shoved behind the refrigerator with the other ones I keep there. It's like I know his every move, where everything goes. He is coming back into the bedroom. His feet stand in front of my closet doors and they're open. It sounds like he is taking out one hanger at a time; his feet twist. The belt of a jumpsuit is hanging down. Must be checking it out, wonder what for? Oh, those deep pockets. He must be feeling in them. Some change rattles. An earring drops on the floor. He bends over and picks it up. When I talk on the phone, I pull one off and usually forget it; I'm always losing one earring. That jumpsuit was so uncomfortable to wear, having to get undressed to go to the john is for the birds. I hate wearing it. So it doesn't get worn much, and then it's not on long enough to need washing. *A bitch to iron, too.* All this imported rayon stuff. Just when the women have finally gotten themselves out of the kitchen and laundry room with microwave self-serve meals and drip-dry fabrics, along come the foreign imports with more stuff to iron. And who can afford to buy USA made, the Dan River cottons we had all those years and didn't appreciate? No matter how wrinkled this new stuff gets, I just *refuse* to iron. Even though it's the style now, it still irritates me to look rumpled. So I end up wearing only the few outfits that don't need ironing. The rest just hang in the closet or lay in my drawers.

Love 'N' Stuff

Herschel's feet turn back towards the closet again. Another hanger. He turns, and it sounds like he is feeling in the pockets again. What was next to the jumpsuit? Was it a jacket? A Sweater? Sounds as if he's taking things out, one at a time. A wadded up Kleenex drops to the floor. He kicks it with his foot. It rolls over towards the bed. I have to remind myself to leave that there. Or he might wonder. *What a slob. How am I gonna live through this?* Anyhow, two weeks, I figure should scare him good. Make him miss me, think about me. Wonder where I am, if someone raped me, killed me, cut me up in little pieces. *I hope he gets scared plenty. He deserves to worry a little.* He shoves the clothes all back to the end of the closet. He's down on one knee, and I can see his elbow as he reaches back into the corner of the closet for the shoe box I keep there full of little junk. He pulls it out. Trying to remember what was in there. Oh, some old medicine I'm saving for when I get brain dead. To kill myself. I decided to save all the old bottles after that old man, Sanders, got life for helping his wife to die. *Alzheimer's. It's so scary.* I'm going to have enough stuff in the house, should it ever happen to me. *I'm not going to hang around this earth when I get good and ready to leave it.* There he goes, rummaging through the bottles. Picking them up and shaking them. "What the hell. How old *is* this stuff?" he says out loud.

The giggles are hard to stifle. But I manage. *Wonder what he thinks they're for?* Some were ten years old already. But he knows I don't believe in throwing *anything* away. Never know when you might need it and then not have it. The refrigerator was the other place things ended up forever.

Herschel puts the lid back on the box and shoves it back into the corner where it was. He stands up. The hangers make a screechy sound that hurts my ears when he pulls back the clothes. The top shelf is lined with shoe boxes. I hear him pull one out at a time and look in every one. There must be a dozen of them. I keep all my shoes in the original boxes with their color and description written in big black letters on the ends. Most are like new. *Wonder why I never wear a pair of shoes out? It's a curse. I never have an excuse to buy new ones.* Alongside the boxes are handbags to match every pair, just about. Now he's pulling them all down, one at a time, pulling out the paper stuffing that retains their shape. "Jesus Christ..." he says out loud again. "What the hell does she do with all this shit?" *I never see her wear any of it, I know he's thinking.* He takes in a big breath and lets out a big sigh. He's quiet. Very quiet. *Wonder what he's thinking?* He closes the folding doors to the closet again. It is the third time since he came home at 5:30 that he went through it. What *is* he thinking?

He goes to his closet on the other end of the room and gets out a hanger. I can just see him putting his shirt on it, buttoning the top button. Good thing I taught him that, to put his dirty clothes on hangers and hang them above the washer. That way they don't get more wrinkled. They go right from the hanger into the washer. Pants too. When they get washed, I take them by all four seams and carefully fold them into several layers and place them carefully into the dryer. One on top of the other. Low heat, always. They dry slowly and the creases in them get set by the time they get tossed too much. Never touch the iron to a thing.

He's taking his pants off now; I hear the hanger as he slips it over them nice and creased. He finally got trained, finally. He already pulled his slip-on shoes off and they are already neatly arranged in his closet. Socks off, I can see his bare toes. They are knobby and full of corns. Never saw anyone tear off their toenails like he does. Sometimes it goes into the quick. No wonder he has trouble with ingrown toenails. *Wonder why he never learned to use toenail clippers like everyone else?* He usually chews on the nails he rips off for awhile, too. *He says he's used to chewing nails from his fingers. No difference.* He closes his closet door and I hear him scratching, scratching. *Must be his balls.*

At the end of the bed, he stops there, and his feet are very still. *Did I make noise and he heard it?* Sometimes my breath catches; an extra little short breath in between the regular ones. A catch-up for my lungs, I think. A funny kind of noise comes out when I do that. But I don't remember doing that now. Although I *could* have; I was so busy thinking about his toes. He turns left and goes around the bed and into the bathroom. Oy. My chest does that thing with air worrying I left something. He goes to the sink and turns the water on. He bangs the glass against the faucet. *He chips more glasses.* It fills up with water. You can tell because the sound gets skinnier. He must be thirsty from the stuff he ate from MacDonald's. He'll be all bloated up now. Serves him right. What a dumb so-and-so. Why doesn't he care about his looks when I'm so careful about mine? He just lets it all hang out, bigger than sin. He was so skinny once, too. Now, he's brushing his teeth. How about that? I didn't know he brushed his teeth before bed. Well, at least he ain't a *total* slob.

He comes out into the bedroom, stops at the dresser and winds the clock, a nightly ritual. It must be after midnight. Can't remember what time it was when last I looked. What, no TV? No, he's pulling the covers back. Up, into the bed with a thud. The springs whine above me, the wood creaks when he moves. I wonder if he's using the bedspread. Or just pulling it off of him. I always fold it up and put it on the love seat on the other side of the bed. But he doesn't care if it gets all wrinkled up. I hear the weight of his body shift into the springs above my head. Groan. *Good thing wood is between us, or he would be sagging right into me. After he starts snoring, I can get comfortable.* Meantime, might as well relax. Nothing else is going to happen tonight, it appears.

The time seems to stretch out into eternity before I hear him snoring. He must have lain there thinking himself into a tizzy, like I do sometimes. Good thing he didn't fall right off to sleep. *Serves him right.* Listening to his snoring helps me relax into the pillow under my head.

By now I'm too tired to care if he hears me. All the adrenaline had me so hyped up, it leaves me drained.

In my dream...

I'm stuck in a coal bin. And every time I move, I get blacker. I have to be very careful I don't get caught sliding into the furnace with the coal going from the hopper. The coal is cold and scratchy. I just know I'll never get the black off of me. So I just forget about it and sit down in it. So dark and scary. And black. And dirty. And the air is stuffy and smells like putrid tar. I feel as though I should cough. Get the dirt out of my lungs. But I'm afraid if I cough, the coal might slide right into my mouth and down my throat. So I keep my mouth closed tightly, and try to forget about the dirt. It's rather cozy finally. The feel of the little pieces of coal against my skin. Every place on my body where it touches me, I feel it rub against me. Like little fingers. Oh, that feels so good. It's been so long since I felt fingers of any kind on my skin. Oh, keep doing that, I keep telling the little pieces of coal... when the squeak of the springs wake me, and I see the sunlight hitting the left side of the bed skirt.

Or, maybe it was his yawning that woke me. He must be stretching and pulling his back like he always does in the mornings. *It's Saturday and no alarm clock ringing! Wonder if he'll play golf?* For a long time, he lay there, turning and stretching. The bed moving above me sends dust into my nose. Must be he's lying in the middle. Funny. He usually hugs the edge, as far away from me as he can get. Helps him breathe, he says. Getting near him is a real trick. Ever since that day. It was like he came home a different man. I just gave up trying to get near him after that. But now that I'm not in there with him, he's sleeping in the middle. So, it must be me. All this time, it was me he was trying to get away from. *Well, I'm away from you now, Buster.* And I'm going to *stay* away. Just you wait and see!

Herschel dresses in his old jeans hung at the end of his closet. Guess he isn't going to play golf since he only wears them to cut grass, usually. The keys rattling and sliding down into his pocket lets me know he plans to go somewhere, otherwise he leaves them in his briefcase. He hates to carry them. He goes into the bathroom and turns on the faucet. While it runs, he takes a whiz. I'm always complaining about his letting all the water waste while he does his business — pee, shit, shower, shave, and brush, as he calls it — while he lets all that water go down the drain.

"Water's free. Got oceans full of it. I'm not worried. One of these days someone will figure out how to get the salt out of it. And then all this measuring will be for naught, you'll see," he said once.

Just as he walks past the end of the bed, I have to stifle a yawn.

In the kitchen he makes a regular racket with the bowls. Must be he's going to eat cereal. The only thing he can think of when he's alone. Doesn't know how to cook water even. And cereal is all that's left in the cupboard. Figure he must've got milk in that bag last night. The silver clangs as he pulls the chair out at the table. Plunk. The scraping noise of the spoon in the bowl. He usually slurps the milk at the end and drinks it out of the bowl. Like a country hog, he gulps down his food. No wonder he has such a big belly. The food never gets ground up. Just sits whole in his belly till something else pushes it on through. The dishwasher is pulled out, I hear. He walks to the garage door and stands there. For a long minute, he's just standing there. I can see the tips of his tennis shoes. They are filthy dirty. He won't let me buy him a new pair. "These are just fine," he says. Ragged in the toes, and the shoe strings have six knots in them. He must be looking at the bed. Wondering whether to make it or not, no doubt. *Bet he don't!* He turns and goes out the door into the garage.

The garage door goes up and eventually the lawn mower starts. *Hurray. If I hurry, I can actually go pee real quick while he's doing that.* My bladder's about to burst when I roll over to the edge and slide out on my stomach, on the bathroom side. Crawling to the bathroom, I can stand up in the windowless john. The seat is up again. *The bastard. How soon we forget.* Down with my slacks, I squat, ready to scoot. Can't take any chances. The toilet roll's getting thin. I listen for the sound of the mower. It's at the other end of the yard. With the windows shut and the air conditioning on, it's safe to flush. Standing up feels so good. I step past the door quickly to look in the mirror. My makeup is smeared all over my face. *What a mess you are, Ella!* The sound of the mower comes closer to the house.

Love 'N' Stuff

Haven't time to do this, I think, and hit the floor. But I'm thirsty so I jump back into the bathroom for a handful of water. The water feels so good on my face, splashing all over me. Better not touch the towel. Can't take the chance, I think, and hit the floor again and crawl back to the bed. This time I stay on my back and scoot under it.

I'm getting hungry. The mower goes out, away from the house, so I reach for the can of fruit cocktail. It's hard to open and when I finally pop it, the darn thing tips and spills all over my chest. I have to roll my head to the side to sip the juice. Finally, I open my mouth and slop it in like a food grinder. *Boy that tastes good*. The empty can and lid goes into the baggie, in the kitchen space. It doesn't make any noise and keeps odor down. Rolling over to one side, I wonder just how long this is going to last? What am I really going to get out of this? I start thinking about how I'm going to come home. *While he's here? Or while he's at work?* Don't know yet what to do.

The mower running into the garage cuts off. That was a quick cut. He must have only cut the front. He's very particular how the house looks to the neighbors. He could care less how it looks in the back, to me.

Next I hear the edger seesawing under the side windows. It hits the house in spots. Warning him about nicking up the paint does absolutely no good. "Oh, who the hell sees that?" he'd say.

"I see it, and it looks dirty," I say. "And if I see it, someone else surely will. Besides, it'll start peeling."

He just shakes his head at me. "Sometimes I wonder if you're from this planet" he says. "Heaven ain't gonna be clean enough for you. You'll probably have St. Peter in the shower before you're up there ten minutes."

The edger stops and I hear him stomp his feet in the

garage. He usually forgets and tracks into the house on this white carpet. The phone starts ringing just as the doorknob turns. I hear his footsteps and see the grass falling on the carpet as he runs around the bed to catch the phone.

"Hello. Hello?" he says. "No, she hasn't. No sign of her. I did what you told me. But I can't tell what she wears and what she don't. You know I travel a lot and I don't pay much attention to that stuff. What do you mean?... No, she don't have many friends that I know of. She had one friend she was thick with who moved, to Alabama, I think. ... No. I don't know her last name. She got married, that's why she moved. Yeah. I could. Let me look for it and see if there is anything in it. Haven't the first notion where to look though. No, it's not in the telephone drawer; I already looked there. But I'll check around. Maybe in the desk. I'll call you if I find anything."

He slams the phone down with a bang. He is really mad. Next thing he'll be tearing the bed apart and emptying the dresser drawers out all over the place. His dirty tennis shoes still all full of grass are stuck flat on the floor and he isn't moving. *Wonder what he's doing?* The ticking of the clock is so loud, it is all I can hear. The quietness is frightening. All I need to do now is sneeze. *That would be a trip.* The giggles want to bubble out of me at the thought of seeing his face. I can see all the grass he has dropped all over the nice white carpet. *How will I ever get it clean?* When I slide out I'll get it all over me and squish it all over the rest of the floor. And you know he'll never vacuum. It'd stay there till the carpet turned forever-green. Have to use the other side of the bed, right in front of the door. *Be careful, that's risky.* He is still sitting there.

Finally, he picks up the phone again. The cord gets wrapped around the bottom corner of the table. "Damn,"

Love 'N' Stuff

he says. It *is* aggravating, having to unhook it for the phone to reach your ear. Almost bought one of those new walkie jobs, but thought better of it. *How could I hear him if he was walking all over the house?* He's punching numbers. *Quiet, heart.* Herschel says, "Yes. St Petersburg. Yes. Do you have the telephone number of Dottie, Dorothy, I guess, Fryer? I think it's near the water. I don't know. Yes. Sounds like it." He's pulling the drawer out, fishing for a pencil. Ten-to-one he's using the cover of the phone book. He'll write on anything: tablecloth, napkins, the table, newspaper, book. "Thank you. Do I have to dial a one first, from here?... Okay. Thanks. He lays the phone down and turns toward the window over the bedside table. You can see the street through the shrubs sometimes, when they are trimmed. He must have the phone in his hand, the new Trim-line, so he can dial it standing up. "Yeah, Dottie? Have you heard from Ella, by any chance?... Not since last week? Well, I don't really know yet. She seems to have just disappeared into thin air. It's the damndest thing. I know you and her gab sometimes when I'm on a trip, and I wondered if you'd talked to her much lately?... Was that the day I missed my flight? How did she sound? Did she say anything unusual... or sound funny? Well, except being pissed at me, what else is new, huh?... What makes you say that? How you mean, depressed?... Oh, she always complains, I think. She's done that since the day I met her, only then it was about not wanting to get pregnant. You know. Different stuff, but the same way... Yeah, I went over to the station. They didn't want to take the missing persons report yet. They say quite often people take off, and then come back after they get tired, or hungry. Yeah, scared. But where could she go without her purse? No wallet, no ID, no money, it's all here. I can't even find any clothes missing. It's as if she just up and vanished.... Yeah, right... While in the shower... Just like her favorite movie. Ha ha.... It scared her so she wouldn't take a shower for weeks.... No, I know it isn't funny... I'm *not* laughing, Dottie. It's just so strange. I think the cops think I did something to her. That's what pisses me to a fare-thee-well. You go ask for help and they turn it all on you. What's a guy *supposed* to do?... Oh, yeah, *have* to go. Just overnight. I've been trying to nail this guy for months, and finally, *he* calls *me*. The ol' man would send somebody else, and then where would I be, come... Yeah. I realize that, Dottie. But I ain't taking any chances. Remember Artie?... Artie who? you say. See what I mean... I'll be in to pick up my plane ticket and per diem money. Hell, maybe she'll show up while I'm gone. Three days should tell it. At least then the cops will process it, put it in the computer. I just don't know what to think. I just never thought anything like this would ever happen to me. You know, as pissed as I get at her... Right. I didn't want nothin' to happen." His voice gets soft.

Is the slob getting a conscience? Feeling bad? Just *feeling* would be good. The cops are giving him a bad time, maybe. I gotta think this one through.

Herschel's saying to Dottie, "No, no. There's nothing you can do, anyone can do. I got all these joints I can eat at around the clock. I'll manage. Yeah, I'll just have to take it all to the cleaners. Do they do shirts, do you know?... Oh, no, I couldn't have you do that, Dottie. Gosh, I owe you my *life* now. Thanks anyhow. I'll see you Monday before I leave for the airport. Yeah. Thanks. Take care. Yeah, I'll be here, I guess. Maybe I'll play golf tomorrow, though. Not much I can do just sitting here, waiting. Later." The phone cord gets caught again, this time he yanks it a good one, and the phone base falls on the floor. He bends down and yanks it with a "Damn," and slams it on the table. He turns around and heads back out towards the garage.

I wonder if he sees the grass he just dropped off his shoes? I reach out and pick it up one blade at a time and pile it into little bunches. Back into the kitchen corner of the space, I'm looking for a Baggie, when I hear the broom in the garage. *Maybe he has promise.* The pile of grass almost fills up the sandwich size Ziplock. Under the bed-skirt, I look to see if there is any more I can reach before he comes back and notices it. Trying to reach out with both my hands at the same time, one acting as a broom the other the dustpan, I'm doing contortions on my side, hurting my hip. My left foot, that cramps, grabs all of a sudden. Must be too tight a squeeze. I rest and try to relax my foot for a minute, roll over on my back with my right arm still sticking out from under the bed when the garage door opens. Back under the bed, I heave a sigh in relief.

In the laundry room, sounds like he's stripping down. All that noise. The keys get tossed on top of the dryer with a clang. Next, I hear the washer. Must be doing a load. Another *first* for him, despite the notes I taped over the washer. How to separate stuff. *Bet he ignores them and throws everything in together.* Oh, well, bleach can fix most things.

I see his bare feet walk past the end of the bed. He stops at his dresser and pulls out something. Underwear, maybe. He grabs the clicker and turns on the ball game. The Phillies playing Cincinnati. He hates Cincinnati. *It was Toni's favorite team. He met a girl from there, once, and ever since he rooted for the Reds.* "One strike... another swing at a high rise ball. McCarthy is a new young rookie." I shut off my ears. The sound of sports makes my stomach ache for my Toni. My mind wandered just then, and I forgot to pay attention to what Herschel was doing, when I hear the shower door slam and the shower start.

He's whistling Bill Bailey... and then he starts singing some crazy words he makes up as he goes along, like he used to do to Toni, when he was little, "Ella, my baby... Won't you come home, sweet Ella... Won't you come home... I cried the whole night long... I'll do the cookin', honey, I'll wash the clothes... I'll even trim my toe... oes... s... Won't you come home, my baby... won't you come home... I'll pay the rent... I'll even get... a maid or houseboy for you yet... Ella won't you please come home."

The TV says, "Do you know where your child is tonight? A family that prays together, stays together. The church of the Latter Day Saints." *Is that Mormon, or 7th day? Or Jehovah's Witness? I never could keep them all straight.*

Herschel is still whistling, *Bill Bailey*. I can see just a foot of the bathroom doorway. He's standing in front of the sink, drying himself. His feet leave the floor, one at a time. The towel falls on the floor; he leaves it, sits down on it. If I got closer to the holes in the islet, I could almost see his face. He's picking at his big toenail, soft from the hot water. He says that's the best time to tear them off. I see his white tush as he bends over his toes. "Ouch, you sonofa..." Must've tore into the quick. When I ask him, why don't you use clippers? He just grunts, and shrugs his shoulders.

"... a fast ball... over the plate... strike one. McCarthy is one of those young draftees that kept the bench warm for several seasons, till he got his chance in the Oriole's game last season. Been showing his stuff in this line up."

Herschel stands up with a grunt. And lets rip roaring gas roll out like a motor boat. "For you, Ella..." he says and lets another one.

It's getting hot and stuffy under here. With the hot flashes especially. Sometimes I feel like an oven turned on Broil for one long minute. My skin turns red, and Herschel notices it if he happens to be looking at me, which is unusual in itself.

He clears his throat, and bellows, "Ella, my darling, Ella my girl... We danced the whole night lo... on... ng . g . g." He walks past the end of the bed, around to the other side, to his own closet. Opens it, and I see his red sweat pants hit the floor. He shoves them back into the corner, out of sight. His feet are still bare. He sticks one into the closet into a rubber thong. And then the other. His closet door closes with a squeak. He walks around the bed to the TV side, takes a jump and lands up on top of the bed with a crash, the thongs flying. I feel the springs bounce down on the wooden board separating us, the coils twisting and turning.

The house is getting into a big mess. I didn't figure he'd need to clean for a couple weeks. By then I'd be back home. Vacuuming might be the way he'd catch me, his one house chore. Sometimes he'd stick the hose under the bed, just for good measure. I could see he never really got any dust that way. The hose would twist, and I'd explain to him how to do it right, show him how to keep the head of the cleaner flat so it would pick up under the bed. But he just shakes his head. "You and St. Peter. He's in for a shock."

Herschel's flipping channels again. Bowling from Dayton Finals Championship. He left that on for awhile. I like bowling. We used to bowl a lot, before Toni. Now, he's always sleeping or doing a crossword puzzle. Ball games even put him to sleep. He'll be snoring before long, bowling is so quiet. Nope. Back to the ball game. There must not have been too much competition in the bowler scores. Without a fight, it ain't interesting, he says. Even on

Jeopardy. He roots for the one with the most money. I never even noticed there was a game going on for money. I just was interested in hearing the right answers, *if you can figure out how to think backwards.* But Herschel gets into all that competition crap. The springs are squeaking as he rolls over to the other side of the bed. He's hanging on the edge, like he does when I get into bed with him. He likes to let his arms fall down and let his hands just hang. I see the tips of his fingers bend, first close, and then relax. Must be doing exercises of some kind. The sound of the ticking clock and the monotonous sound of the ball game mix into my head making me very sleepy. *Just a cat nap... for a minute...*

Through the blur of white snow, I see myself in the mirror... smeary makeup. I should wash it, clean my face. Too dirty, I think, as I sink into that other world...

I'm going up the stairs again. It's the same house; I live upstairs. The stairwell is echoe-y. Inside the house, I look out the windows. Where is everyone? It is so quiet. Next, I'm in the back yard in the same house. There is another house in the back, in the back yard of the one I live in. It blocks my view of the garbage can across the way. Down the alley I hear the ragman yelling, "Rags... Rags..." I feel terror inside and run back up the stairs. I am little and my short little legs take forever. Into the closet I scram. Way back into the dark, where it is safe, where the rag-man can't get me. In the dark, all alone, no one can find me. Not even nasty ol' cousin Carl. He won't be able to drag me by the hair to the curb, like he keeps saying, where the rag-man will come and stop his horse with his wagon full of junk. Carl says, See there, he can take you away in there and no one will ever find you. In the corner, I huddle in the dark in the hopes that the rag-man is gone. Gone. Gone.

The sound of snoring wakes me up. It is dark. The nightly news is on TV. My back is aching from being on it too long, but I'm afraid to move very much. Starting at the bottom of my toes, I begin exercising. Tighten. Relax. Tighten. Relax. I move upward to my calves. Tighten. Relax. My thighs. Tighten. Relax. I get to the pelvic area, pinching my buttocks tightly together. Then relax. This forces the air out, up into my chest cavity. The air goes deep into my middle. To be quiet, I have to be careful to breathe very slowly.

Herschel is only inches from me. *I wonder if my aura is overlapping him?* What a silly thought. Auras. I don't know much about them except what I saw in a movie once. During the art festival, a psychic showed up at the mall. She told me I had a purple aura. *The highest one was white, same as Jesus and Ghandi had.* When I told Toni about it, he asked me how much I paid her? Twenty dollars, I said. He laughed. "Yeah, Ma, You got a purple aura alright. If you'd have paid her fifty dollars, you probably could have gotten a white one!" I didn't really believe in them after that. Everybody's got a gimmick. *Wonder if I could get a gimmick?* I wish I was smarter and understood more about life and things, sometimes I feel so dumb. *When your kid knows more about auras then you do.* It must be his generation. But this psychic said that auras were as old as man. That Jesus believed in them too. Wonder why it never mentioned them in the Bible? Or maybe they were in there somewhere. *How would I know?* At least I don't ever remember ever hearing about them in Sunday School as a kid.

In my exercises, I'm up to my pelvic. I get stuck in my pelvic every time I do them. It is where I start deep breathing and feel my *uttermost parts*. Oy, what names people concoct for that part of their anatomy. *Weewee* was what I called it until I was five. Before that, I remember calling it my *Tinker*. Where did I get *that* name? Tinker. Maybe I was trying to say "tinkle," but got mixed up. I was always getting mixed up when I was little. And no one ever would explain to me where I got off the right track. But it was always somewhere in the thinking stage, before it actually came out in words. *Wonder, do other people have thought problems like I did?* My Tinker was feeling very sensitive at the moment. It was no doubt because I had to pee. Now that is a real fancy word. Pee. I can just see it in a jar, at the doctor's office. It is burning to come out of me right this minute. And Herschel was still snoring like a buzz saw. The TV was still blasting. *How could he stand it so loud?* Back to my lower regions. Pull in the buttocks, suck in the middle, let the air out of the chest cavity, breathe deeply, let the lower regions relax. *O god, I could go for sex right now. After I pee.* Oh, god. Now, what?

It is times like these I would reach over to Herschel when he was sound asleep and start with him. Sometimes it would work. Sometimes he'd pull my hand away and turn over and sleep on. *Wonder what he'd do if I did that right now?* He'd shit. Think I was back from the grave or something. Then it would be that necro-thing, with a corpse. How yuckie. Maybe he'd like that. Never could figure out what he really likes, never says much. He acts like that part of him don't exist – the unspoken area of life.

My buttocks are tightening again. *That feels so good.* Up to my rib cage, I can feel my breasts expand when the air fills up the lungs. *Wonder how much he misses me not having big breasts?* I always felt a little left out in that department. But you know, some of those big-chested dames ended up looking fat as they got older, like one big boob. So I'm glad, in a way, I had less to start with. At least you can still tell where my waist line ends and the boobs begin.

The phone rings and Herschel makes a startled noise, "Oh. Uh uh." Sounded like he might be sharing my same thoughts about sex. *Wonder if that is really so?* They say after you live together so long, your thoughts run together and you almost know what the other is thinking. The phone blasts the third time. *Why doesn't he answer it?* I want to poke him and say, "Answer the phone, Herschel. Are you gonna let it ring all day?"

He says, "Yeah, Hello.... No, uh uh, she ain't here. Who is this?... You're kidding, when? Thursday? You saw her Thursday? Here? What was she like, I mean." I feel the bed move like he's rolling over to the edge. His feet are hanging over the edge. "What time exactly was this? You say she told you to come back next week? What kind of stuff? Clothes? She was giving you stuff for the homeless? Oh, yeah, I guess she has it around here somewhere. What kind of stuff did she say she was giving you?... Well, let me tell you, I ain't seen her since Thursday night, well Friday morning when I left for work.... She's not here. Gone, disappeared. I think the police might be interested in talking with you. Would you mind giving me your name, is it Jay? Hello. Hello. Sonofabitch. Hello. Hello." He slams down the phone. The TV blasts, *A Tampa man was found stuffed in the trunk of an abandoned car. His body looked to be dead for about three weeks. The remains can be identified at the county coroner's office. That's about all there is. And now to the weather."* See, I knew it was safer under the bed.

"Jesus," Herschel says under his breath. He's getting

up. He flicks the channel to another ball game. The NY Yankees are playing the Baltimore Orioles. He flips the channel to some pretty orchestra music. I love that. *Leave that on*. He leaves it on for a minute as though he hears me. Wonder, would it work? Maybe I could practice thinking for him. *Herschel, go look in the front closet. Herschel, go look in the front closet. There's a bag there, Herschel."*

He gets up. I watch as his feet sink into the carpet. His bony toes. He goes into the bathroom. The water runs, he makes noises with it, gargling. Oh god, he isn't getting a sore throat is he? Oh god. No. Now what? He gargles some more, and then spits. Are you gonna clean the sink now, Herschel? *Clean the sink Herschel. At least rinse it, okay?* He's taking a whiz. What a loud whizzer he is. There isn't anything wrong with his *stream,* like they say in the doctor movies. The toilet flushes. He is yawning very loudly; I think he's bored, *hope so* at least. "Oh shit," he says.

Now what?

He stands in the doorway of the bathroom, up against the door frame and rubs his back. It is a habit he has. He says it feels good. But it doesn't work for me. My butt sticks out too far, the way I'm built. I can't get close enough, he says. He walks over to the bed, and sticks his feet into the rubber thongs. Flip-flop flip-flop flip-flop, he walks past the bed and out of the bedroom, into the hall.

Around the corner, into the kitchen, the refrigerator opens. "Shit," he says. He sounds disgusted about something. Probably he's hungry and hates to have to fix it. He comes back into the bedroom. He opens my closet. The zipper in my handbag goes rip. He's getting change, it falls into his pockets. The dollars I left in there purposely. *Probably took them too.* The purse hits the back of the closet shelf. He is mad, I can tell, the way he is throwing

Love 'N' Stuff

things with all the "Shit" comments. He goes over to his closet. I can't see higher than his ankles, but I don't think he's wearing anything on top. He runs around the house in his birthday all the time. I get mad at him and run and get a towel so he won't stink up the furniture. *Stink in furniture is impossible to get out.* He gets so mad. "For Christ sakes. Can't a guy just live?" So I'm *sure* he is wearing nothing now. That would be like him. All the things I don't like him to do. The hangers click. Must be, he's going out. *Good. Then I can go pee.* He goes back to my closet again. Out comes my purse again. It hits the bed with a loud thud. "God damn bitch," he says. "Shit." He must be looking for money. *Write a damn check, you ignorant jerk.* Oy. Sometimes I wonder how he made it to fifty years of age. What a dumbkin. When we make love, I call him that. Sounds as though he's looking really good this time through my wallet, the zipper on the inside little pocket, where I keep my ID and driver's license. *What is he looking for?* Must think I've got money hid like I used to, before I lost my wallet, with over five-hundred bucks in it. That was the last time I hid money. "See, if you'd a left it in the bank, you'd still have it," he said.

His feet flip-flop to the door. I hear keys rattling in his pocket, so he must have clothes on. He must be reaching for them as he opens the door. The door shuts loudly, and I hear the car door slam. Sounds like it is *my* car. Oh, that was it; he was going for *my* keys. Gonna check out my car. The mileage is put down in my new (for disappearing) wallet. That way I can see how far he drove. I've been thinking about starting a mileage check on *his* car. But I never get a chance. He keeps his car locked, even in the garage. I did have an extra set of keys. But he put them in the fire-proof safe box. He has the combination written down in his little black book. For emergencies. He might see me getting into it, so I pretty much leave his car alone. But he helps himself to my keys anytime he wants to check out the engine. So he's out "checking the engine" when I hear the garage door go down.

Over to the edge, I wiggle out from under the bedskirt. The TV is blasting away, still. He never turns the darn thing off. It drives me crazy. *Don't dare touch it now, either.* He left it on the ball game. At least it lets you sleep, the ball game does. I get up on my knees, but I stay still. *Gosh. Oh, gee. How long can I take this?* Like a cat, I stretch. Yawn. Up on my feet feels good. I remember the window. It's dark. The TV light might give a shadow, so I stoop down real low and slip into the bathroom. This time I pull the seat down. I'm just too stiff to squat. My legs would not hold me up. It feels so good, I don't want to hurry, but I better. He might just have gone for tomorrow's morning paper. He does that. Buys another paper, for the crossword puzzle.

Hunger. Fruit again. That might not be such a bad idea. Good for the gas. *I'll get you yet, Hershey Baby!* The toilet paper is well past the middle. If I get another roll out, he'll surely see it. Well, I have to use toilet paper. I just gotta. A body has limits to what it can put up with. I'm feeling pretty low, just now, wishing I'd never done this fool thing. *What if I just wait for him and just tell him?* I toy with this for all of one minute. Naw. He's too mad right now. *I gotta wait for him to feel really bad for me.* I pull my slacks up and zip them shut. *They are on the loose side. Ain't bad, huh?* One way to lose weight, not that I needed to. *Want to lose weight, just move under your bed!* Wonder how many fools would try it? I turn the faucet on real slow and reach for the water. It feels so good on my face. Boy. *Sometimes*

Love 'N' Stuff 91

little things do mean a lot. Yeah, they really do. Some water, I drink out of my hand. It makes me more thirsty, so I drink another fist full. *Better watch that. Never know when you'll get to pee next.*

I hate to have to get back under already. I could wait for the garage door; I always have enough time. I climb up on the side of the bed. The TV throws a light on me. If someone was outside the window, could they see me through the curtains? The heavy draperies cover most of the window. As I lay back on the bed, I think how good this feels, just for a short minute. The garage door startles me and I jump up with my heart pounding like hell. Like a panther, I hit the floor and scoot my legs under the bed all in one swosh. I'm in up to my neck when the door opens. Twisting my head to get it under the bed, I hit my nose. *Turn your head sideways next time!*

Herschel is flip-flopping into the bedroom. Oh god, I'm beginning to panic. The bed-skirt is stuck to my shoulder. Quickly, I smooth it down and am caught in a crooked turn; the kink in my neck hurts like hell. Herschel comes around the bed and turns the TV off. *Thank god. At least I can have a minute's peace.* I'm winded from rushing, but I hold my breath in. Herschel flip-flops back out of the room. The kitchen chair slides, papers crunch. Food, and a crossword puzzle... *like the back of my hand.* The clock's ticking. Ticktock. Ticktock. Ticktock. God, how empty this house is.

The phone rings. He gets it in the kitchen so I can barely hear. He must be walking into the family room with it. Sometimes he stretches the cord so far it looks like it is losing its curl. I tell him he'll ruin the cord. "Get another, for christsake," he says. He's talking a long time. I can't hear a word. Back in the kitchen, I can hear him say, "Yeah. That's what I been thinking. She must've had something going....

Well, she ain't got any money in her wallet like she usually does, I mean, she never goes without a couple hundred tucked away. I looked through the whole damn thing and she ain't got *anything* but a few ones and a five. That ain't like my wife, Harry. She's always afraid the bank is gonna close down and leave her with no money. A thing she has about banks, from her old man.... I wonder the same.... You think so? But Harry, listen to me, what makes you think that? Huh? I know she's a dumb dame, but not *that* dumb.... Oh, okay, I see what ya mean. Okay. What do I look for?... She don't use nothing like that.... Hey, she's *over* that, she don't use nothing no more.... Okay, I already looked in her drawers. All her shit is in there, man, *all* of it. I can't know what this dame uses. Who gives a shit, you know? I mean, do you know everything Mandy uses? Bu— ull shi—it. That's all I gotta say. Bullshit. Well, I ain't thinking like that. I think she has a friend somewhere. This guy calls and says he was picking some clothes up for the homeless. And when I ask him his name, to talk to the police, he hangs up. That makes me wonder. You know? I mean, there's a guy for every dame, right? And, hey, she ain't fat or ugly. She's just dumb, and a cleaning bitch. She's so clean her pants don't even stink, I think. Not for long anyhow. Ha ha."

This golfing buddy — who I never yet did see, just talk to on the phone — is *some* creep. Herschel is steamed already *before* this guy calls. He get's quiet for a long time, listening, and saying, "Yeah... Yeah... Okay, Harry. I'll keep you posted. Naw. I ain't thinking like that. Not yet, anyhow. Wait till the three days is up and then we'll see what the cops say. Just gotta wait it out."

He slams the receiver down and comes back into the bedroom. He walks fast this time and heads straight for the

Love 'N' Stuff

bathroom. Every drawer in there he opens, rummaging. I can tell he's making one big, grand mess in my drawers. Makeup, fingernail polish. He opens the medicine cabinet. He moves every bottle. *Nothing is missing. Nothing. I know I got him. Thanks, Harry. Friends like you, my husband needs!* Must at least wonder have I got another somebody? Is he mad? Because he has to take care of himself. That's the only reason. He hasn't got a jealous bone, not before Harry called anyhow. How about these male crumb bums. They think just because *they* do it, we gotta.

Herschel's back in the kitchen, at the table. Back to numb-nuts pacifier, his crossword. The paper bag rattles again, must be eating something. Donuts. I won't ever let him have donuts. Especially for dinner. And that's when he likes them. For dinner with milk. What a dumbkin. *I'm missing looking at his beautiful, sun-tanned face.*

The night is horrible with his sleeping on and off. He's rolling and tossing all over the bed, keeping me awake. He slept too long this afternoon. So did I. Wish I could get out from under without him hearing. What am I gonna do all night now? Couple times, he flips the TV back on. First time, it's *Saturday Night Live*. He hates that show. A bunch of jerks getting paid for jerking off, he always says. He flips it off. The night drags on. I'm trying to plan how I'm going to reappear. I haven't figured it out yet. *Too tired to think about this, and I feel sick. Oh, god, what if I throw up?*

Thoughts so strange come into mind... I am nowhere, going nowhere, am I really nothing? *Just a lump?* I don't know this person inside... Sick, yucky sick, I doze off...

In a small box, an assortment of pills are all mixed together. Usually I can tell by the feel of each one which it is. Bonine for a sick stomach could make me sleepy also. They're easy to feel in the dark because they are big and flat, ready to chew. I have a jug of water with a bent straw in it so I only have to turn my head slightly to drink out of it. I have to be careful to not hit the bed board or the drawer slots above. Sure as all get-out he would be able to feel that. But I couldn't take a chance and start puking, that would be the end of me. I turn to one side. My hip is below the middle of the bed so I have plenty clearance. I feel along the carpeted floor. The pill box is a flip-top and easy to get into, an old sewing pin box that must be twenty years old. My finger is on the flip-top button when he rolls over right directly above me. I can't risk his hearing the box open, something I forgot to check out. I'm lying still, waiting for my stomach to settle. Not enough to eat, must be. I really need to eat. Something dry. A cracker. But all I have is some short pretzel sticks. The little thin ones. They sort of melt in your mouth. But they are on the other corner of the space. I'm stuck now, until he starts snoring. Just have to lie here and breathe, breathe, breathe. From my surgeries, I know deep breathing helps the nausea. *Inhale in the nose, exhale through the mouth.* Finally, I pull the waistband of my loose slacks down below my belly button. That helps a little.

Suddenly, the bed starts to move. It is loud and squeaky above me. *Oh, my god, he isn't. He isn't! Oh, my god!* The springs are making noise now just over my head. He is really going at it, when suddenly he takes a flying leap, up and out of bed, and runs to the bathroom. *He's cussing, I know, I can just hear him in my ear. That is when he bites my lip, my ear... just before is when he acts as though he knows I'm alive, a part of him. He feels for me all over. The only time he touches my skin, ever. Only then. Oh god, and*

I'm missing it. Oh god, why did I do this?

The tears well up into my eyes. Oh, god, I can't cry. That would fill up my head and then I'd really be a mess. I roll over onto my back so the tears will go into both ears, instead of just one. Maybe they can drain out through my throat. Maybe. Sometimes it works. But not usually. I get a stuffed head for a week after I cry. It's my sinuses.

I hear the toilet flush, finally. Oh god, I'm sorry baby. I love you so. Why do you make me do such stupid things just to get you to let me know you know I'm here? I get a little mad thinking these kinds of thoughts. Then I hear the toilet seat go down with a bang. He is sitting? Oh god. He must really be upset. He gets the crud when he is upset. Sometimes he has to get right up and take one, after sex. It really upsets him. What a bummer of a mother he must've had. Poor guy, why I bought him that new book, *The Joy of Sex: A Gourmet Guide to Love Making*. But he was too embarrassed to even look past the pictures, just put it in the bookcase.

I hear the toilet paper roll turning. *Oh, god. Don't use it up, Sweetie. What'll I do? Why didn't I think about that?* How could I forget such an important thing? The toilet flushes again. Sounds like he is at the sink to turn the light on. I can see his shadow moving on the bed skirt. He must be doing something at the sink. What? Looking in the mirror? His shadow turns a little, but he is very quiet. I hear the comb and brush set. The comb? He's combing his hair? *Oh god. What next?* I hear the water faucet. The glass is filling up with water. The water is still running and he is brushing his teeth. Spits. Gargles. Fills the glass up with water again. *Boy he must be thirsty. Eating all that salty stuff that I don't ever let him have. Serves him right?* He'll have bags under his eyes now. Maybe that's what he's looking at. He's always afraid he is going to get thyroid problems like his family all had. But I tell him, "It's just salt, Baby. Don't worry. You just eat what I tell you and you'll never be sick from anything. It is all that junk you eat when I'm not around."

I'm getting a stiff neck from lying on my back with my head turned in a half-screw off my body. I turn my head back and look up into the dark. The bed above me smells like wool, or something. Some kind of material I can't place. A funny smell. First time I noticed it. *God, I'm hungry.* I hear the light switch go off in the bathroom. He rubs his feet together before he gets into bed. *Haven't heard him do that in a long time.* It was something his mother taught him to do because he liked to go barefoot as a kid. *Thought he stopped doing that after I told him it wasn't necessary.* If he goes barefoot, I make him take showers now.

When we were first married he hated taking showers. He kept telling me he was allergic to the water. "It always makes my head fill up with shit," he'd say.

I would just laugh and tell him that was a big lie.

He had an embarrassed giggle. We were living in that two-story townhouse with the bathroom upstairs. He would watch TV until the very last minute. That night I knew he needed a shower something fierce, so I started in on him. He was flat on the couch in his boxers. I went over to him and started to pull them off. "Come on now, Hersh. Time for a shower like a good little boy."

That made him real antsy. "Hey, get outta here; leave my underwear alone."

"Aw, Sweetie. Is you embarrassed? How come you're embarrassed, huh? I seen you before."

Then he really turns red. His shorts are almost to his hips and he is holding on to them with one hand and

Love 'N' Stuff

pushing me away with the other. Somehow I manage to get my head under his hand and stick my tongue into his belly button. *It's an outzie, unlike my own, which is an inzie.*

That did it. He gets his hand on the top of my head and shoves it clean off him, and grabs his shorts and pulls them back up, and jumps off the couch. He is still red and embarrassed, I can tell, but I think he is just acting mad. He runs to the stairs and up he goes, two at a time. Next I hear the bathroom door shut and the shower is going.

I run up after him and stand by the door to make sure he gets in. He always tells me how he used to turn the shower on and stand outside it to fool his mother. *Well I ain't his mother, and I ain't gonna be fooled.*

The soap hits the tub, and he cusses, "Damn."

Now he has to wash his hair too, I'm thinking, if he had to bend over to pick up the soap. Good thing. I want to go in there and sit down on the john, and watch him, his beautiful body. I want to so badly. But I know he's already a little pissed at me, so I better leave him alone. *He is getting clean. That's enough for one night.* Why does he hate to get clean, I wonder? I know I stall and put off taking my clothes off for a bath. *Do you suppose it is the getting naked part that is so upsetting?*

All of this so long ago, and I'm thinking about it so hard, I barely notice that Herschel is above me, sawing logs like thunder in a lumber mill. I have to smile to myself. My Herschel. *My sweet baby. I love you honey; please love me back.*

Please, God, please, if you never give me another thing in the whole world, just please make my husband love me again. I've waited so long, so long. Please, God.

When I was little, I would always look out the window at night at the stars and say: I wish, I wish upon a star that someone will look at me, into my eyes, and say to me, Ella, dear heart, you are special, or maybe just *see* me.

That other world that always awaits me in sleep, I'm there again, driving a car. I come to a four-way stop. There is a bunch of commotion. The cops are looking for somebody. It surely isn't me, is it? It seems I have a long ways to go on this trip. The map shows where I've been and where I'm going. If I hurry, I might be able to get to the southern part, of some state (is it Arizona?) before winter comes and freezes me in. Cops come over to the car, one on each side, a flashlight in each window. Yikes, I'm so scared. My heart is not going to live through this, getting caught.

One cop says, "Lady, you find a body anywhere?"

I say, "What? A body? You think I look like a lady cop?"

They laugh.

I laugh.

Somehow the joking gets me out of the jam because they flag me on with their flash lights.

Next, I am on a very dark road, no lights anywhere. It hits me like a bolt, What body? I start wondering if it's in the trunk of my car? I want to get out and look, but in the dark, I'm really too scared.

Waking up, I have a weird, guilty feeling, as though I really *had* a dead body hid, someone that I killed. *But who?*

Herschel is still snoring away. I have to get some food into my stomach. Maybe that's why I'm having bad dreams. Or is it from a full stomach you get bad dreams? Can't really remember any more. I begin to slide sideways very carefully and reach for the Baggie in my little, very little kitchen. I slide my fingernail into the zipper-lock. For some reason, it doesn't want to give. Finally, it snaps open. I feel for the pretzel sticks, several, and close the baggie very quickly so they don't fall out. I am careful like that. Rarely do I have accidents of things spilling. Not since I was a kid and spilt that white shoe-polish. My ma yelled and yelled. "Don't you have any sense," she 'd say. "You put the top on immediately, right when you finish. That way nothing will get spilt." So I would wet the cloth with shoe polish, screw the top back on tight, then when all the polish was used up on my rag, I'd have to open up the bottle again. But it was better than getting yelled at twice for spilling. Once it got all over the coffee table. And my ma had to get some special stuff to clean it up. Almost ruined the table — at least she kept saying it did.

I put the pretzels into my mouth, all three of them, and closed my lips around them so they wouldn't make noise when I bit into them. Of course, if I just let them sit there in my mouth long enough, they'd almost melt. But I'm too hungry to wait. Instead, I bite into a big chunk of them. *Boy, they taste good. Maybe I'll get three more of them. Once a person starts eating, you find out how hungry you really are.* I could've managed, until I took that first bite. Wonder why? *Now, I'm thirsty.* To reach the water, I have to slide another foot. It's right next to the flashlight.

Maybe I could read awhile, I'm thinking. To do that, though, I have to stay on the other end, where the shade blocks the light. But Herschel's snoring anyhow, so I reach and stretch real hard, and get the light into my hand. It's one of those big flashlights, one you might use to flag down traffic when your tire goes flat. It was ten bucks. This experiment was adding up. *That's something I could do sometime, when I'm bored, add up everything.* Right now I should try out reading, while he is snoring.

Gone With The Wind. It was so long ago that I read it and loved Scarlet because I know just how she feels. Maybe it will give me a hint on what to do about Hersh. A ways into it, before she really believes there is going to be a war, I have a page turned down. I'm trying to get comfortable and let the book lay on my chest. I put my knees up. That always rests my back. Sometimes I turn on my side to get relief. But then I have trouble holding the book open, so I start out on my back. Scarlet sounds like she has the same kind of trouble I have, same kind of hurt feelings all the time. Reading about her wakes up all the fight in me. Seems as if the women all have so much to do to keep things going. *Why is that,* I wonder? It doesn't seem as though men have changed much either since those bad-off days.

Why do us women always have to be the one to do all that taking-care-of stuff? It just isn't fair. I get so tired of having to worry whether Herschel is full, warm, clean, happy. *Isn't happy a stupid word? What does it mean anyhow?* Happy is when you get what you want. But what you want is never the same two minutes in a row. Just like myself. One minute I want to make Herschel suffer. The next minute I want to hold him in my arms and make all his hurts and upsets go away. *Now, which one would really make me happy?* Oy. What else can I do? Such a quandary of things I'm stuck with to worry about. And I never seem to get any answers. Take this experiment, for instance. I ask myself, *Just what the hell are you going to get from it?* If he never finds out I wasn't really gone, then maybe it'll work. Just maybe. Have to wait and see what happens tomorrow. Suddenly, I realize I have only read two sentences, so I close the book. *It is just not my night to think about somebody else's war, I have enough with one of my own.*

Love 'N' Stuff

Off goes the flashlight, and I shove it back into the corner, where a place was made for it. Wonder if my feet are ever going to get warm? Can't reach them to rub them without hitting the board between me and the box springs. Thinking about my toes reminds me of my exercises, where I start at the toes. *Tighten toes. Wiggle, wiggle, let them feel as though they are so loose they will fall off, like Raggedy Ann toes. Be a Raggedy Ann all over.* I close my eyes and let the dark be a cover that stretches over me. I feel red and white wash all over me as I listen to the ticking of the clock. Ticktock. Ticktock. Ticktock. Ticktock.

Sun hitting the bed skirt wakes me up. I try to see my watch. *Ten o'clock.* I listen to see if Herschel is still sleeping, too. I hear nothing. I can't move, and if I don't, I feel I am going to die. My back feels like it has a knife stuck into it, so I start stretching all my muscles. *Wish the phone would ring so I'd know where he is. Now what? Where is he?* Who would call him on Sunday morning? Toni? Oh god, I keep forgetting Toni can't call. Why can't I remember that? I still think about him being my sweet Toni. Oy. Maybe Herschel's friend, Harry? Maybe he'll come over. I never saw him. He is just a guy at the golf course. Don't even know his last name. Only his voice, when he calls for Herschel.

The garage door opening gives me a start. The car engine is running in the garage. *He's coming back?* Oh god, did I sleep. Never even heard him get up, open the door, leave. Nothing. *Oh god, why am I sleeping so sound? Never do I sleep sound, never!* The inside door at the end of the hall opens and I hear something that sounds like a bag hit the floor. He is doing something in the garage and leaving the door open, because I feel a breeze, a draft. *How can it be this cool this late in the morning?* The wind is starting to really blow. Must be a storm brewing. Only time it blows at all on the Gulf side of Florida; it is usually hot and muggy. *Wonder, does he know enough to turn on TV weather?* Sounds as if he is wiping his shoes on the carpet. *Guess I did teach him some manners. His ma never did, that's for sure. Yes, just a few things sunk into his dumbkin brain.* The wind catches the door and it slams. "Jesus Christ," he says aloud. The sound of his voice is so good. Never thought I'd miss hearing that. He doesn't say much else but cussing or complaining. Telling me always I'm so stupid. "Ain't you got no sense?" he asks me sometimes.

Now he is in the kitchen rattling the bag of stuff. Next I hear him pull open the cupboards. He pulls the silverware drawer out. All the rattling. I hear the click-clacking of the knife on the plate. Coffee? Instant is all there is, for emergencies. *What emergency? We don't get drunk any more to need it.* Wouldn't let him have it anyhow. Drink tea, I always tell him. And he hates tea, so he drinks milk. It sounds like he is sitting down to the table with the paper rattling and the click-clacking of the silver against the china. He must be drinking coffee. He likes tons of sugar in it. That's the one reason I stopped him from using it. Afraid of getting diabetes. He must be reading the paper. That's the only thing he likes to do on mornings he's home. Read the paper and drink coffee and eat donuts. Except, I don't let him have that anymore. Fruit instead. *Eat your fruit, Hersh, honey. So much better for you than those empty calories.* Don't you know donuts are cooked in fat? I tell him.

"No," he says. "Aren't they baked in the oven?"

"No," I say. "You drop them into hot fat and cook them same as French fries or onion rings. See, why you shouldn't eat them?

Love 'N' Stuff 103

"No wonder I like them," he says so smarty-pants.

Yeah, that's what he's doing alright.

I'm wondering if I could use the bedpan. Have to go so bad my bladder is starting to hurt. I roll over on my side and pull my knees up. It helps a little bit. *I could almost get up and pee and he'd probably never hear. Naw, I better not.* I try to doze again. Sleeping makes the time go by fast. *Sleeping is all I can do, I guess.* I look at my watch. It is twenty to twelve already. Almost noon. Guess he isn't going to play golf. That's something. I'm beginning to feel good about that. If he gives up golf, I know it's important. I'm enjoying that feeling, so nice, to think he cares about me, like in the arms of Jesus. *Safe in the arms of Jesus.* That funeral song, for Toni. Wonder how anybody thought that up. Safe in anybody's arms feels good, I guess. I feel the warmth and the safety hug me up all over. Even in my cramping toes, I feel warm and good. For a minute.

The ringing phone startles me. I have to remind myself every time I wake up under here why I'm here. *One of these times I'll remember.* The chair slides on the kitchen floor. Herschel is talking, "Yeah, Harry. Naw, I slept too late. Had a bad night." *You liar, you had it good, you liar.* "Well, if you want. What time?... Okay, maybe, if the wind dies down. I hate losing balls. I'm down to my last dozen. Ella always gets them for me at that discount place, but she must've forgot." *I didn't forget, you bastard. Why should I remember your balls when you don't even remember my birthday, or nothing?* "Let me figure out what I'm going to do.... Naw, I ain't heard nothing.... Tomorrow. I'm going to do it tomorrow... Yeah, I know, I was supposed to but... Maybe I'll go after, get a later flight.... Okay." Clunk goes the phone.

He comes back into the bedroom. He has his light tan loafers on, the ones he wears when he wants to look really spiffy. I don't see the bottoms of his pants; he must have on shorts. He walks into the bathroom and takes a whiz, and drops the seat. *Must've forgot and did right.* The toilet flushes and he comes back out whistling. Can't figure out the tune, a slow tune. Can't figure it out.

He walks on past the bed, but stops at the door. *Oh god, he must have seen something.* I hold my breath. He turns around and comes back into the room. Right at the corner of the bed, he is standing, still whistling. Then he stops and rattles the keys in his pocket. He must have some change in there too. He goes to the bedside table on my side of the bed, where I keep nail polish and a box of Kleenex, an old pair of glasses. He has the drawer open and I hear him moving things around. *What's he looking for?* He shoves the drawer shut, then pulls the bottom one open. *Gee, what do I have in that drawer, anyway? It's so long since I went in there.* He is doing something bent over. I can see his one foot is up, off the floor, resting on the other toe. I hear a bunch of stuff moving in the drawer. Then I remember I left that old address book in there. *Carrie. Oh, god, he's must me going to call Carrie.* He walks around the bed to the phone, sits down in the chair. I hear him pick up the phone and punch in some numbers. He's talking. "Yes; Is this Carrie's house? Yes, this is Ella's husband, Herschel. Would it be too much to ask to speak to her? I got a problem here... Thanks." He is whistling: *I could have danced all night. I could have danced all night. And still..."* Yeah, Carrie. Herschel Goodlove, here. Ella... You *do* remember. Listen, I hate to bother you on a Sunday morning, but when is the last time you heard from Ella? Would you mind telling me?... You haven't? That long, huh?

Well, I came home Friday night, and she wasn't here.... No, she never came or called yet.... Yeah, I went to the police and they said even if I filled out a missing person thing they wouldn't act on it for three days. Then they started in on me. Questions like you wouldn't believe. And I walked out on 'em.... Yeah. Can you believe it? Yeah.... Ah, I did look. I can't tell anything is missing. Of course, I wouldn't know, I'm gone so much. I never know when she gets anything new or what.... You think so? Why? Did she say something to you?"

Carrie must be telling him about all the threats to do myself in. I went through that once. Started thinking about all the ways I could do it. We talked about it. Carrie tells me I need to see a shrink, and that's when I tried to go, a few times and he gave me the *I'm OK* book to read. That's when I figured out Hersh wasn't anymore OK than me.

Herschel is saying, "You really think she might've? What bridge? Oh my god, you don't *think?*"

The shock in his voice is really making me feel good. He really does care about me. See there, he does. He does.

Herschel is saying, "Well, I guess I better go to the cops and tell them about that. They might want to talk to you. Where do you live in Alabama? How many miles is it?... Oh yeah? You think they will do that? Well if they do, will you call me and let me know? You can call collect."

This phone bill is going to be out of the sky. This experiment is going to cost plenty.

"Okay, Carrie. Thanks for talking with me. 'Preciate it... I had no idea she was thinking things like that. No idea. Guess I was gone too much, huh? But it's my job, you know? What's a guy to do?... You think so? What kind of thing? I mean, we have sex every week, just about.... More than that? You're shitting me, at my age?... Oh, really, they do? I thought she was getting it plenty. I know some guys who don't bang their wives but once a month. I figured I was over-sexed." He's laughing. "Just never know about these things," he says in his cute, teasing voice.

I'm beginning to squirm. I feel red hot jealousy at the sound of his voice, talking to Carrie. *That little hussy. Where the hell does she get off, talking sex to my husband?* I want to jump out from under the bed, grab the phone, and break it in two.

"Thanks again, Carrie," he says, and lays the phone down in the cradle so softly I'm not sure it is really hung up.

Maybe he is going to make another call?

He is whistling again. I've grown accustomed to your face. We both loved that movie. *My Fair Lady.* Saw it three times. At least I loved it. He said he went just to please me. But he learned the songs quick enough. Oy. I feel all tore up inside. One minute wanting to kill him the next minute I'm wishing he was in my arms.

He's talking on the phone again. "Ah, yes. This is Herschel Goodlove. I came in about my wife the other day. Well, can't I just tell you this over the phone?... Okay, I'll be right over." He slams down the receiver. "Sonofabitch," he says, and walks very fast around the bed. He has his keys, I can hear, and the garage door opens, and the car starts.

When the garage door closes after him, I roll to the edge of the space. I have only a few minutes to get myself cleaned up. I get up on my knees first. I am so stiff I can hardly move my legs. My back is caught in what feels like a permanent cramp. Have to do some stretches to loosen up the ribs. I stand up and get very dizzy. *My head. God, I hope I don't get sick.* I hurry to the sink for water. I need water badly. A whole glass goes down, and then another. In the mirror I see my hair standing straight up in the back. I'm

Love 'N' Stuff 107

trying to pull it down, but the ends are frizzy and need a brush. I go into the drawer for it, and notice how clean the bristles are. Then I remember I cleaned them with ammonia just last week. I get the brush and start on the back, for the little tight snarls. All of a sudden, I have to pee so badly, I lay the brush down on the sink and quick run into the toilet room. The seat is okay, and I just make it getting my slacks down. *God, my bladder is not holding too well. It's not coming out very good.* I feel a stinging sensation when I cut off the pee. It burns again when I start. *Oh, god. Now what?* The toilet paper is down to about a third of a roll. *Have to figure something out about that.* I only use a few small squares. *Can always wash my hands.* I flush the john and pull up my slacks. The dizziness hits me again when I stand up. Back in the sink area, I see I left the drawer open, and the brush is full of my hair. *Now I have to clean the brush and where to put the hair?* I wad it up and stick it down into the bottom of the trash bag, inside the can. It is empty. Still has a fresh liner in it. But my hair is so fine, he won't see it. Back at the sink, I splash cool water on my face. *It feels so good. I wonder if I have enough time to brush my teeth?* I'm looking for the old toothbrush in the back of the drawer, the one I left in there on purpose. I squeeze the toothpaste onto the brush. The brush hurts my gums. *But at least I am alive to feel it. I could have been dead, if it wasn't for Carrie.* I rinse the brush and wipe it dry and put it into the back of the drawer. I have to rinse the sink and get all the toothpaste off. When I get up close to the mirror and look at my skin, it is all dirty and bumpy looking, from the carpet pile maybe. *I need a good facial and makeup job. Not used to going to bed without cleaning my face. Tomorrow...*

It is past noon already and I haven't really had breakfast. I tiptoe into the kitchen. The newspaper is spread all over the table. Herschel's coffee cup is setting next to the instant coffee jar. *The little shit. Give him an inch.* There is the bag of donuts, too, and I go and look inside. There is one left. *Boy, it looks good. Chocolate, with nuts all over it.* I don't dare. I go to the refrigerator. He has a gallon of *whole* milk. *Oh, god, the cholesterol. This is going to be his death.* I pull the jug out and open it, and put it to my lips. *Just a swallow. Just a swallow. It will make my stomach feel better.* I didn't take enough to notice. I pull out the refrigerator bins. There were a couple apples in there. Three to be exact. *Do I dare?* I don't think he thought to look in there. I take one out and bite into it. It tastes so good. The skins are too hard to chew, I usually peel them. But I know I don't have time to do all that, so I take it with me into the bedroom and climb up onto the bed. I'm chewing the apple. *Wonder if I should call Carrie and tell her? So someone would know? Would she keep a secret? Naw, the way Herschel laughed with her. Never trust your best friend, is what my motto is.* I'm down to the core of the apple when the garage door opens. I hit the floor with a thud and slide my feet under first and remember this time to turn my nose to the side. I'm under good when the door opens and I hear talking. Men's voices.

Herschel is saying, "Naw, she don't wear makeup anyhow. Not even lipstick. My wife don't use all that shit." No makeup? My ears are not hearing right. I put makeup on every morning of my life. The same lipstick for twenty-five years. A soft melon color, by Revlon. In fact, that is the color, Melon. I have three tubes going. One in my purse. One in the medicine cabinet, and one in my makeup kit. No make-up?

The other man says, "Where did her friend say she talked about going to jump?"

"Oh, she said they didn't really map it out real good. She more or less just let her talk about it so she wouldn't do it, and the doctor helped. The doctor. I should find out if the doctor knows anything."

"Yes, that would be a help. But if it is a shrink he might not tell us too much. You know, all this privacy stuff."

"Come in here and you can see for yourself that she didn't take anything." Herschel steps into the bedroom and opens the closet door.

I can see a pair of black shiny shoes. A cop alright.

"See, there's her purse," Hersh says.

I hear the shuffle of the bag coming off the shelf. "I already looked through it. Everything looks like she was here ten minutes ago. I can't tell nothing."

"What about the check book? When did she write the last check?"

"Can you believe it's a week since she used it?"

"Is that normal? How many checks a week does she write?"

"Oh, I don't know; she always has money. I give her my pay, two times a month, and she takes care of everything. If I need money, I just tell her and she gives it to me. Not much though because I travel a lot and I got the company's money. I ain't asked her for any in a couple months."

"What about deposits? When is the last deposit she made?"

He says, "Let me look. Here. Look at that. Like clockwork, every payday. Every two weeks.... That's strange. She usually has a bigger balance, I thought."

"How *much* bigger?"

"Oh, three or four grand. This here is damn close to

the minimum, think it's fifteen, or is it two thou?"

"Now maybe we're getting someplace."

"You think she was planning something?"

"Could be a mite suspicious."

"I can't believe she was smart enough to do that, I ain't kidding you. She ain't the smartest of dames. Except she's good at getting the stuff she wants. She saves for things. A penny here, a nickel there. Like the bed in there."

"Yeah, I noticed. Some bed all right. Well, we'll check out the bank tomorrow and all the other things you gave us. You said she didn't pick up your suit on Friday like she was supposed to, right?"

"Yeah, I had to go get it. It's in the car, I just remembered. Better bring that in. Gotta wear it in the mornin'. I only wear suits when I travel. The rest of the time I just wear jeans and shit. You know. The boss don't care how we look at home. It's on the road he minds we look good."

"What do you do, again. Sell?"

"Naw, I don't sell nothing. I just try to interest people in what the company's selling. I'm a tree shaker, not a jelly maker."

They laugh.

"You know, another guy follows up behind me and closes the deal. I just find the clients that I think might be interested."

"What is it, again. What?"

"It's a line of radios. We sell radio systems. You know, short wave. Stuff like that, like your police radios. Something like that, only these are special channels. Secret."

"Oh, you work for the government?"

"Yeah, sorta," he says. "Got a thing going now, with

Love 'N' Stuff

this hostage business."

"Oh, some *big stuff*, huh?"

"Not big, really, just tricky dealing with the oil slicks."

They laugh again.

I'm feeling the blood trying to get back into the arm I'm lying on. I try to pull it out from under me, but it is stuck. I'm caught in just the wrong spot so I can't move. They are talking about radios as they walk back into the kitchen. They leave the closet doors open and I can see the box of pills I keep back in the corner. *Wonder what the cop will think about that?*

Herschel is saying, "Want a cup of coffee?"

"No, thanks. I'm all coffeed up for one day," the cop says.

I hear them walk around, into the other part of the house. Hersh is telling the cop all the rooms, "This is the family room. I watch TV in here most of the time.... Yeah, she sits in here with me and does her knitting stuff.... Yeah, there it is over there. She's making some mittens for my golf woods. The ones I got are full of holes. So I asked her and she started them the next day. But she only has one done so far. I need four, one for the putter. Do you golf?"

Mutters an answer I can't hear. They are out on the porch looking at the pool. Can't hear the words. But they are laughing again coming back into the house. "Well I think we have enough to go on for the time being. I wouldn't worry about her quite yet. She might be just gone out for a pack of cigarettes." and laughs.

"But she don't smoke."

"That's a saying that means she left, skedaddled. Flew the coop."

"Oh, that. What makes you think so?"

"It's just the whole picture. She's got it too good to do

anything to herself, the way I see it. She just wants your attention, maybe. You know, a little TLC."

"Yeah, I guess she might, at that," he says. He sounds really confused. I can just see the wrinkle in his forehead. The tic in his upper cheek that appears when he is disturbed and thinking.

When the door closes, I hear a car start up and the garage door shuts down, and I am alone again. The silence in the house is deafening. I want to get out and walk around but I'm too tired to move all of a sudden. I close my eyes and think, *It'll be over soon. Soon.*

That was how this all began just two nights ago. It is now Sunday evening. I have been dozing, and I wake up to the sun setting over the kitchen table. The light plays eerie shadows all the way into the dining room, where I'm still perched, leaning to one side, against the wall next to the china-buffet. My neck is so stiff, I can hardly turn it. I don't know if Herschel is still here or not. I want to get up and pee, but I hear the TV still has the ball game on. *Maybe he's asleep.* I think that maybe if I go through the living room, into the other hallway, into Toni's room, I can duck into that closet if he comes. That closet has room to hide me, behind the roll-away. But then how do I reach the light switch, by the door? Oy. All this stuff I never figured out before I think up this silly scheme. But I have to pee, so I tiptoe real quick over the thick white carpet, into the foyer. The floor is white marble and I have to be extra quiet walking across it. I stick my head around the corner to be sure he is not in the family room, and it is empty.

I slip across the hall into the bathroom. The toilet is in the tub area with a sliding door. There is no window, so when the light is off it is pitch dark in there. I don't like that

Love 'N' Stuff

part about it. Why I never use it. I have to have lots of light; I hate dark anything. But now it is a godsend, so I slip into the shadow and feel for the john seat. It is down. *Thank goodness.* I am sitting there doing my business when the doorbell rings. *God, this is getting to be grand central station.* I just have to stay put. I'm in the dark. *Who's gonna come in this bathroom, huh?* I tell myself. I decide to finish quick, pull my slacks up, and then sit on the seat, dressed. That way I'm ready to run if I have to. Sitting on this john with clothes on reminds me of what Toni told me he saw once in a public men's room. There was a cop sitting on the stool like this, waiting to pinch weirdoes. The cops hang out in the public rest rooms, and just wait until they hear someone in a not-so-nice act, then they come out and grab'em. What a puky job. Sitting on the can waiting your life away. Just like me now. How do I get into such predicaments?

I am thinking so hard I don't even hear Herschel come to the door. But I hear it open, and he says, "Yeah, I don't want any. Oh, for a good cause, huh? And I suppose *you're* the good part, hey?" he says joking.

It must be a cute young thing or Herschel wouldn't waste his time. He says, "Okay, how much?" I hear the change in his pants jingle. He says, "I have to go get some more money, if you wanna wait."

I hear him walk back through the house. He is shaking the vase in the center of the kitchen table I keep change in. I forgot to clean that out. He comes back through the house, the door of the bathroom is up just a few feet from the hall that goes into the foyer. Even if I'm standing up, in the sink part, he couldn't see me. "Here doll," he says.

What'd I tell you?

"I think I can spare a buck and a quarter for a dish like

you."

I hear this tiny little voice. She must be a Brownie selling cookies. You hate to say *No* to a little kid; I usually peek out and don't answer the door because I don't know anything about scouting stuff.

After the door closes, the footsteps fade away into the other part of the house. It must be getting time for *60 Minutes*, I think. Herschel never misses it. I half listen, unless it is about a movie star or someone interesting. Who cares about some Real Estate jerk trying to swindle somebody? People are so gullible. Not me. I figure *everyone* is out to get my money, that's why I'm so careful. Never trust nobody; that's my motto.

My stomach is really empty. I feel like it is touching my back bone. I feel weak and I think I need to drink some water. Didn't I hear somewhere if you are ever stranded, you can get along without food, but not without water? I haven't been drinking enough. I reach for the faucet and turn it on very easy, slow. But I forget it's the one that makes a wrenching sound if it gets turned on just right. I hear this sound in the pipes. *Oh, my god. He can surely hear this.* I have only got one little fist full of water and I have to turn the faucet off. I bend over to drink out of my hand, and I hear what must be the garage door slam. *Oh, thank god. Now I can flush.*

He must be hungry. I listen for the car. He must have washed the car or something, or cleaned it out. He does that on the street in the shade where it is cooler than the garage, he says. I tiptoe into the living room and through the curtains I see him get into his car. He is dressed fit to kill. Where the hell is he going now? I wonder. I see him take off and I don't remember hearing the garage door close. I run through the kitchen, to the back door and open it a crack. Sure enough, the garage is wide open. He must've forgot. I wonder, should I close it? I think, maybe I should. No neighbors know anything about it, so why would he find out? He'll think he closed it. So I stick my hand out into the garage and reach for the button. I hear the door go half way down and stop and go back up. What the...? I stick my head out and my car is sitting half way out of the garage. He must've been doing something in it. He can't see so good in the garage. He always pulls the car out half way for light. *Now what?* I tell myself I better get back to my roost because, with the garage door left up, I won't hear when he comes back. The engine to his car is so quiet you can't even hear him pull into the garage.

I go to the sink and fill up the glass with clear water from the cold faucet. It is lukewarm. That's the one thing about Florida, you never get cool water from the tap. The sun must bake the whole damn ground. I am so thirsty, this time it tastes good. I drink two full glasses. I belch a good one. If I don't do that, I get sick. I try to bring up another belch. Empty gas. That's what Herschel calls it, empty gas. I do some stretches with my arms as I walk through the back hall again and see the laundry room is one big mess. He has dirty clothes thrown all over the place. As though he just stands at the door and tosses them, and who gives a darn where they land? I want to get in there and clean it up. God, how bad I want to but instead I go on back into the bedroom and into our bathroom.

It is almost dark. He missed *60 Minutes*. He must've had someplace special to go to miss that, I think. I don't take the chance of turning a light on either. I go to the sink and turn on the faucet. I splash water all over my face and reach for the towel, and it's not there. He must've put it into the laundry room and not got another one. Darn. I hate to dry sticky. But at least it is cool. I take one look at the outline of my hair, all stuck up on top, and aloud I say, "You look like you just crawled out from under a rock." The sound of my voice, speaking after two days, sounds and feels very strange. I clear my throat; it hurts when I swallow. I go back to the bed. I hike myself up on it to sit, wishing I could just lie down and wake up as a princess somewhere, with a handsome prince who really loves me. But if I think that way, I will cry, so I have to stay mad.

I slide down on my knees and slip back into the space that's now home. For the first time, it feels better under there than outside. At least I am safe.

The house is so quiet I feel like I'm dead. The clock is stopped. No TV. All I can hear is the sound of an occasional car out on the main road, behind our house. The tall wide shrubs keep the sound down so that it isn't very noticeable, usually. I try to find a way to be comfortable. My back is really getting sore. I'm getting tired of trying to find a place for my arms. Without thinking, I stick both hands inside the waste of my slacks and am surprised to find how loose they are becoming. They were on the tight side anyhow.

My stomach is getting empty so I feel around for some Gerber's baby food. Someone told me it was a good way to diet. I found a small jar of meat and a plastic spoon. I twist the cap off, and it makes a pop. I have to remember not to do this when Herschel is here. I smelled it. It must be lamb. It has a greasy feel to it and sticks to the roof of my mouth. And it needs some garlic. *No wonder babies make such faces.* I'm lying on my back, and I'm afraid I might strangle. I do that sometimes for no reason at all. Sometimes I will swallow wrong and a drop goes down my windpipe.

Love 'N' Stuff

Drainage from my sinuses unexpectedly drips down and gets into the wrong pipe. That's all I can figure. In fact, that was one worry I had about doing this. Wouldn't that be a fine howdoyoudo, if I choked to death under here? *Wonder how long it would take to find me?* The thought of it struck my funny bone, after all the fun Herschel made of me over the diaper stinky-poo left in the back bedroom trash can. Wouldn't that serve him right, though? I could just see him sniffing all over the bedroom thinking he had lost some dirty socks. *Wonder how long it takes for a body to start stinking?* So I'm careful eating. Very quickly I'm feeling stuffed. I reach my finger inside the jar to see how much I've eaten and it feels as though it is half full. The whole jar didn't have more than a hundred calories so this wasn't really enough. *Every time I cut my calories back too sharply, I end up getting sick.* I hadn't been drinking the orange juice I had in little cartons all along the end of the kitchen space. Reaching around for one, I punched it open with the point of the straw that comes with it. *This is tricky, having to turn my head to get the juice to stay in my mouth.* Now I'm really filled up. I set it next to the empty juice can above my head. I feel like there's a lump in my chest. The food feels stuck, didn't want to go down. *Guess I should get up and walk around some more.* For some reason, I just don't have the pep. I roll over on my other side. The pillow's soft and doesn't give me much support for my neck that's getting stiff. The quietness reminds me of that day Toni didn't come home. It was after the big storm and the electricity was out all over. *He must be holed up somewhere and couldn't get to a phone.* He was good about calling if he couldn't keep his word. When the phone rang that day, I just knew it was him. This woman says on the other end of the line, "You Ella Goodlove?"

I hate that when people call up and ask you who you are without telling you who *they* are first. That's gotta be nervy. "Just who is *this*?" I say, letting her know that.

She says, "I'm a friend of Toni Goodlove. He gave me this number to call his folks if anything happened."

My stomach does a regular somersault whenever Toni's name is mentioned in that way. "Whadaya mean, anything happened?" I say very nervously.

"Then, this is his mother?"

"I say, "Yes. Yes. This is Ella Goodlove. What's the matter with Toni?"

"Well, Toni. He was staying at my place. I gave him a room, you know, to help him out, and I don't see him for a couple days. I don't like the looks of it. He is so friendly and comes and talks to me when I'm cooking, n'stuff. You know what I mean?"

"Yeah. He's like that."

"So I knock on his door. When I don't get an answer, I go and get my keys to look. When I open the door, there he is, out like a light, sprawled out on the bare bed. Right on the *bare* mattress he was sleeping. And I *had* sheets, plenty sheets."

"What do you mean, *out*. Drunk? Or what?"

"Well, the first thing I do is go over to him and shake him, and he doesn't move. His eyes are a little open, like he is peeking through the lids. He just wasn't looking right. I am scared to stay in there. But I also hate anybody snooping around my property, you know. You never know what somebody is gonna find. So I decided to try to wake him up. He is in this sweatshirt with a hood, that's up over his head, and he has his hands in his pockets. I try to get them out of his pockets, but I can't move'em. Then I see his color is not so good. I feel his face, and it is cold. Cold."

I am getting so upset. "Hurry up, already. Where is Toni, and is he alright?"

"I'm sorry," she says real nice and sweetly. "Well, I think it was too late. But I called an ambulance anyhow. The medics came and gave him oxygen, but it didn't work, so I ask them to take him. I don't want any stiffs left in my house. After they left, I finally found your number…"

Somewhere down inside me there was a scream trying to get out. I felt like every ounce of blood in my body was trying to get out my eardrums. But I can't let myself do this, I have to find out where Toni is. My sweet Toni. So I take a big gulp and try again in my nicest voice. "Please ma'am, tell me where Toni is."

"Oh, that. Yeah. They took him to the county place, it's at the back of the big new hospital. They have a morgue in there."

At the sound of that word, I just lost it. I wanted to scream and curse every terrible word I ever heard in my entire life. They all crossed my mind like a speeding train. I wanted to spew them out at this horrible woman. But all I could do was stand there with the phone in my hand while the very life drained out of me. I couldn't think, couldn't even remember if this wretched woman had told me her name, or anything.

I just stand there, and she is saying, "Hello… Hello, Mrs. Goodlove? Mrs. Goodlove. Hello?"

She finally hangs up and I am standing there holding a dial tone… that finally turns into a squeal… and then nothing. It was that kind of quiet I hear now. I'm ready to doze off, and I shut my eyes. I haven't got any reason to keep them open.

I hear the noise of a car engine and garage door. I open my eyes and it is pitch dark. The door to the garage is opening and I hear this thud in the hall. Then the door closes. I hear Herschel jiggling his keys. They make this loud clunking noise. It sounds like they fell on the floor. "You sonofabitch." I hear Herschel bellow, "You sonofabitch. Now why'd ya go and do that?"

Oh, oh. He's been out drinking. *Oh, no. What have I done?* He hasn't had a drink in over five years, since we buried Toni. *"Oh, god, no..."* The tears want to come into my eyes. They feel hot. My eyes feel hot, but I can't cry. That would really be the end of me. And if Herschel's drinking? *Oh, god, couldn't you leave well enough alone, Ella? You stupid broad."* Those are the very words Herschel says to me. And it's his voice saying them to me again, in my head, and I am not answering. I just want to die. But I have to listen...

Sounds like a grocery sack being picked up. Next I hear Herschel making this big commotion. Sack noise. The shuffling sound of his feet, the keys rattling. There is this loud carrying on in the hall, and Herschel is cursing. Every word in his big-boy vocabulary seems to come out his mouth. In the kitchen, there is a loud thump. Maybe he fell onto the kitchen table? No, he hits the floor. No question about that sound.

The quietness now is almost more than I can stand. I'm thinking, I gotta get up and take care of Herschel. *Go take care of Herschel,* I'm telling myself this over and over, but I just can't seem to make myself move. I know I can't let this change things, no matter. So I tell myself, *It will all be over soon, real soon. And then you won't have to do this anymore. Soon, Ella, soon.*

Love 'N' Stuff

Sometime in the night, Herschel wakes up and I hear him walking past the end of the bed and go to the bathroom. He is taking a whiz, and he says aloud, "You sonofabitch. See if I ever lift this goddamn seat again for you. You... you... you goddamn bitch," and I hear him break into sobs. I hear him fall down again. He is bawling like a freaking baby.

I think, *Cry, you bastard. Cry. You ain't never seen tears yet, Buddy. Not even a little bit."* I turn my head to the other side and wipe the tear that is caught in the corner of my eye. I try to stop listening then. *Let him go to hell,* I think. *Let him go to hell.* And I shut my ears to what I'm hearing. *Go to hell.*

In the wee hours of the morning I hear Herschel climb into bed. He is finally snoring like a lion. I go back to sleep myself. It's getting so the weirdness of my dreams is no worse than the awake times...

I am back inside that house that keeps coming back. There are windows all around it. I can see outdoors and it is dreary looking. I think to myself, It's going to storm. I better close all these windows here. They are all open. I start going around the house trying to get the widows closed, but the rain doesn't wait for me. The wind starts blowing. Raining. Blowing. The windows are sticking. I can't get them closed. The wind is coming into the house and making me very cold. Very cold. I am so very cold, cold...

The phone ringing wakes me up. I hear Herschel roll over and reach for it. He says, "Hello.... Oh, yeah, Dottie. What the hell time is it, anyhow?... Oh, god, I overslept. Thanks for calling; I'll be in soon.... No, she's not here. I did the report thing yester.... They think she did something to herself... or had a friend, maybe. They were a little nicer to me this time. I don't know what they're thinking. Who can tell about cops? Jesus. Hey, let me get going here. Yeah, would you? Gee, that would be great. Get me on the noon flight. That'll get me into DC before the afternoon traffic. Thanks." Herschel slams the receiver down and it must miss the base because it makes a crashing noise and slides off the table. He is cussing again. He cusses when he is mad, the doctor told me. *Yeah, I know he's mad. But not near as mad as I am.*

Herschel gets his suitcase out he keeps on the floor of his closet. He is walking around the bed, back and forth, putting stuff into it, cussing in between. He uses his electric shaver in the bathroom. He must be too hung over to use the straight razor. He told me that once when he was drinking. When he first quit, he switched to the electric because he started cutting himself too badly, from the shakes. So he must be feeling shaky today. *I couldn't care less. It is all over for me now. No love. No affection. No sex, is bad enough. But the booze I'm not ever living with again; I've made up my mind.*

Herschel walks over to the phone. He has on his new shiny Florsheims, the black ones so he is wearing his blue suit. He must look like hell in his eyes with all this crap he has been eating, and now the booze. He's punching the telephone buttons. He says, "Yeah. This is Herschel Goodlove again. I just thought I'd remind you I am going on a business trip. Couple days or so. And you can get me through the office number I gave you. They will have my hotel number as soon as I get there. I'm staying at the Arlington Marriott, in DC, in case you need me after hours. I'll check in with you though, from there, to see if you heard anything. Well, I figured if you had, you'd've called me.... No, no sign of her. I got a little drunk last night, but I would've remembered if she called, or anything. Thanks."

The door closes with a horrendous bang. I hear the garage door go down after him, and I think, *I can get up now. Move around. It is my house again.* But I know I have three days, so I don't hurry. I doze off again. *I have plenty time...*

Back in time, the cops are all over the place. My ol' man is holding me in his arms. The room is smoky and the house is dark and smelly. I look around at everyone and wonder what is going to happen to us. Then a cop tells us to sit down. "Over here on the couch," he says.

We sit down on the funny feeling couch. It has a high back with wood carvings all across the top of it. I sit down next to Pops and the cop pulls up a chair from the dining room and sits in it. He has this long board with a bunch of papers stuck onto it. He starts talking, "Now, Mr. Cahill. Did you say you were moving at a slow rate of speed?"

"Yes," says Pops. "I saw her, and she was walking very, very slow. So I slowed down, but I thought I had time to get by her. I was only going about five miles an hour. Hell, I was almost stopped."

"Yes, well, she says you were *stopped. That's why she reached for the car, to help herself across to the other side. She doesn't see too well, and she says she was very surprised when you kept going."*

Pop says, "I just can't believe this, Officer. This old lady walks into my car, and tells me I run into her. For Christ's sake, look at where she fell, will ya? I am already past her before I hear this thud."

"Yes. She has very poor eyesight. This we have documented by her sons. I don't think there will be anything further on this, I just have to get your sworn statement. So if you'll just sign it."

I see my dad writing his name on the big, long paper. And then in walks the doctor with his black bag. His monocle glasses are pinched to his nose. He looks at Pops. "My patient has a broken hip. She somehow thinks she was using your car for a cane," he says, and laughs.

Pop says, "Look doc, if there is anything I can do for her?"

"I think she'll be alright. I'm having her put in the hospital, but it was inevitable. Her other hip was barely healed. Too much stress on the good one. One of those things." He tips his hat at Pop, winks at me, and says, "Little cutie." I don't like how it feels in that house. It is creepy, stinky, and I want to leave. I tell my dad, and he picks me up again and carries me down the big high steps. I ask him, "Are we going to get in trouble, Poppy?"

"Not with the law," he says, "but with your mother, probably. Trying to explain this." And then he is silent. Silent as now. Silent...

It is the quietness in the house, the stillness, that awakens me. There is no clock ticking. *That's why he overslept.* I am sore all over. I slide to the edge of the white islet bed skirt. The little holes in it not only give me a little air to breath, but they let me see through. At the bottom it is scalloped, so all of that together gives me extra oxygen. But I feel like I have been sleeping in a heated house in the

Love 'N' Stuff

middle of a snowstorm. Blizzard. When the wind blows so hard the crack at the top of the bedroom window is even too much, so it gets closed. And before long you are feeling headache-y, dry nosed, all around drowsy. That is how I feel as I get myself up on my knees. As I do stretches, my arms and legs feel as if they are made of wood. The circulation is so poor that they are like ice, an unheard of condition in this hot, muggy climate. The dampness makes the condition feel worse. Resistance to pain is not one of my best qualities. It has only been in the last couple years that I even know I have a body. I never used to feel hunger, or any other malady. Never a weight problem, because eating has always been the last thing on my mind. It just has never been important. But I am smart enough to know that I have to get some better nutrition in me these next couple days, somehow. *Soup. Chicken soup. Maybe I'll make some.* Then I think about all the odors. Herschel does have a good sense of smell and I don't want to tip him; I need some more time. Sticking with the bouillon and Jell-O that kept me alive for a month after the gall bladder surgery when I was too sick to eat anything else, is the best way to go.

Finally, I get on my feet. It is an eerie feeling. It is as though I am a ghost. And in essence that is what I have become. I always did feel like a nothing, a nobody. But I could always look in the mirror and say to myself, *Hey, pinch yourself, you are alive. It is just all in your head, this nobody stuff.* But finally I had become a real live ghost. It was almost humorous, if I could only laugh.

In the bathroom, my bladder feels the heaviness, and the release of its contents sends sharp pains into the lower regions. I decide I have to check for bleeding. The sliding door between the commode and the sink area has to close so I can turn on the light. There is very little toilet paper left. Yellow, to match the gold wallpaper and gold toilet fixtures. It has a dark appearance to it. I look into the toilet and see a pile of mucous, striped with blood. *Oh god, not another stone. No wonder the pain was so sharp. What now?* I think I will have to call this all off and go to the doctor. But then I remember, I have that whole prescription left from the last time. Herschel got it filled and I was supposed to take it. But the sulfa made me so hyper, I just couldn't handle it anymore. And the blood and pain had stopped, so I stuck it away at the top of the medicine cabinet. I decide that is what I will have to do — and drink more water. I knew I had set myself up for something like this. *But I didn't want to live anyhow, so what's the use.* But for some reason, I still feel like there has to be something better than this, something has got to change. Him. Me. All of it, and so I go to the medicine cabinet and find the sulfa. Bactrim, it says, the best thing for bacterial infections, the kind I usually have. The doctor says, "It's not unusual for women your age. At this time of life, it's the lack of estrogen. Use the vaginal estrogen cream at least three times a week." But it cost so much, I let the prescription run out. I decide I will have to open my tight fists and get it refilled. It beats this kind of mess, pain, then to add to it a kidney stone. Passing it is almost like having a baby. Anyone can tell you who has had both. Now I take a Bactrim and drink down two glasses of water, right then.

When the pill hits my stomach, within minutes, I am sick as a dog. I decide to lie down on the bed for a minute. Just a minute. *Oh god, it feels so good.* The sun is out bright and the stillness in the house feels like a blanket of snow over my tired, achy body. Soft and exactly. After a few minutes the nausea goes away, and I decide I have to go eat, but I remember something about not eating with this

Love 'N' Stuff

medicine. I go back and read the label. *Take 1 hour before meals, or two hours after eating.* I figure I have a good hour to wait.

Into the bathroom I drag myself to take a shower. I feel like a hog ready for market. There is no towel. I go into the laundry room to see where it is. *I'll just use the old one.* But he already has put it into the dryer but forgot to turn it on. *Oh god, the clothes are going to mildew.* On goes the dryer; he won't remember that he didn't do it. *I'll get another towel because it can get washed and back on the shelf in time.* In the front closet, out of the bag of clothes for the homeless, I get out another pair of slacks and shirt. (I have underwear under the bed.)

I'm going through the kitchen, rounding the bend with the clothes in my hand when the front doorbell rings. Because I'm standing right in front of the dining room window, I have to speed it up. The shears over this window keeps anyone from seeing in but I am not sure they couldn't see a shadow moving. I hit the floor and crawl back and over to the edge of the curtains, under the draperies. Peeking out, I can see it is the Real Estate lady that keeps coming by to see me. She caught me on a bad day once, and I blurted out that I was getting ready to leave my husband, and she never forgot it. Now I have her visiting me at least once a month. *She'll go away. But I have to be quiet till she does.* I hear the screen door close and I know she has put something inside, for me to read. Now I wonder if I should go look. If I do, and she happens to call or something, and Herschel says he didn't find anything, then what? But what if I leave it there, and she writes on a note to me about leaving him? Then what? I wonder what to do. I'm afraid to go look yet, though. She might come back. I decide to go ahead and take my shower and then take care of it. *At least I can look and see if she wrote a note. If there's no note, I'll just leave the Real Estate stuff for Hersh.*

The shower is still running and I go into the laundry room to check and see if anything is dry yet. But, nothing. From the linen closet, I take the clean towel out and head for the bathroom. Lousy is how I'm feeling. *Maybe the shower will perk me up.*

Inside the shower, I feel the hot water hit my shoulders. God, it feels good. My skin is starved for something to touch it. *Anything.* But about all it gets is a stream of hot water. My skin must think it has one friend, at least — the hot water. The soap is down to a skinny piece. I forgot to start a new bar and Herschel never remembers to tell me it's out. My new soap is under the bed, and I don't want to drip water all over to go after it, so I use *his*. It makes a little bit of lather, but sometimes I get rashes from it, if it's Irish Spring. Have to take a chance. If it is, I will just have to itch for awhile. My hair is so ratty, I figure it can't look any worse, but at least it will be clean, so I suds it up three times from the Head and Shoulders. There is plenty left for Herschel; he won't miss that.

When I get out of the shower, I'm feeling a lot better. The bathroom floor is carpeted with the same white carpet that's in the rest of the house. But I don't worry about dripping, ever; I dry myself off with the wash cloth first inside the stall, so the towel never really gets damp. But it's the idea, I have to have a towel. So I wipe off, but I think the towel is so clean and dry, I can fold it up and put it back on the shelf. The old pair of slacks, that are broke in the clasp, lets me see how thin I am getting. *No matter. Who is gonna see, huh?* I decide to wash all my clothes so I can put these I have on, back into the bag. Herschel never looked in the bag anyhow, I don't think, so what's the difference?

Love 'N' Stuff

This whole situation is getting to be too much, but at this point, I am stuck with it. What else can I do?

In the kitchen, I go to the sink, get a cup of water, and put it into the microwave. It gets hot, and the bouillon is melting. Sitting at the table, looking through the newspaper, I read about the taking of the hostages all over the front page. *I can't believe this is happening in America.* I sip the bouillon until it is gone and I feel better.

The package of Jell-O from the cupboard I put into the plastic bowl of hot water and stir it, to take under the bed with me. *Herschel is going to be gone three days, so don't worry.* I wonder if I dare take the car and go somewhere? *Nobody knows us or about anything, so maybe I'll do that. But it is better if I do it at night. Not as likely to be seen.* I get a little energy from thinking about where I will go tonight.

In the bathroom, I look at my hair. *Guess I better put some curls in.* My hot rollers are the quickest. While I'm waiting for them to heat, I turn on the TV. Phil Donahue is on real soft, and he has on a couple of lesbian women who are married and raising a kid. The audience is really mad at them for being such bad examples to the kid. But the kid comes on over the telephone and tells them they are wrong. She has *two* mothers that love her and she feels very lucky, as they are better than most. She is a teenager and says she thinks the audience is not very fair. She says, "How do you think I feel to hear you complain about my mothers? I love them you know; you don't have a right."

My rollers are hot so I put them in. They are so heavy they will hardly stay in my hair. But they do leave some curls, so I spray them good with hair spray. *Wonder if I should've done that?* But I think, *It will be three days, so it won't matter.*

What a mess, hair all in the sink; I clean it up. After the curlers are put away, my face all on and teeth clean, I am ready to go back to bed and sleep all day. But I think I should move around. *Better for the bladder.* The timer on the stove is set to remind me to take the Bactrim, one hour before supper.

After Donahue, Mike Douglas, another talk show, comes on. He has some funny stuff on sometimes, musicians too, so I leave that on for awhile. This pretty black lady, who knows six languages, is talking. She has a funny name, Maya Angelou, but she sounds so kind, a soft voice, and I listen. They are discussing how all of us hate changes, especially big ones. She says, *"My grandmother always said to me, Get Steppin'. I am here now, all of me. Everything I am, was, am not, was not, whatever, here I am. When I leave here, I will take all of me, but I will leave the chair. Give it up! It was good while you sat in it, but leave it behind you. Don't hang onto it. Don't say, I paid for this chair, it is mine; I won't let anyone else have it. Foolishness! Give it up. Go on, all of you, to the next place, to the next chair. Get steppin'."*

Her words are soft and sweet like marshmallows, and they stick. I turn off TV and decide to do some needle work for awhile. Cross stitching keeps my fingers busy. I'm wondering, *Could Herschel possibly be my chair?* Wonder what he is making of all this? *Where does he think I am? Who is he seeing?* Thinking of *her* makes me angry. Every time I stick the needle into the cloth, I think, *You mean so-and-so. Why don't you love me? I take such good care of you. You'd've been dead long ago, just like your old man, if it hadn't been for me. I'm the one that feeds you correctly, keeps your clothes clean, your house clean. You can't even love me a little?*

Love 'N' Stuff

By now, I am getting lonesome to talk to someone. *Who can I call?* I get this idea that I could call a hot line for troubled people. Once I wrote the number down and stuck it in the recipe box; Herschel never goes in there. The needle work is back just like I had it, under the knitting in the basket on the floor next to the TV Guides and stuff, and I go into the kitchen. It is an 800 number. *Better not talk right here in the kitchen. Too close to the windows.* Back in Toni's old room that has Venetian blinds, I sit down on his bed next to the phone and dial the number. It's busy. Lying back on the bed, I am looking at Toni's picture. It is of him in high school, a big picture, blown up to poster size, from a friend on his birthday. It was such a nice gift, thoughtful for a kid to do. She was one of his first girlfriends. Cheryl. Cheryl was red headed and so sweet. I was sure they were going to end up together for good. But Cheryl's old man didn't like Toni *at all*, so she had to make up her mind: Does she want to live at home without Toni, or be thrown out with him? She was an A student. When she comes to the house to talk it over with me, I tell her that she has to make her own decision. But that no matter what she does, whatever her dad might say, no one can take away the love she and Toni have for one another, even if they were to not see each other ever again. "Loving someone makes them *forever* in your heart."

Poor baby, she is bawling, and then she hugs me, and says, "I wish you were my mom; I love you so much." I hug her and tell her she is like the daughter I never had. It is so hard to let her go out the house that day. It was over for Toni and her; she was too smart a girl. And Toni, he just was too stubborn to see what he was doing to her, with the stuff he was into. *Oh, Toni, my baby. What did I do wrong?* I feel like crying again.

Then I remember the busy 800 number and dial it again. This time it rings. A young man answers. He sounds to be in his twenties. *Same as Toni would be now. Oh god, can I talk to him?* I ask him, "What's your name?"

"Michael," he says.

I say, "Can I call you Mike?"

"Sure," he says. "Anything you feel like. How are you today?"

I say, "Not so good."

Then Michael says, "What's *your* name?"

I say, "El (I think real quick.) Ellen. Ellen Smith."

He says, "Okay, Ellen Smith. What's your problem?"

"Well, I have this life," I say. "It looks like a good life from the outside. And nobody would ever believe how it truly is. But it really is awful. And I just don't know how to get out of it, or change it."

"Tell me about it," he says.

"Well, this guy I'm married to, I'll call him Herb. Herb is a hard worker. He always brings in the money. Gives me the checks. Only asks for very little for himself, except that he loves golf."

"That's good," Mike says. "At least he gets some exercise."

"Yeah, that's true," I tell him. "But the trouble is — he don't do it with me. *Nothing* with me, in fact."

"Does he sleep with you?"

"Oh, that. You mean, sex? Well, once in awhile."

"No, I meant *sleep* with you. You said he didn't do *any*thing with you."

"Oh. yeah. Well he does sleep in the same room, in the same bed. But it is like he ain't *there,* really. Since... since... See, he hugs the edge of the bed, gets as far away from me as he can."

"And you feel it is *you* he is trying to get away from?"

"Well, I *know* it is," I say. "It's me he's trying to get away from, because when I ain't there, he sleeps on my side of the bed. Right in the middle, really. Can you figure that?"

This Mike says, "In other words, when you aren't there, he misses you?"

"Oh, no. I don't think *that* at all. Do *you* think that?"

"Well, why else would he go over to your side of the bed when you aren't there?"

"Maybe. Oh, I don't know. I never thought of it like that before."

"Well, sometimes we interpret other people's behavior through our own feelings. See, *you* are feeling rejected. So you think *he* is rejecting you. When it is really your own rejection you are feeling?"

"Now, wait a minute. Let me get this straight. You mean it is just in *my* head? His hugging the edge of the bed?"

"No, I didn't say that. The *reason* he is doing it is in *your* head. Can you see that?"

"Well, not really. But if you say so."

"Just think about it."

"Okay, Michael. I think I'm too tired to talk anymore."

"Okay, Ellen Smith. Feel free to call anytime. If I'm not here, someone else *will* be."

"Okay, Mike. It was nice talking with you."

"Same here," he says, and we hang up.

It's time for my Bactrim. I reset the timer on the stove to ring for my suppertime pill. The two glasses of water I force down is so putrid. Florida water always tastes like the ocean to me. But Herschel didn't buy any spring water. I can never carry the big jugs so I always let him buy it when he goes. Today I have to settle for the fishy water. *Why do I feel so tired?* I haven't done anything to feel tired. I should feel like a cat out of a cage ready to pounce, but I don't. Very tired, and I think, *Wonder, is this medication working?* I have to wait an hour before I can eat. Having to watch the clock for something puts me on pins and needles.

When I was little, I couldn't wait for the hands on the clock to move, why sometimes I would push them ahead. One time for a birthday party I was supposed to go to on a Saturday afternoon, I was so excited to get dressed up that right when I get out of bed, I put on my best outfit. My ma laughs at me and tells me I am going to get my dress dirty by the time for me to leave. I ask her to show me on the clock when that will be. On an old broken-faced clock, she moves the hands forward from nine o'clock to two o'clock, and then puts them back and winds it up so it is ticktock-ing away. I think, oh, no, it is too long to wait. Two o'clock is forever away. Right then I decide to fix things so I can leave early. It was a boy's party; I will never forget it.

After about a half-hour watching the dilapidated clock, I get tired so I put it up to ten, just a little push. My ma, she is reading one of her silly books, and the day was just too boring for words. She told me to "play with your toys now, and be a good girl."

Into my closet where I keep things, I get out the box of tinker toys. I always like building stuff, especially into a tower. Getting it so high, I think it is almost to the sky. I am so excited. I run into Ma to tell her, but she gets mad at me for interrupting her.

"Go knock it down and build it again, then I will look," she says.

I am so mad. I go look at the clock and it is fifteen

Love 'N' Stuff

minutes before noon. So I push the hand way past twelve to the one. And the big hand is after one, too. I wait a little while, and when it is moved a little, I creep back into my ma, and I tell her, "Ma, I think it is time to go to the party."

She says, "Oh no, it can't be. I only just sat down here. Go play."

Then I get the clock and take it to her.

She takes a look at it. "Oh my, god, I am a slow reader today. Must be my new glasses," she says. "Go get washed up and don't mess up that dress. It is all you got to wear that's nice today."

While brushing my teeth, I look into the mirror and see they are really white. I like the taste of the toothpaste. A little gets spilt on my chest, but I get a rag and wipe it off. It's dry, I think.

But my ma sees it and screams at me. "What'd I tell you? Be careful. Well, you'll just have to wear it; that's all there is to it."

She has a peanut butter and jelly sandwich and a glass of milk at the table for me. I ask her, "Ma, ain't you hungry?"

She says, "No. I'll just have my coffee till your father comes home. Then I'll eat with him." She sits down at the table with me, with her coffee. She is looking out the window, daydreaming. I want to talk to her, but I don't know what to say. It seems no matter what I pick to talk about, she yells at me anyhow. I just sit and chew my sandwich and drink my milk. I want to hug her, she looks so lonesome, drinking her coffee, looking out the window. *Wonder what she is thinking about?* Maybe Pops? But I don't dare ask. Sometimes she screams when I ask her anything. So I push my plate back and wipe my hands and face with a napkin she put there, and I say, "Thank you.

May I be excused?" I have to always say that; one of her rules. Ma says if I don't, we might not have anything to eat next time. If I remember, I always say it.

She nods, gets up and goes to the closet, and gets the present she wrapped up for the party. I didn't get to see it before she wrapped it, but she said Tommy would like it. I take it and she pats me on the shoulder.

"Thank you, Mama," I say, and take off out the door.

She says I have plenty time to get to the party. It is two streets away and I have fifteen minutes. She says, "You don't even have to run,"

I decide to skip instead. When I was a kid, I always liked skipping; it made me feel so light and loose. If I could just skip higher in my steps, I might get picked up by an angel cloud and get where I'm going faster. Real high skips in the air; I am doing good. No cracks either; break your mama's back, if I did, so I don't.

At Tommy's house, it is all closed up, no doors open, nothing on the porch to play with. When I ring the doorbell, no one answers. The porch swing looks inviting; I sit down on it and push with my feet. I really get into it. The swing is really going high. I am even pumping, and all of a sudden I hear this loud crunch. In the back of the swing, the chain comes lose at the ceiling and the swing falls at the end, and I slide down the swing just as it hits the back railing of the porch. It makes a loud thud and scares me. As I jump off of it real quick, the swing slides down off the porch railing, and the chain is hanging on the floor, on one side. I am *really* scared now. I quick get my present and start down the porch steps just as Tommy and his mom and dad drive into the driveway.

Tommy yells out the window at me. "Ella. Ella. Hi."

Tommy's mother is frowning. I think she already saw

Love 'N' Stuff

the broken swing. "What are you doing here already? Huh?" she says and looks at the present I am carrying.

Tommy gets out of the car and runs over to me and takes the present.

His mom says, "Wait a minute, Tommy. The party is not until this afternoon. It isn't even lunch time yet." She says to me, "Does your mother know you are here?"

I say, "Yes, she does. Isn't it time?"

His ma looks at her watch, and says, "No. It's only eleven o'clock. Three hours before time. Give her back the present, Tommy."

He says, "Oh, Ma, can't I open it? Please. Pretty ple... ease, Mom."

She frowns at me, and says, "No Tommy. Give it back."

He does, but he shakes it hard first to hear if it rattles. But it doesn't. I already shook it and so I knew it didn't.

I think I have to go back home, and my ma is really going to be mad so I decide to walk the other direction for a ways and see what is there. After walking a long time, I finally come to a busy street. There are cars and stores and buses. I wonder if I could get a ride on one while I am waiting? When the bus stops, I get on behind the other people waiting. The bus driver says, "You with someone, Miss?"

I say, "Yes, my mom is already on, back there," I point.

He turns around and people are standing in the isle of the bus, so he says, "You need to stay with your mother, Sister. You'll get lost."

Towards the back of the bus there is this pretty lady who smiles at me. I make-believe she is my mother; it is such a good feeling. We ride and stop and ride and stop. Finally, the lady speaks to me. "What's the name of your street?"

"Oh, I can't remember. It is close to Whitehall. That's all I know. (Whitehall was the street Tommy lives on.)

She says to me, "You missed your stop. Go tell the bus driver you need to get off and get back on the other bus going the other way."

I say, "Thank you," to the lady. Always I remember to say thank you. I walk up next to the driver and I whisper in his ear, "Mister, I am supposed to get off; I missed my street."

He says, "Okay. But you damn kids are going be the death of me yet." He stops the bus, and lets me off right in the middle of the block.

I get off the bus and it is a strange street. There are some stores at the end of it, and a tavern. I walk to the corner and look across the street for a bus stop. Over there is a bench and a big yellow bus sign on its back. In between the cars, I cross over right in time for the bus going the other way. I wave at the bus driver, and he stops. I don't have any money. I say, "I missed my stop and I have to go back to Whitehall street."

He says, "Where's your transfer?"

I say, "I don't have it; I lost it."

The driver looks real disgusted. Then I smile at him real sweetly, like I do sometimes when I am afraid. And he says, "Oh, alright, get on. But hurry it up, will ya?"

I get on and stand by the driver.

He says, "Yeah, you better stay right here so you don't miss it again."

We stop a couple more stops and finally I see the corner, where I first got on, coming up. I tell the bus driver, "This is the street."

"Do you think I don't know that, little lady? You think I got this job on my looks?" he says real loud and laughs so everyone in the whole bus can hear.

He finally stops, and I jump off.

I'm still hanging on to the present for Tommy wishing I knew what was in it. I am crossing the street and shaking the box next to my ear, and a car screeches its wheels and stops real fast. The man yells out the car window, "Hey, kid. Watch where you're going. You're gonna get killed one of these days."

I run the rest of the way, to the other side.

What is in that package? There is a high curb to sit on, and I decide to slip the ribbon off and peek inside; the ribbon can go back on after. Very carefully, I open the paper. Inside is a wooden airplane to put together. *Oh boy, I think. Maybe Tommy will let me help him do it.* But, then I think, *Maybe I could start it now?* I see the wings and how they fit into the engine part, and I try to stick them in each slot. But there is nothing to hook the wheels to even with all the pieces left, and some glue. The part I have started, I put back into the box and decide it is harder to do than I thought. The paper goes back on alright, and I lick the tape again hoping it will stay stuck. The ribbon fits back on it okay, too. A little messy looking job, but Tommy won't care when I tell him what it is.

I start walking again. Back at Tommy's house, it must be three hours by this time. Up the stairs I can see the swing is still broken, and I get scared and go back down the steps. I wonder if I should go to the back door instead?

Around to the back, I hear Tommy's dad in the garage monkeying with some dirty daddy stuff. When I peek into the door, he is bent down over this noisy thing he is holding and doesn't hear me, or see me. There is this wooden thing that sometimes is in the street to block cars, only this one isn't painted yellow. It is just plain old dirty wood. I have to stretch my legs to get up on it; it's a little high for me. I am on it good, when the machine Tommy's dad is working on, stops. Tommy's present is bumping on my swinging legs; his dad hears the sound and turns around. "Mercy above, child, what are you doing here?"

"I am just waiting for Tommy's party," I say.

"Well, you are a little early. Didn't we tell you to go on home for awhile?"

"Yeah. You did, but my ma ain't home. I couldn't get into the house," I say. "So I came back"

He looks at his watch, and says, "Well, come with me and see what Tommy's mother says about it. Maybe you can help her with something."

I am really excited now. Getting to help a grownup lady with real stuff.

He takes me by the shoulder and pushes me through the back door, into the hall. He yells, "Martha, this kid is back. Here. Come and get her."

Tommy's mother comes to the top of the back stairs and sees me and gets that same frown on her face. "Why are you back here already?" she asks.

When I tell her the same thing, she wipes her hands on her apron and motions to me, "Come on, then; I guess we'll find something for you to do. Tommy is taking a little nap so he doesn't get too tired. That's what you should be doing. Would you like to rest on the couch, downstairs here?"

E-gads, what now? I think, but it is better than going back home, so I say, "Alright. I guess I can."

She takes me into the living room where the carpet is thick like grass and leads me to this brown velvety-feeling couch. It is so soft and fuzzy. I never felt one so soft before. She says to me, "You don't have accidents any more, do you?"

"Accidents?" I don't know what she means.

"You know, pee your bed, ever?"

I get embarrassed. "No, I ain't no *baby*," I say.

She laughs. "I'm sorry, I didn't' mean you were, but it wouldn't hurt you to use the bathroom, just to be sure."

She takes the present from me and you can tell she notices it is messy. But she looks back at me and doesn't say anything. She puts it on the dining room table where there are some party stuff, some hats and blowers. "Here, come with me. What's your name?"

I say, "It's Ella." Then I add "May," to it. Ella May sounds more grown up.

"Well, Ella May, I guess you are just anxious for the party to start. It's hard being a little girl, isn't?"

I am really feeling good; Tommy's got such a nice mother and daddy, I want to stay there forever. I look up at her, and say, "Can I be your little girl?"

"She says to me, "I'm afraid your mom and dad wouldn't like that."

I say, "My ma wouldn't care at all. She'd probably like it."

"Well, but what about your daddy?"

I think a little bit, and remember how quiet and sweet he is with me when we are away from my ma. So I say, "I think he could get used to it; he would want me to be happy."

She laughs a little, and opens the bathroom door, and says, "Go ahead and use the bathroom, and we can make-believe you are my little girl for this afternoon."

While I'm sitting on the commode, I'm looking all around this pretty bathroom. Pink or blue is everywhere. There are white swans all over the pink shower curtain, and the rug on the floor is thick, thick blue. It comes right under my feet, and all over the floor. We don't have no rug in our bathroom, just a little teensy one. And it's over by the bathtub. So my feet get cold at night when I get up to go. This rug goes all the way back to the wall, behind the commode. I'm wondering how the rug got all over that way, *Do they bring this whole floor into the house with the rug on it already, or do they make it that way in the store?*

Pretty soon, Tommy's mother knocks on the door. "Are you all right, Ella May?"

"Yeah," I say, scooting down in a hurry. "I didn't have to go."

As she opens the door, I just make it pulling my panties up.

"Well, it never hurts to be sure, does it?" she says.

"I guess."

She tells me to rinse my hands with soap.

The faucet is round and silver, not a square white one like we have. I turn it on. The water is warm, too, and I wash my hands extra good, sudsing up a storm since she is standing there watching me.

Finally, she says, "My, Ella May, you had dirty hands. Where have you been?"

"I was helping Tommy's father, out in the garage," I tell her without thinking.

She looks at me very strangely and frowns again. She doesn't say anything but leads the way back into the living room, to the soft velvet couch. "You lie down and rest a few minutes. The party will be ready to start before long."

I am so excited. I start to put my feet up on it, and she says, "Oh, I think you can take your shoes off for the time being." She comes over and pulls them off without unbuckling them.

My dress is all dried where I spilt the toothpaste. Only a little spot, but no one would know it but me and Ma. I put my head on my hands, the way I like to sleep; I like that better than a pillow.

"Close your eyes, just a few minutes," Tommy's mother says.

"And so I do."

The doorbell ringing wakes me up, and Tommy's running through the living room. "Ella, I saw you *sleeping*," he says with a silly laugh.

I get up and put my shoes on real fast. Must have dozed off because I couldn't remember anything.

The door opens and Tommy's boyfriend comes in. They start giggling. I feel funny. So I go into the other room and look for Tommy's mother. I remember then she said I could be her little girl for one day, and so I call, "Mama. Mama. Where are you?"

She comes out of the pantry and sees me, and says, "My, Ella May. You were sleepy, weren't you? You slept a long time."

"How long? " I ask.

She says, "Nearly two hours. Well, that's good. Now it's two o'clock and time for the party to start. You'll feel much better now."

"Thank you," I say to her, "Thank you for being my mother today. It's fun."

She says, "Well, if you say so."

The doorbell rings and then a bunch of noise and screaming kids come rushing into the house. She takes me by the hand and we walk into the living room together. Everyone is looking at me, and I feel like I am the birthday person all of a sudden.

That was such a nice day. The touch of her hand inside mine felt so good, I didn't want to let it go. But I had to when she gave me the balloon from off the table to hold. I was the only one with a balloon, and I felt so special. Everyone came up to me and asked me how come I had a balloon and they didn't. "It's special, just for me, for the party. You'll just have to look at mine," I tell them. The boys kept trying to take it away from me, but I hung onto it for the whole time. Even when we played Pin-the-tail-on-the-donkey, I wouldn't let anyone hold it for me. When I think about it, I can still feel that special feeling from the party. Whenever I see a balloon now, I want to cry I get so excited. Maybe *that's* what I need to do, go buy balloons and blow up a whole room full of them so when Hersh comes home he can't even get in the door. Wonder what he'd do? I think, *Naw, Hersh would just grunt, and say, "What the hell are these balloons doing all over this house?"* Forget that idea.

It is time to eat lunch. I go fix more bouillon and sip it, still thinking about the balloons.

The whole day is something else. I feel like I am living in the store window. Being careful of everything I do, not to forget to leave things the same, or touch anything that Hersh left, is hard to do. I want to clean up the house, where he left things all over it. But I know I can't, so I feel like I'm in someone else's house. I don't like that feeling at all. Back under the bed I go, where it is mine again. I am so tired anyway. I get my pillow just right and I think, *Now I can relax, maybe I will feel better after I take a nap.* My back doesn't hurt as bad and I am peeing all right, so I think I will get through this yet.

When I wake up, it is dark. I roll over and try to

remember what day it is and what I'm supposed to do now. I slide out from the space and I hear some cars out on the street. I can't see my watch to see the time and the clock is not ticking. The electric one is in the kitchen. I get up and go to the bathroom and see on my watch that it's after eight o'clock. I remember I missed my Bactrim. I get one and take it. I have to wait an hour to eat.

While I am waiting, I go into the family room and flip on the TV. It is Archie Bunker. Edith is screaming at Archie, "No I don't have to do what you say, Archie. I am a person too," she says; she is trying not to cry.

Archie's eyebrows go up, and he says, "Awe, Edith, why do you gotta act so, that way? Huh, Edith? You ain't acting yourself."

Edith says, "Wait and see, Archie. You just wait and see. I am Edith, not Mrs. Archie."

Archie says, "Oh, Edith, you never was Edith before. How come all of a sudden you gotta be this new person? I like the old one better."

Edith says, "Well, I don't. I'm not going to let you tell me what to do *any more,* Archie."

"Stifle, Edith. Stifle."

Edith turns around and presses her lips tight together and walks into the kitchen like he didn't say anything. In the kitchen, she is alone and talking to herself, "Stifle, he says, stifle. I'll show him, stifle." She puts an ice cube in his coffee and stirs it around. "See if you like cold coffee, Mr. Stifle," she says, and takes the coffee back into Archie.

Archie's face lights up into a big smile. "Now, that's my Edith," he says and accepts the cup from her. He takes a sip and his face drops as he looks up at her in such surprise. "This is *cold,* Edith. You forgot to heat it?"

"No. Archie, I didn't. If you want it hotter than that,

there is the door to the kitchen. Be my guest," Edith says and turns to clear off the dinner table.

Archie just looks up at her through his eyebrows and sips on the cold coffee.

It makes me think, *That is what I gotta do with Herschel, gotta stand up to him. I gotta tell him where to go, I just gotta.*

It is dark outside and I think I can go out somewhere for awhile, in the car. I go and get my purse, but there is no money in it. My car keys are not in there either. *Now what?* I say to myself. *Where are my car keys?* I lay the purse on the bed and go look in the closet, the laundry room, the kitchen. Then I wonder, *Maybe he left them in the ignition.* I go out in the garage and peek into my car. No keys. I figure, it's just as well. Back in the house I put my purse up on the shelf. *I would just get in trouble anyhow. Maybe the cops have my picture on a wanted poster. That would be a fine howdoyoudo.* Go in to buy something and have the cops show up to arrest me.

"Arrest me for what?" I hear myself asking.

"You're under arrest for being alive. We thought you was dead. But now that you ain't, we'll, you're under arrest."

In the kitchen I make some more bouillon to take into the family room, by my needle work, a wall hanging. I put TV on. Dean Martin's doing his roast for Danny Thomas. Orson Wells, that big, big man, is doing his turn. I remember him from *Cat on a Hot Tin Roof* with Liz Taylor. The line in the movie I always remember is, "When the marriage is on the rocks, the rocks are right here," and pounds on the bed. It makes me think about my Herschel. I don't like thinking about this. I turn off the TV and pick up my needle and thread and stick it in and out. In and out. The design is a house with words under it that says: *The ornaments of a house are the friends who frequent it.—Emerson.* I wonder if I studied him in school? I can't remember who he was. That guy who was a fairy? Who wrote poetry, I wonder?

The first time in a long while I think about being called Ella May. Tommy started calling me that when he wanted to tease me after the party. "C'mon, Ella May. What ya doin', Ella May, huh? Ella May is a dope. Ella May is a dope," he'd say. I hated him after that, but I so loved his mom.

The words all done in red are cross stitches, and they're about finished. Black is better for the name, I think, so I put it up.

The air in the house seems heavy and the quietness is more than I can stand. It makes me want to go to sleep. I finish my bouillon, wash my cup and put it away. Time to turn in. I crawl under the bed and find my pillow waiting. It feels, and even smells, good. So quiet. So, so quiet. Sleep comes so fast I don't have time to think about where I am, or why.

In my dream, I am talking on the phone, and I'm trying to get off. In confusion, I finally hang up. Orson Wells is there, bare chested, and grabs me, picks me up and squeezes me tight to his big, huge chest, and says, "Why do you hem and haw on the telephone? Just assert yourself and say, I want to hang up now so I can fool around. At once, things seem to feel orderly and lovely inside of me.

The first morning sunshine wakes me up, and I am still feeling the warmth of those big arms. A smile creeps into my whole body, all the way to my toes. It is like a spring of warm water bubbling over me, washing away my guilt and questions, soothing all the aches. I think about how huge Orson Wells is, big enough to hold all of little ol' me.

As I fall back asleep, I think about him telling me to *ask for what I want,* and right now what I want is to crawl back into those big, strong arms...

It is early morning. I know it is morning because the birds are singing. It is light out, and I roll to the edge. I feel like singing too. I have to go to the john, and the pain is gone. I try to remember what day it is. I feel like I have been in a terrible blackout, hardly remembering anything. It seems that I have turned into somebody else. Although it is difficult, the muscles are so stiff, I get up on my feet. I stretch my arms and legs, pull my body to the left, then to the right, twisting myself until everything hurts, but it feels good. The sun is trying to shine through the clouds. Florida always has clouds, it seems; they are never very far away. *My life?* But today I feel like the clouds are gone forever. I want to sing, to run, to be happy with somebody. And then I remember that I am a ghost, that I am disappeared, and I hate it. I have to think carefully. I don't want to get myself in trouble. Herschel is gone. *Yes, where is he?* I try to remember. *Maybe I could call his secretary, Dottie. Wouldn't that be a kick in the head?* I have to think this through. After I finish my early morning rituals, bathroom, face, hair, change my clothes, I go to the kitchen and open the refrigerator. It looks as though it belongs to a bachelor. Nothing in it but left over french fries and onion rings. *Wouldn't that taste good for breakfast?* I'm hungry for fruit. I see there is some orange juice left, quite a bit. I pour a tiny glass full. He bought the wrong kind, from concentrate. It's never as good as the freshly squeezed. But Herschel never reads labels, I don't think. When I close the door, a piece of

Love 'N' Stuff

paper flutters to the floor. A note from Herschel he must've left on the refrigerator:

Ella,

if you come home, please call Dottie and ask for my phone number and call me. I am in DC.

I love you, Babe.

Please don't go away again. I miss you too much.

Love, Herschel.

I am really touched. I already feel good, and that just sets my heart on fire. *What should I do?* I think that he will be really mad if he finds out I did this to him. *I just can't tell him.* What jumps into my head right then is how he was when I told him about what I had done that day in the motel, when he took me along.

He had a special trip come up over in Arizona. Never been out west. So he says, "Come and go with me. No sense staying here, alone." I get myself ready and pack some summer cool things and we catch a non-stop flight to Tucson. His convention is in a small town south of there, Sierra Vista. It has a big Army base where Hersh is trying to sell some radios.

It is a beautiful place. Mountains all around, but there are no big trees. Just small ones, and not any grass. It is a strange place. We drive for a few miles south of Tucson and it is nothing but little hills full of sage brush and rocks. *How do people live here?* Herschel says this is where they make Westerns, movies. I never was too much for them but Herschel loves 'em. He'll pick a Western over anything to watch. Once we were coming around a bend and there is a jack rabbit in the road that has ears the size of himself. Herschel gets all excited when he sees it.

When we finally get to Sierra Vista, it is earlier in the morning than when we left Florida. No matter, with four hours time difference from east to west coast, it is already dinnertime in my stomach, and I am hungry.

The one-street town has lots of fast food places. Herschel says there are all kinds of men floating around here all ages and to be careful. "Some of them might try to get friendly."

I look at him, and laugh. "You're kidding, Hersh. Friendly? With the likes of me?"

"Hey, you ain't half bad," he says to me.

I am feeling pretty good. But I ain't believing his kind words. I think it would be something if that really happened.

He puts me in my room at the Ramada Inn, which appears to be a hotsy totsy place, better than Holiday Inn or HoJo's. I have my own big bed and I can watch television all day, or go out shopping, or whatever I want, Herschel says. But I don't feel like paying for a cab just to go looking, so I take a walk around the place. There is a pool and there are people in the chairs, sunning and reading. I decide to go get my book and act the way I see them all doing. I really don't like the sun; I just like to look like everyone else, and everyone else seems to like the sun. I don't understand it. It burns your skin, makes you sick, and peels — then you look like hell. I don't know about people. My swimming suit, that Herschel insists I take along, is a black jobby, one piece. The strap goes around the neck, back is bare to the waste. Herschel picked it out himself and brought it home. I have all kinds of suits from when we first moved into this pool

Love 'N' Stuff

house, went crazy buying them. But I never get anything sexy, he says, so he picks this one without me even trying it on. I'm wearing it this morning and carrying this old ratty-looking pocket novel that I picked up at a garage sale, just to have something to read. Looked exciting. It's *The Exhibitionist* by Henry Sutton, from back in the '60's. The title sounds really risqué. I sit down in a lounge chair, far away from anybody, and I open the book. I am so sleepy though, because I woke up too early, to the Florida time. I never went back to sleep, so by midmorning, I am so sleepy I can hardly keep my peepers open, but I am trying.

The book is open as though I'm reading and somebody sits down right beside me, in the next lounge. I wonder why this person has to pick one so close? I suddenly get embarrassed and look at myself through their eyes. I see veins in my legs. "Old bag," I hear them thinking. I see flabby arms, "What a hag," I hear them say. I see bone-white legs and feet, dry wispy hair, a few greys here and there. But I have nail polish and toenail polish on, and my face is on, for the second time today, after Herschel left. He never sees me do it; he would freak out, I guess, if he saw all the stuff a woman uses. Keeping the illusion in place with him is what I try to do. Someone told me once when I was a young girl: *Never let a guy see you put the face on. That way they think it was their lying eyes that saw you looking not-so-nice before.* Anyhow, I'm sitting in this lounge trying to keep my eyes open, at least to find out what this *Exhibitionist* is like, hoping it will give me a few pointers or sexy ideas for Herschel. I am concentrating on all of this when I hear a voice say, "Hey, have you got any matches?"

What a jerk. Hasn't he got a better, more subtle, way to get acquainted? I act like I don't hear him. I'm staring at the book, as though I'm really into it, and I turn a page.

This time he clears his throat and says it again.

I look up.

A guy, almost right on top of me, is peering into my eyes. He is so close, I'm a little shocked. He is smiling. He looks about the age of Herschel, in his late 40's maybe. He is in great shape. He doesn't have any flab anywhere in his jockey swim trunks. *Oh god, this guy likes his body, I can tell.* He has very blue eyes that seem to reflect the water and the mountains and the warm dry air. They are smiling with that devilfish look in them that says, "Hey, Babe, you wanna dance?" Only, of course there was no dance floor, but I mean, if there was... He's looking at me waiting for me to answer. I'm a little tongue-tied. I shake my head, and say, "I'm sorry, I was dozing here, the time change. What did you say?"

He says, "Yeah. I'm getting my bearings too. Just flew in from Boston. I wondered if you had a match, but I was really just trying to strike up some conversation. I have some time on my hands, and I thought you looked like the kind of person who would be fun to talk to."

I am embarrassed now. With my sunglasses off I take a better look at him. His hair is naturally curly thick, and getting grey at the temples. He has a short and stubby mustache under a little bum of a nose. *Guys with mustaches look a little silly, I say to myself. I guess they think it makes them look debonair. Each to his own.* Aloud, I say, "I'm not much of talker, though. I guess looks are deceiving."

My glasses are back on, and I open my book. Never even started reading the darn thing, but I open it up to the middle.

He says to me, "You don't have to make believe you're

Love 'N' Stuff

reading; I can take a hint. Sorry I bothered you, I was just lonesome, that's all. See you around," and gets up to leave.

Now I'm really feeling bad. What is the harm? I am out under the open sky, where the whole world can see me. And he hasn't exactly asked me to do anything bad. I close my book and to his back, I say, "I didn't mean to be rude. I'm just not used to talking to strange men, or strange anything. Not that you're strange," I add and laugh. "I stay home a lot, and I didn't know what to say, really."

He sits back down and looks at me again with those big baby blues. Right then I remember my father for some reason. He had such big soft eyes like that, and they always looked at you like he was seeing through you into tomorrow. I get a little nervous, but I decide, I got a right, too. So I try to relax. I feel my toes in the one part of my mind, while the other part is trying to look cool, as though I'm used to talking to the big, bad world every day.

He says, "Where you from?"

"Florida... today." I say a little timidly.

He lets out a big belly laugh, "Well, where were you from yesterday?"

"Oh. I mean... We just flew in from there, where we live now. But we really come from the Northeast, originally. From a small town outside of Pittsburgh."

"Oh yeah? Where exactly? I've been to Philly."

"It's between Philly and Pittsburgh," I tell him.

"Well, welcome to Arizona. I'm a native Arizonian. A real *strange* bird," he says and we both laugh. "Most everyone here hails from somewhere else. But I never could find a place that made me feel as comfy as this stretch of God's paradise."

"Oh, so you really like it here with all the sage brush?"

"Yeah. I'm a desert rat. I can spend days scrounging

around in the tumbleweed and rocks. There's nothing like it"

"Oh, really?"

"Hey, you got some time?" he says all of a sudden. "Do you want to see my desert?"

I think this guy's koo koo, but I am curious.

He says, "You got tennies with you? Something to walk in that will protect your feet?"

"Yeah, sure, I always bring some. Uh, what kind of time frame are we looking at here?"

"What do you mean? When do you have to be back?"

I say, "Well, my husband is planning to have lunch with me in about an hour. And after that I am free till dark, whenever that is. He is going on some kind of expedition, out in the mountains somewhere."

"Oh, in that case why don't we meet after lunch. At the bar? And bring a hat, if you got one. The sun gets a little hot about two o'clock. I'm James, by the way," he says and sticks out his gorgeous hand.

I stick out mine, "I'm Ella," I say, and we shake.

He has a gentle touch. He takes my hand in both of his and rubs the top of it. "God, what soft skin. What do you use on it?"

"Nothing in particular, just dishwater" I laugh, embarrassed.

He finally lets go.

It is a warning. I think he is warming up my heart through my hand. I think to myself, *Ella girl, this one is a tough-y. You better not do this.*

He gets up and says, "I have enjoyed talking with you, Ella. And I am looking forward to giving you the grand tour of my desert. It will be a day you will never forget." He smiles as he turns and goes into the motel.

Love 'N' Stuff

My watch tells me it's time to get dressed for lunch. I don't like to run around in my swim suit unlike some do. My cute cover-up is an orange terry cloth jog with a zipper that is slanted across my body in the shape of a green stem. At the top of it is a white rose bud. It feels good to wear it. I am walking into the motel to go to my room, and I hear the loudspeaker call my name. "Ella Goodlove. Please come to the front desk. You have a message, Ella Goodlove."

At the desk, the clerk says Herschel called and canceled lunch. "Go have a ball," is the message. "Tied up till late tonight."

I'm really upset. He promised me he would be here for lunch. *But what can I do?* He says he has to work, so he has to work. Herschel is the kind of guy that gives his super two-hundred percent. It's a little irksome. Me, I get two percent, if I'm lucky.

I'm back in my room changing my clothes when the phone rings. I answer it, "Yes?"

"The voice on the other end says, "Ella Goodlove?"

"Yes."

"This is James; we just met at the pool."

"How did you know my name and room number?"

"I just heard it over the loud speaker."

"Oh, well I guess you did. That was my husband, canceling lunch. He's tied up."

"Well, how about we *start* with lunch, then, Ella Goodlove?"

"Okay," I say. "I'm game, I'm very hungry"

"Good. I've got a neat place to take you. Ten minutes?"

"Okay. I'll try to hurry."

My newest cotton safari pants I just bought for this trip are white and have a bunch of outside pockets, for going into the jungle. I get my socks out and put on the pink Nike's. The sexy white t-shirt, that has a picture of a teddy bear on it, makes me smile. The bear has his arms outstretched, saying, *I NEED A HUG*, trying to give Herschel a hint. I wonder if it is too much, but it is all I brought that is cool and casual. *What the hell. This guy already knows I'm married.*

We are in his car. He drives us down a gravel road. The dust is flying everywhere. There is a house here and there, and chicken coops. A very large trailer home with a porch built on it is parked way back off the road. He turns onto a dirt road, to the trailer place. In front of it, there is a small sign on the ground, with a big rock holding it that says,

Pepi's Slumgullion.

"This is it," he says. "You'll love *Pepi's*."

We go up the steps and inside it is real cool with booths along both sides. There are swinging doors to the kitchen and you can smell the aroma of food. There is no one else there; we are all by ourselves. Soft guitar music is playing in the background. James says, "We are early for lunch. Pepi serves all afternoon. He makes the meanest Margarita."

"What are *they*," I ask. "I see them in the movies. Are they good?"

"They are so good you won't even remember your mother's name?" He laughs.

"I would never forget that," I say shaking my head.

It is one of those afternoons when time gets lost. I am sipping on my Margarita and the food is so good I can't get enough. But it is James. He is so nice, I can't help but feel like a beauty queen with him. He takes my hand always, when he talks serious somethings. He rubs the tops of my fingers, one at a time, and the smile in his eyes say things my heart wants to hear. I am feeling so relaxed, so sleepy, I just want to curl up in a ball... in someone's arms... and take a long snooze.

Hey, Ella," he says. "You look too sleepy-eyed to go traipsing about. Maybe we can make it tomorrow?"

"That sounds like a winner to me," I say, yawning.

Then things get a little fuzzy. I remember getting in the car and his driving through town. He pulls into an apartment complex, into the back of it, and when he turns the key off in the ignition, it was the silence I remember. The silence.

Next I remember being in his arms. He was so sweet. He whispers in my ears, both of them, sucks on them, puts his hands in my hair. I'm feeling so warm and good I want to stay there forever. He is touching me, all over my hungry body. I want him to not stop, to go everywhere I got skin. I tell him that. "Go everywhere I got skin," I say.

"You got skin where nobody else has skin," he says sticking his tongue into my ear.

I am so heated up I can't help myself.

His hands are all over my legs. He is rubbing them from my toes up to my knees. I want him to go higher. *Higher*, I am telling him in my head. I feel the soft touch of his hands on my thighs. Outside, all around, and then somehow he gets to the inside. His smooth, silky hands move up so slowly I think I will die before he finally gets to the spot. I can't stop myself from moving, just a little. *Come closer*, I am telling him with my legs. I put one over his hips. I'm feeling like putty in his hands as he pulls at my safaris, his soft warm... I want to... want to... Oh god, he is into me. He is going... God, it is as if we were made together... I am moving, he has me by the behind... He has hold of me and is moving me onto his body... *He knows this stuff, down pat.* He has me just right. I'm caught, locked in his grip.... My control let's go.... No stopping in me... Go. Go. Go, I whisper, go, go, go. Don't ever stop, go. Go, oh, god, go...

The breeze and stillness wake me up just as the sun is going down over the mountains. James is lying next to me in somebody's bed, resting his head on his elbow. He says to me, "You know you are beautiful when you sleep?"

I am awake in a flash then. I am in my birthday, just like James. He has the body of a god. *He must work out every day.* I'm embarrassed for my flabby skin hanging out. He says, "Not everyone sleeps graceful. But you, you're a guy's dream come true."

I wonder what he is getting at? *Does he want to go again?* So I ask him, "What you got in mind, James? Is this the desert you wanted to show me?"

"Now, do I detect a slight tone of bitterness?" he says raising his eyebrows. "You didn't enjoy that very much, did you?" he says with a slight snicker.

"I think it was fantastic."

"I think?" he says. "I *think*?"

"Yes, I can't remember everything. Just the first orgasm. How many did I have?"

He laughs. "You are the kind that counts?"

"Oy. What else have I got to do?" I say with a smile. "What else have I got to do?"

Back in my motel room, I am showered, clean. In the mirror I see my old flabby skin, and I wonder what the

Love 'N' Stuff

guy saw in me? *James, what a smoothie you are!* I know I've been had, and I loved it, what I could remember of it. *Those Margaritas.* I am beginning to feel a little bad now, for Herschel. *Wonder if he can tell when he looks into my eyes? Have to remember not to let him do that.*

Room service brings me half a chicken and apple pie a la mode, my favorite desert. The news is on, and I don't even hear it. I am in a world of James and skin and soft mellow tongues in my ears. I want to keep this day inside me forever. *Who cares why or what for?* I just want to keep my legs locked until kingdom come. I don't have any remorse; I only feel like heaven peed in my belly. I want to savor it, suck it into my middle, deep into my lower most parts. For the first time in my life, I have an orgasm with a man inside me. *Finally, I'm a woman, the way Phil Donahue's show talks about.* I know I am okay, now. *I don't care if Herschel ever comes home.* I am finally okay. Me, Ella May, a regular, everyday kind of person, a whole woman.

Ready for the sleep of angels, my body is like a feather, floating.

In my head, I am young again in one of my Christmas pageants. Learned words stay etched forever in my child brain.

In yonder sky...

I feel the bright lights overhead and some are at my feet, red and blue spots pointed up at me. The dark out in the room has sounds of coughs, throats clearing, all are waiting for me to speak. In my six-year-old voice, the sound rings out loud and clear:

In yonder sky I see a star;
it is the star of David.
In yonder sky I see the promise;
it is the star of love.

The star of love... The star of love... A promise... The star of love... Promise... in yonder sky. The star of love... Promise of love... in yonder sky...

Before I decide to tell Herschel, I think he'll understand. At least I try to explain it to him that I never feel quite whole before. No matter how hard I try, it just never happens with us. Maybe because I love him so much, I am more afraid, especially to let him know.

He says to me, "You mean, you been acting all along?"

"Yeah, sorta. Oh, don't get me wrong. I always love to have you touch me. Just having your anything next to my anything feels good. It just never gets any better than that, and I've been told it should. They're talking about it right on TV, on Donahue, that a woman can have orgasm right along with her husband."

"Well, how come you didn't *tell* me?" he says, a little hurt, but more angry.

"Herschel, there are some things a wife just can't tell her husband. And until I know I am okay, normal, I'm afraid to let you know. Now that I know it, I can quit worrying about myself. Don't you see how happy this makes me? How else can I tell you?"

That was the beginning of the end with us. At least we had something going before. But I see then that I made a big mistake. A man, he has so much pride. It really isn't me, or my allegiances, it is who? When I tell him it is a guy I met at the pool, "an angel," I say.

He winces. "Gosh, Ella, ain't you got no suave? At least you could've picked someone a little higher classed."

"Like who?" I ask him. "Just who do you think is high classed?"

I got him there. He just shakes his head and goes into a quiet like I didn't know about before. And that is when I start thinking about being disappeared. I think maybe if he misses me, the way his note sounds, maybe it will bring him back to me. I don't know. I just know I can't tell him the truth. Not now. I have to play it out.

I want to clean the whole house so badly. Cleaning is my salvation. If I vacuum, but don't move anything, at least the dust will stay down. He won't know the difference, but I will. Once, when my pop was so sick, that time, I went over for a week. When I came home, Herschel was so proud. He had vacuumed and everything put away, nice and neat. But you could write your name on any piece of furniture in the house. I show him, and he says, with such shock, "Well, I never even saw that." We still laugh about that sometimes. He says, "If you don't go around writing your name on things, you don't never gotta dust!" *Better be sure to leave some dust somewhere that he might look.*

To keep my hair clean, I put it up in a scarf, the way I always do when I work around the house. Somewhere the energy comes while I am trying to figure things out, how to come back to life. I clean out under the bed. When I see the bedpan, I have to laugh. *Just how the hell was I thinking I was going to use this thing? Where was my head when I planned all this?* But I have to put it all back right now, just in case of emergency. I remember to take my Bactrim; the bladder business seems to be doing okay. I am drinking lots of water and I start eating the tuna fish and baby food meat I got hid. All the empties from my food I have to wash good with soap to keep the odors down, in my special Ziplock trash.

Since I put in a whole day, I am feeling pretty good and

I know I will sleep like a baby. Sometimes I put on the radio in the day for awhile, but I have to be careful not to change the dial. Herschel keeps the ball game station on with music only in between the sports. But anything is better than all the quiet. I do my laundry and remember to put the towels back into the dryer like he left them. The mess he left in the laundry room is hard for me to leave, but I manage.

About ten o'clock I decide to crawl into my space. What a bummer, I think. This has got to be over with soon. Maybe I could even sleep in the bed, just for tonight. Herschel isn't supposed to be back til tomorrow. But I am already half asleep and too tired to move.

I am sawing logs real sound when the garage doors wake me with a start. I quick use the flashlight and see it is two o'clock in the morning. I say to myself that this is luck I didn't sleep in the bed. Something must've told me, *Sleep on the floor, Ella.* I am going over the whole house in my mind. *Did I forget anything?* I had such a good day. Sometimes when I'm happy, I don't see everything. "Overconfidence" is what Herschel calls it. He says I get euphoric-like, thinking I'm a god or something, and breeze right over top of stuff. I'm really worried I did that. But there's nothing I can do now, so I just breathe deep and slow, trying to feel my toes.

Herschel makes a big lot of noise coming in. I wonder if he is drinking again. *Oh, no, don't start that again. I can't live through that any more.* He slams the door and the brief case hits the back of the closet wall. He comes into the bedroom and I hear something hit the bed, over me. The light in the hall is so dim I can't see his feet very good. He goes to the bathroom and into the john. The toilet seat is up just as he left it. Except I did clean the john good, but he

Love 'N' Stuff

won't know the difference. The toilet paper roll I changed to one half full, he won't notice that much difference. He is in the dark, I think. Boy, he must have to go. He slams the seat down and flushes, being very loud. The bathroom light goes on, so I can see his feet, finally. He has on his dress shoes, the nice expensive Florsheims, and it looks like his best suit that he only wears to special events. *Not to ride on the plane.* I wonder what is going on? I hear him start to undress. He comes back around the side of the bed and opens the suitcase. The zipper gets stuck and he swears "goddamn Sam." I hear the zipper finally snap. I wonder if he breaks it or just fixes it? I don't know. But I can't do anything now; I will fix it later. He is going back and forth to the closet, hanging up his stuff.

He goes to the laundry room and I hear him open the dryer. He turns it on and starts the washer. He must have some dirty stuff. Maybe he played golf and got caught in the rain. One time he came home with a suitcase full of wet dirty stuff. It was the smelliest mess. He said he didn't think anything could happen to it in just three days. I had a time getting the mildew out. I beg him never to put wet stuff in a suitcase again. He says he will just throw the stuff away then. Which makes me very upset. "Herschel, don't you have no responsibility about you? Can't you think for yourself?" I say to him. Now he at least is doing his laundry. That is something my being disappeared has done. Taught him to do his laundry.

He is in the kitchen. I hear him going through all the cupboards and the refrigerator. He pulls the bin out this time and I hear him biting into an apple just when he walks back into the bedroom. He is standing at the end of the bed and is chewing for a minute. Then I hear him go back into the kitchen and run the disposal for the apple core.

Sometimes he acts like he is alright. Can take care of himself. This being gone is good for him. Makes him do more for himself. I have to figure out a way to be gone and stay being alive, not a ghost.

He comes back into the bedroom. I left the bed spread the way he had it, pulled up over the pillows all in a wad, even though I cringed every time I looked at it. He pulls his clothes off and throws them on the floor. Must be sleeping in his birthday again. He does that a lot when he is real tired, and hot. He is sawing logs in a hurry. And I am thoroughly confused. *What's going on?*

The clock is ticking. He must've wound the clock when I wasn't paying attention. But it sounds good. At least it is not so quiet. I feel better though, having Herschel back, above me. I can almost touch him. Feel his aura, anyhow. I go to sleep feeling his aura, whatever color it is. It could be black, for all I know about auras. If he sets the alarm I know he is going to get up early in the morning for something.

The alarm goes off and he jumps out of bed with a groan. Sometimes, when it rings, he screams. Luckily, I am not real sound asleep. Or when he screams, I scream from his screaming. It is not so funny us scaring each other like that. One of these days when we get old, we are going to both flake out like that. The old ticker has a limit on screams in the night. He picks up the phone. I hear him punch the buttons. He says, "You okay?"

I don't like the sound of his voice. It is too cozy, too quiet, too sweet.

He says, "I had to leave. You don't understand. It's over. But I had to tell you in person.... No, she's not back and I am beginning to worry now. This just ain't Ella.... No, you don't understand. Ella and me, we got things... Toni... You just wouldn't understand, if you didn't have a kid die on you. It's not just one little thing. There are lots of things. You and me, we was good for a few minutes, huh? No. Don't even try; it wouldn't work. You gotta believe me. No. ... Don't say such things, she ain't dead. She ain't." His voice gets all crack-ly, and he is almost crying. "Naw, just a cold," he says into the phone. "Okay. It was real. Take care. See you around."

Herschel is dressed and gone in half an hour. He is in a hurry to go somewhere. I am glad because I have this knife stuck into me, my heart. The sound of his voice when he spoke to her, the gentleness. *I knew he had a cookie. I just knew it.* And now I know I can't tell him the truth. I have to play it out good and long, so he knows for sure I was really disappeared. I wonder just how long the cookie was on? I know it was some time after Arizona, so I guess I can't really complain. Got it coming, he would say. *No doubt.* Well, maybe now we're even. Maybe now we can start on the same rung of the ladder. I always felt before we were one off from each other. For the first time, I feel even with Herschel. It is a big relief, but it doesn't make the knowing hurt any less.

    I don't know where Herschel is going now, so I think I better rush to the john and right back. I scoot out and do my business fast and splash my face with cold water. I drink a big glass of the putrid water and run and take a peek at the clothes in the washer. He has all his underwear and pj's in there. He started taking pj's on trips a while back. Not like him. He doesn't wear them at home. I always wonder about that. And he only wears the tops sometimes. That is strange too. But no lipstick or anything so I can't figure it out. This time I know he has been with her so there is no reason to look any further.

In the kitchen, I quick get a package of Jell-O and run the hot water into a cup over it. It is yucky, sticking to the sides when I stir it, but I drink it. Then I wash the spoon and cup and put it back on the shelf. I take the empty Jell-O packaging with me for my own personal Ziplock trash. This feeling that has come over me, that I should hurry, is making me anxious. I don't know where he is, but it is too early for work. *What is he up to?* Getting back under my space and wait is all I can do.

It is fully light out, a little after eight o'clock, by the time I hear the garage open. The car shuts off. In the garage I hear his voice, and he is talking to someone. He comes into the house, still talking, "You mean this guy has been charged with six women so far? What makes you think? I don't see the connection at all. Ella, she don't talk to strange..." Herschel stops in the middle of the sentence. "She don't usually talk to strangers. No, I just don't think she would let someone into her house like that."

"But you said she let the boys from the homeless shelter."

"No, I never said she let them *in*. She could've handed the stuff to them through the door."

"Well, that's just how this guy works, apparently. He befriends women and gains their sympathy somehow, and next thing you know, they are gonzo."

"So how does this stuff, she was giving away, figure into all of this?"

"We got it figured that he gets appliances that would bring in more money, along with the clothes. And sells them, down at the bus station. He has been seen by several with different things. Toasters, fans, waffle irons... anything

Love 'N' Stuff

that plugs in and can't be checked to see if it works."

"Well, she supposedly gave him a waffle iron. Here, let me go check."

They are in the kitchen, opening all the cupboards. Herschel is saying to the guy who sounds like a cop. "I don't know where she keeps anything, I swear. I am lost in this house. One of these days, I'm going to rearrange things so I can find them."

Be my guest, Buddy. I'll find a way to give you plenty time. Nothing makes me more angry than when he talks about my way of keeping house. *Who does he think he is?*

Herschel is saying, "It looks like it must have been on this shelf. There is an empty space here," he says.

"Yeah, could be. No waffle iron then?"

"No, it's not here."

The cops say, "Think. Is there any other place she might have put it?"

"The only place might be the garage."

They come down the hall and I hear them go into the garage. The shelves inside the built-in cupboards are full of left over paint and turpentine and a bunch of junk Herschel saves in there. "No such luck," says Herschel.

The cop says, "If we can put our fingers on the stuff your wife gave to this guy, do you think you can identify it?"

"I'll try. I don't always know what she's got," he says.

"Doesn't sound like you and the missus is too cozy."

"Yeah, I know. I travel all the time and I pretty much let her run things at home. I just never was a home body, you know. The old saying, *A man's home is his castle* is a bunch of crap. It's the *ol' lady's* castle, and as long as what the ol' man wants doesn't conflict with what *she* wants, it's okay. I got tired of fighting the problem. The only place that's my castle, is my office. Nobody goes into my desk and when I close my door, no one opens it. There ain't no place in this house I could shut a door to Ella. She even comes into the bathroom when I'm taking a shit, I ain't kiddin' ya. This dame is where she wants to be *wherever that is*, that's why I just ain't buying your theory. It just don't figure with her ways."

The cop says, "Okay, but we gotta check everything out. If you'll get me a sample of her handwriting, a good picture, and let me see her clothes closet so I can get sizes of her clothes, I'll be on my way."

Herschel and the cop are standing in the hallway, between the garage door and the bedroom door. I can hear them very well. They step into the bedroom. Herschel opens my closet door and says, "Well this is her closet; help yourself."

The cops start pulling the clothes out by the hangers, one at a time. "Looks like she is pint size. This here is a size three petite. How tall did you say she was?"

"She's not quite five feet, about four-eleven."

"Okay, we got that."

It sounds like he is writing something. Herschel says, "Over here by the telephone, she wrote all these addresses in this book."

"Hey, do you mind I take this with me, make some copies, and you can pick it up later today, if you like, if you need it."

"Sure, go ahead. I can always look stuff up."

They start to walk around the bed and the cop stops in front of the bathroom. "What did you say was the color of her hair?"

"Dark, real dark. She has Cherokee Indian in her. One of her grandparents was almost full blooded. She looks Indian, very small boned."

Love 'N' Stuff

They stand there a few minutes. Herschel says, "How come you're stopping here. What's in the bathroom?"

"I'm just thinking about your saying she doesn't wear any make-up. And I see what looks like powder all over the sink."

They walk into the bathroom. "Ah, is that what that is? I thought I just needed to dust or something. How did you see that way in the other room?"

"A cop gets trained to look for things. Anything you tell me that doesn't sound right, I gotta question. And no woman in today's world goes without makeup. You know, my daughter took this beauty course to teach her how to use makeup so no one can see it. It's an art. She spends an hour at the mirror so that when she turns around it looks like she isn't wearing anything but her natural face. And I suspect that is what your wife does."

"I'll be damned," says Herschel like he is really shocked. "There so much I'm learning about my wife these last few days. I don't know where I've been. It's like I didn't even see her before, she had to leave for me to know she was here. Wonder why that is?"

You're just a normal guy. Don't be too hard on yourself. Life with a woman isn't the easiest thing in the world," the cop says almost with a resigning tone, as though he wishes he didn't have to live with a woman either.

"What else was it, now... a picture?"

"Yes, something recent, if possible."

Herschel starts out into the hall. He says, "Let's see, I'm trying to think where I'd find that, maybe back in Toni's room. There is one with him."

"Toni?"

"Yeah, he's our son. He died a few years ago."

"Oh, yeah? How so?"

"OD'd. He was found in a rented room, in his bed, dead."

"That must've been hard on the Missus."

"Yeah. We ain't never been the same since, either one of us. It's just not the same." Their voices start to get fainter as they head into Toni's room.

I know the picture they are going to get. It was with Toni at his first high school play. He got a small part as the milkman in *Our Town*. He was Howard. He only has a grunt or two and one line. But he was so proud to be picked. He doesn't even look like my Toni after the make-up and the clothes they put on him. I have such great hopes for him to maybe do something with this new interest he has. Herschel thinks it is sissy and he won't even go to the school to see it. He says it's his "traveling" that kept him from it, but he could've fixed it, just one day, to be at home. I never forgave him for that. Toni was so hurt. But he doesn't let it show when they take the picture of us together.

I hear Herschel and the cop back in the kitchen talking. "Don't let anything happen to that picture, now," says Herschel. "It's the only one I got of the kid, and Ella, too. I'll have to look for one more recent. But she looks just like that. Her hair is a little longer I think. Bigger, it seems to me."

"I'll tell you what, why don't you come into the office and let our artist do the hair up like you think is more up to date. They can do that you know."

"Oh, I ain't into hair, let me tell you. I couldn't even tell them. It's just more puffed out, or something."

"The artist will be able to do it. Why don't you give me a call later on this morning, see if I can line you up so you don't have to wait. I know you are busy."

"Yeah, I gotta get into the office. I came home a day early. I had this thing come up... and I had to get back."

"Okay. Let me take this stuff in and see what we can come up with."

The house is quiet again after Herschel closes the garage door. I keep trying to listen for the car to start. But nothing happens. I wonder what he is doing in the garage? I hear something hit against the house. Sounds like he is going through that cabinet out there. *Wonder what he is looking for?* It's months since I was out there. Not a clue what he is after.

Pretty soon he comes back into the house. He comes into the bedroom, into the bathroom. He must be washing his hands. He comes back out and hops up onto the bed; the phone buttons are getting pushed. "Dottie? Yeah, I had something come up about Ella, so I came back. No, it doesn't sound good. They are talking serious business. They think it wouldn't be a bad idea to dust the doorknobs and some places around the house, for prints. So I had to be here. They are coming in about a half hour. I never thought such a thing would happen to me... I just can't believe it... Naw, I won't be in till after lunch. Tell the ol' man if he needs me to call me here. I have to go into the precinct to meet with the artist too, later on this morning.... Yeah, thanks... Yeah, I'll be fine. Just have to get my thinking straight.... Okay."

After Herschel hangs up, he sits on the side of the bed a long time, not moving. His feet are dangling, so I know he is sitting right on the edge. Sometimes he sits that way, with his head resting into his hands, with his elbows propped on his knees. *Wonder what he's thinking?* Inside, I am getting a little upset now. I wish I was up in the attic. The heat and the insulation would be better than having a cop find me. I am getting nervous. Finally, Herschel gets up and walks around the bed into the hallway. He opens the closet door and I hear his briefcase snap open. He must have something in there. I hear it fall back into the closet. Next he goes into the laundry room and fools with the washer and dryer. I can't tell what he is doing, besides making noise. He's not moving too very fast, like he was this morning when he got up.

Into the kitchen, I hear the TV in the other room go on, some talk show, Merv Griffin, or Phil Donahue. You can tell it's a talk show, because it doesn't have any background music like the soaps. That background music gives me the creeps, as if something is going to happen all the time. Keeps a person suspended in air and grabbing on every word. Why I stopped watching them when I had Toni. Couldn't get anything done, ever. I was walking around the house, tiptoeing, and I hate having anything run me like that. It was as if I was a puppet on their string. So I cut the string, you might say. It is so long ago, I can't even remember what I watched. *One Life to Live,* or some such thing. What a joke, one life to live but different every day. What a farce. Nobody really changes their life much, I don't think. Look at me. I'm no different under the bed as on top of it. Still scared. Still listening to every word, watching every move Herschel makes. His shadow. Only when he is gone do I have any real freedom. And then it is not really freedom. I'm forever trying to be careful he doesn't find out anything he wouldn't like. Never really free... even disappeared. *What am I going do?*

Love 'N' Stuff

Herschel is going to the front door, to let the finger printers in, I guess. I can't hear them way back in here. They are in there a long time, and then I hear there is three of them, I think. Herschel is saying, "Now I don't know where you'd get nothing but her prints on anything, as I went all around the house looking for things more than once. Take her closet. I must've been in there a hundred times already since she left. The only place might be the piano keys. She is the only one who plays it since Toni, my son..."

"Okay, let's get a set in there," says a high squeaky voice. Sounds like a little old man. They must turn around as I can tell they're in the living room, the drapes absorb the sound. I wonder what kind of mess they are going to make in there on my white rug? Something falls on the keys. They are in there a while, and Herschel comes back into the bedroom and opens my closet again. He has someone with him, and he takes some boxes off the top shelf. He is saying, "This might be something. I only took the top off these boxes; I didn't touch the shoes. These here patent leather jobbies should give good prints, huh?"

"Yeah," I hear the woman say. "Good choice. The glasses in the cupboard. Do you want to come and show me the ones you have used most recently, so we can get a single print of yours?"

Now I am really scared. I remember washing and putting the small juice glass back after I used it. That could only have my prints on it.

In the kitchen I hear Herschel say, "Yeah, I think this is the one; I used it for orange juice. Yeah, this is the one."

I hear noises; Herschel is very quiet. My heart is pumping up a storm in my chest. I don't know what they are going to find. They are there another fifteen minutes or so and I hear Herschel say, "Anything you need now, just holler. You going to let me know as soon as you get them processed?"

The front door slams and it sounds like the roof is vibrating. The humidity must be making the door stick again. I hear Herschel coming back into the back hall and the phone rings. Herschel gets it in the kitchen. I hear him talking very softly into the phone. All I can hear him say is, Ella this and Ella that. I don't have a clue who he's talking to. He hangs up and I hear him go into the laundry room. He is fooling with the clothes, I think. I hear the dryer go on and he comes back into the bedroom and sits next to the bed, by the phone. He pushes the buttons. "Yeah, Sergeant? You said to call you about the artist. Okay. I'll be right over."

It is the sound of the silence that drives me nuts. The clock's ticking is the only thing that keeps me remembering I am alive. I slide out from under and head for the bathroom in a hurry. I figure I have about a half hour before he comes back. I do my business, brush my teeth, wash my face with cold water. It feels so good. Wakes me up. I am so hungry. I go back and reach under the bed for a can of fruit cocktail. The juice goes down first, and then I turn the can upside down, into my mouth. I am too hungry to look for a spoon. I get it all over my face, but that is alright, I'm going to clean up anyhow. I go to the bathroom sink and rinse out the can. There is a piece of red maraschino cherry stuck on the edge of the sink. I can't get the darn thing to go down. Finally, it washes away, and I quick put the can into my Ziplock trash, under the bed. I am down on my belly reaching under the bed when the garage door opens. I can't remember if I left the bathroom okay,

Love 'N' Stuff

but I don't have time to check. I am under the bed in a flash.

Herschel comes into the house and goes right to the phone in the kitchen. He is talking softly again. I try hard to hear, but I can't make out a word. He must be facing the other way. He talks a long time and hangs up. He goes into the hall closet for his brief case and I hear his keys go into his pocket. He must have been using my car keys all this time, I think. He comes back into the bathroom and does his business. He flushes and puts the lid back down. It is becoming a habit, I guess. He walks back out into the hall and I hear the door close behind him. The exit noises I have become used to have now become routine. I know when he is completely gone.

The stillness in the house is what makes me move. I slide out and go into the kitchen. I look for any notes, to give me a hint. All I find is a sheet of doodles, circles over circles of doodles he was doing on the last phone call. *He must've done a lot of listening on that one.* My curiosity is so strong, I am dying. I think I know every little thing Herschel thinks and does, what he doesn't do, and this new thing has got me stumped. I wonder right away if he has a new girl? *He gives one the shaft, maybe it's because he met someone new?* My mind is going a mile a minute. *I gotta find a way to reappear. And soon.* But I'm worried now, with the cops involved. I have to think this out.

I walk around the house. Just walking, I'm watching the clock. If he took his briefcase, he's gone to work, and if he's gone to work he doesn't have a cookie — unless, of course, she's at work. I have to think. The dryer buzzer sounds; the clothes are finished. Automatically, I walk towards the laundry room, until I remember I can't touch anything. I want to take charge of this whole affair, get it over with, but I'm stuck now. I don't know where to start. *Wonder, should I leave the house really now, and come back as if I was gone all that time?*

On the spur of the moment, I decide to get all the stuff out from under the bed. *I am going to have to really disappear; that is the only way.* I have a collapsible bag I found at a garage sale, folded flat. I pull it out and reach under the bed for all the stuff, the Ziplock trash, the mirror, the flashlight, books. The Kleenex, the extra toilet paper, the stack of clothes, underwear, the pillow, the blanket, sleeping bag. I roll the bag up and take it into the closet in Toni's room and stick it down behind the rollaway bed with the pillow. It doesn't show and he'll never know it wasn't there all the time. The stuff in the bag is not heavy.

Five-hundred dollars in cash and an extra house key, I've stowed. A small make-up case, a nylon windbreaker Herschel threw away out of his golf bag. It is just to keep the draft off if the air-conditioning got too cold somewhere. I go to the bathroom and check my face. My hair could stand a few curls, so I quick plug in the hot curlers. It is all set up to use; I leave it that way. I am looking under the bed again, to make sure everything is clean. The shade I made, tacked onto the inside of the bed, is nothing anyone would ever find, until they took the bed apart, so I leave that there. *I can get that later, sometime...*

The hot curlers are ready and I put them in all over my head. By the time I get the last one in the first one is ready to come out. I need some hair spray, but I don't dare use it. I have a red paisley silk scarf inside the small bag and I pull it out, tie it around my head and into a bow under my hair, on my neck. It makes me look like a Gypsy. I always liked that look with big round earrings. In my dresser, I pull out some big white ones. The scarf has just enough white in it to make the earrings stand out. *I probably could use a darker color lipstick one of these days... But that would blow Herschel's mind for sure, since he thinks I don't wear any.* I put on another thick coat of *Mellon*; it feels like wax and stops the peeling skin from not wearing enough the last few days. I go into the bottom of the other end of the closet. Inside is an old handbag. I have another small shoulder bag. I pull it out. It is tan, sort of khaki color, and it blends into my washed out jeans and tie-dyed t-shirt. I pull out an old shirt of Herschel's that he never wears. It is under one of my jackets in the back of the closet. A narrow striped, heavy cotton shirt I wear on top, as a jacket with the sleeves rolled up. The loafers I have on are really Indian moccasins. They are soft and feel like heaven to my feet, the closest thing to being bare footed you can get.

In every room, I take a good look now. I unplug the hot curlers. The hair I dropped, I blow real hard out of the sink. The toilet is flushed all the way, and the seat is down as he left it. The bed skirt is hanging straight all the way around. In the kitchen, I don't see anything out of place.

Now, which door should I go out of? I can't go out the pool side door, because it has a sliding latch from the inside. Not the garage door because I don't have a clicker. The only door is the front. It leads out the front walk between two fat cedar trees that almost cover the door from the street. In the yard is a shade tree that has branches very low to the ground. The front doorway is almost hidden from the street. I think I better get going, quick, and get lost somewhere before he comes back.

Going out the front door, I feel for my key in my jeans' pocket before I close the door. I have my purse hanging from my shoulder and the other bag in that hand. When I pull the door behind me, it clicks shut. I slip past the shrubs, and go around the corner of the house, through the back yard, towards the tall hedge. I walk as if I'm supposed to be there. When I get to the shrubs that separate the backyard from the busy road behind our house, I take a deep breath. In the hedge there is an opening worn, from people walking through it, and I hear someone coming with a dog. The pooch is barking and coming in my direction. I know I have to move in a hurry so I don't look as if I'm sneaking. My head is down, and the dog, a little shaggy thing, is pulling on the leash to get near me.

The owner says, "Pootsy, now Pootsy. Come back. Pootsy."

The dog gets chained in by the lady walking him.

I look up at her, but grab my bag and pull it in close.

She says, "Sorry. Pootsy *loves* people."

I smile and say, "Don't worry about it." Walking past her, I'm going the other way so that my back is to the oncoming traffic, the direction in which Herschel would be driving if he were to come home just now. Up to the end of the block, I cross over and go down a block before I turn back towards the main drag, towards the big shopping mall that is two blocks from our house.

Suddenly, I feel like I am free, free. I can't believe the feeling. I have a few thousand dollars I've siphoned from Herschel's account, into a new bank in my maiden name, Cahill. For ID, I have an old driver's license and library card. I feel as if I just unloaded one hell of a burden. My stomach is so empty, I can't wait to eat. French fries, onion rings, a quarter-pounder, and a chocolate shake. Something to fill me up. *After I get my stomach full, I will figure out where to go next.*

The thought of going home suddenly doesn't seem the least bit inviting. Maybe I can find a room, get a job, wait tables, buy some new clothes, meet a friend... *No more chains, beds, fears, have to's or should's.*

I am so excited, I start to run. French fries cooking fills the air and spurs me on. I am a kid again, on my best day, and if I think about it hard enough, I can even remember two of them. *Maybe I'll go down to the beach...*

Suddenly the picture above our bed, of the two sailing ships, flashes into my mind. The thought passes through my brain somewhere, click, that I am the sail almost hidden, nothing more than a shadow of the first. As I am running, chasing the aroma of food, I can see the second sail slowly pull out on its own, into full view. *Funny, I never noticed how tall she is...* As if my mind has angel vision, I see her now, that second sail, as she heads out over the horizon, *alone.*

~ ~

TOO MUCH IS NEVER ENOUGH

ALLEGORY

Once upon a time, in a small island country, there was a little orphan girl who was poor, homeless, and had no shoes. She walked the streets in her bare feet. But she was very beautiful. When she grew up, her beauty and tenaciousness, coupled with the contempt she had for the poverty of her youth, led her to become the wealthy first lady of the land. Although she could have anything she wanted, she surrounded herself with many, many shoes. Rows upon rows, closets upon closets of shoes. But still her feet felt bare as she found that *too much is never enough.*

Her name was Imelda Marcos.

~ ~

THE WHITE MARBLE DOORKNOB

FICTION

It's just one of the things I remember about Gramps, my granddaddy. He'd say to me, "Sissy, when I was a little girl..." and I'd say back to him, "Naw, Gramps. You ain't never been a little girl, now was ya?" He'd just smile at me and pull on his whiskers like he was thinking, *You'll find out. You'll find out.* The sun could rise and set purple if I wanted it to. He'd say something like, "Say-rah, do you want a purple sky? Just say it; Gramps'll get it for you. Me and the guy up there is on speakin' terms, you know." I knew he was joshin' me. But the turning-into-a-boy thing... Gramps *was* wearing a dress in that picture, on his mama's knee. The only one I'd believe over him was my ma, when she came around.

One day Gramps and me is out gaddin' about town in his shined up DeSoto. He says to me, "Say-rah, can you keep a secret?"

"What's a secret?" I ask. "What does it look like?"

"Well, a secret is something that has its own special place in here," he says thumping his chest. "The place has a lock and key on it so nobody can steal it from you."

"Awe, Gramps, how can you lock up your insides with a key?"

"Lemme show you," he says as he swings down a side street. We drive a little ways off the main drag before he slows down and stops. At the back of this big empty lot, with grass growing up your sunshine, sits a little house with a tin roof on it that's rusting. "I keep telling her she needs to get a new roof," he says to himself. "But she likes the way this one sounds when it rains."

"Who?" I ask him. "Who lives here?"

"You'll see. It's my secret."

So we walk back though the grass on this worn path. It's for certain we ain't the only visitors to this secret house. When we get to the door, the screen's pulled and curling out, like someone tore it to get to the white marble doorknob inside. "Gramps," I say. "I ain't never seen a white doorknob like that before. How come it's white?"

"That's a classy trademark," he says. "It tells you a thing or two about the one who put it there. Not no cheap rusty tricks for this one," he says.

I'm standing there, eyeing this white, shiny doorknob just inches from my nose, when the knob suddenly turns.

Gramps is rocking back on his high-boot heels and winks. "Remember what I told you now. Mum's the word," he says and puts his finger to his lips in a mock shush.

I turn back to the white doorknob; it stops turning, and the door opens just a crack. I'm looking into the dark and seeing nothing inside. Then I hear Gramps say softly, as though someone's sleeping and he doesn't want to wake them, "Alva. This here's Say-rah, my grandkid."

The door opens a little wider and I see a woman with the brightest red, curly hair I'd ever seen peek her head around it. She must've been holdin' on to the white doorknob inside, but she lets go of it when she sees me, and the white knob takes a quick twirl backwards to a dead stop. It leaves a silence in the air, a quiet that makes you afraid to breathe.

The door doesn't move, so Gramps takes things into his own hands. "Alva. It's okay. Say-rah here, she don't do nothing I don't tell her. And I told her it was secret."

"You sure?" comes this tiny little voice. "I ain't ready for no trouble. Can't keep the grass cut now," she says with a big sigh.

Love 'N' Stuff

"Yeah, I'm sure. Say-rah here, she's a good kid. She's gonna turn out just like me. She don't pay no attention to the meetin' folks either," he says like he's king or something.

This Alva person grabs the outside edge of the door with her hand. Her fingers are full of fancy rings like I never saw before. Even on her knuckle finger, she's got a big red stone the size of a cherry. On the middle finger is a wide, yellow-gold wedding band. It stands out so plain and pretty. I'm taking all this in while Gramps and her get close enough to whisper to each other. Finally this Alva says in a big voice, "Yeah. Sure. Just like that Betty dame. She was in and out so fast the sheets never got warm."

"You'll see, Babe. You'll see," says Gramps in a soothing voice, looks at me, and winks again.

She holds the door open for us and says, "Come on in then, I guess." She turns to me, "Say-rah, did you say?"

"No, I didn't say," I answer with a silly look just like Gramps does sometimes. It's how he gets the upper hand with people when they talk.

Alva stands up real straight. She looks at me with a hard stare. The look in her eye makes me decide maybe the way Gramps does don't work too good on her. So I quickly add, "But you can call me that, if you like."

It must be the right thing to say because she wilts a little into herself and reaches for my shoulder. "Say-rah, you got any friends?" she asks. Feeling my protruding bones, she grabs hold of me and pulls me over, into the light. It's a lonely bulb hung from a wrinkled cord that has different color wires strung and twisted in it all the way to the ceiling. The light is dim, but it's enough to let you see the old rickety round table under it piled high with books and newspapers. There's a pair of clear, plastic-rimmed glasses laying on top of the mess.

"Friends? What do you mean friends?" I ask, not really understanding such a question. I got Gramps, and my ma once in awhile, and the sissy-pants social worker who always says she's come to see our Rembrandts.

"You know, Say-rah. Girl friends your age, or even boyfriends. Some little girls like to play with boys. What about you. Do you like girls? Or boys better?"

I look up at her like she's daft. It ought to be plain to see I ain't no sissy pants goin' to meetin'. My dander don't get up too often; Gramps says it don't pay. "You cain't fight City Hall," he says, "and if'n you owe them money, *they's City Hall!*" I can't tell yet if we owe this Alva person money. So I decide to play her silly game of Question and Answer. At least for a while. So I say, in my most formal and polite voice, "Yes'm. Either one'll do. For a time. Too long of anybody ain't no fun."

She lets her head fall back into a loud he-haw laugh. "Oh, you are a smart one," she says. "Am I going to have fun with you!" She turns around then, and walks past the table into the dark corner where an old fashioned refrigerator stands. It's painted a shiny, light apple green. You can see where the brush strokes missed a few spots and dried that way. This Alva pulls at the big silver handle that has speckles of green paint dotted all over it. "What'll you have, Say-rah? A glass of cider or rum? I got both."

Rum is something I know about but never tasted. Gramps says it's okay only if you don't have sour mash. And since she offers, I accept. "Rum'll be okay — if you have enough," I add to be polite.

She rears back her head and laughs again just like before. "Well just how much rum do you anticipate drinking? Huh, little lady?"

"Oh, no. That's not what I mean." I look at Gramps and he's shaking his head, smiling.

"See. What'd I tell ya, Alva. Is she something or is she something?"

"Yeah, she's something all right. Something," she says looking away, out somewhere past my head.

Alva finds an extra chair with one lame leg on it in the back room and sets it down to the messy table. "Here now," she says. "Have yourself a good one."

The rum tastes like rotten raisins. But I don't say it. I'm not about to let on.

"The first one's always free," she says.

How much is the next one? I want to ask, but her and Gramps are into looking at one another. It's a quiet look that must have mountains of words down under it. You can tell. Gramps is already sitting in the other chair, right next to Alva. In the light you can see her bright red hair roots are as white as the marble doorknob. She has curls, though, all over her head. I wonder about them. Not that I'd ever want *my* hair to curl like that; I'm just curious how she does it. So in between their staring at one another, I venture a question. "How do you get your hair to be so curly?"

She looks over at me and a smile starts in the corners of her eyes and spreads into every line and crease in her face. "Well, it's like this... When my mama gave me life she threw in the curls for good measure. She said it never hurt a woman to be pleasant to look at; men all *love* curls, you know."

"Oh? I didn't know," I say self-consciously reaching up to feel the back of my straggly, straight hair. "But I ain't going to be no woman anyhow when I grow up. I'm going to be a *man*, just like Gramps. He said I could if I really wanted to," I tell her.

Alva frowns at Gramps and purses her painted-on lips in a shame-on-you look. "You didn't tell this youngin such nonsense, did you George?"

Gramps looks at me and winks again. I take that to mean, what he's saying is a lie — just for this particular occasion. "Honestly, Alva, I cain't remember exactly the circumstances of our discussions, but I was telling her she can be anything her little heart wants, even if it be a mean ol' man."

It's the tone in Gramps' voice that undoes the winkin' just then. He must know it too, because he reaches over and pats me on the head. Alva's watching him when he turns back to looking at her, and I'm busy trying to figure things out – which don't take any time at all. Seeing the way Gramps looks at Alva and her bright red curls makes me want to do or be anything that would make Gramps look at *me* in that same, same way.

~ ~

A CHILD'S WISDOM

MEMOIR

While living in Boston, JoMarie, our six-year-old granddaughter, came to us all the way from Florida. Accompanied by her grandfather on the plane, she was to return alone, via Non-Stop — in the care of the stewardesses — and did. A giant trust, our daughter had placed in her eldest child, in us, "in God," she said. On the first morning of what turned out to be JoMarie's only extended overnight with us, she cried at breakfast while talking to her mom on the phone. Afterwards, I explained that it is too bad that often good things in life, happy and fun things, are accompanied by something sad or unpleasant. "Look at the beautiful roses," I said. "Their stems are full of prickly thorns."

She thought awhile and then looked up at me, and in a very matter-of-fact tone, she said, "The thorns are probably just protecting the roses."

~ ~

VACATION INTO HEAVEN

FICTION

"There is an ambush everywhere from the army of accidents; therefore the rider of life runs with loosened reins."
—*Persian Proverb*

The night it happened, it had been one of those dreary, fall New England days when gloom hung from the skies like a weeping willow tree draping itself over everything — my aching heart, my searching soul, my freshly permed hairdo turning frizzy from the damp sunless air. The top of my head looked like a nesting site for a wild bald eagle from all the peroxide. I'd fought the wispy grey in my once-lovely dark-ash-brown with just a Loving Care rinse until Linda Evans, swinging her bleached, silver tresses at the camera, breathlessly announced from the tube, one time too many, "You can be anything you want to be..." But a Martha Washington was not who I wanted to be just yet. All that snow on the mountain, my husband teased, might necessitate a jump-start to fire the furnace. So I set out to cover my thwarted drug store, vanity inspired efforts, with color, and more color, trying, I am sure, to hide who I *really* was under the rainbow coalition of my Grandma Molly locks.

All weekend during the arduous campaign I had waged to fight off the willies – while Hal's fighting Irish slaughtered the team in red, or was it black? — I could hardly keep my sweater pattern straight as the knitting needles took off in a frenzy. Looming before me was another week of being alone in an empty house shining of Daum crystal, carved teak, and sad -– longing to be held — rag dolls I continued to purchase on every trip. Hal was a devoted husband. And because he asked me often to accompany him on his cross country treks for The Company, he had convinced me not to take an outside job. But this time, for such a long overseas trip, he hadn't invited me along, so here I sat at McDonald's on a Monday night devouring a Big Mac, eating only a few of the limp colorless fries that had caught my nose off guard when the punky teen behind the counter smiled down at me from under his scalp of green porcupine-looking spikes.

At least the place was clean. Hal hated to eat in here because the kids climbing all over the seats made him nervous. Not that he didn't like kids. Carrie and Cassidy, our two granddaughters living in Florida, had wormed their way into his heart and still called him Grandpa Owl from their baby-talk days. I hated being so far away from them and their generous hugs. But I'm sure Hal didn't realize how lonesome I got – their visits all I lived for. Coming here to McDonalds sometimes, gave me a feeling of still belonging to that world of yesteryear when life had direction, cooking had purpose, and thoughts of touching made my bosom swell with love for my young children – instead of aching with feelings of abandonment.

So I wasn't in a hurry to leave as I watched the last toddler being scooped up by her very young jogger-father and pulled through the swinging iron door, out into the heavily gloom-laden night. I stood to follow, but as I slid my empties into the bulging container marked *Thank You,* I realized the extra large decafe I'd been sipping – an excuse to linger, a peeping Grandma Molly — shot a wincing reminder to my bladder that public rest rooms were named such for a reason. So I headed for the door that had Little Bo-Peep on it. As I rushed through it, I came face to face with a young teenage girl who jumped at my entrance as she hastily adjusted the swinging lid on the large plastic-lined trash can.

I did not realize how young she was at first, her profile was almost completely hidden by her long, dark straggly hair that hung into her face. She appeared small but thick around the middle when she grabbed her shabby car coat and pulled it closely around her. She deliberately avoided eye contact as she flew past me out the door I was still holding. It struck me instantly that she must have been a street person like I'd encountered sneaking into the hotel rest room in DC recently, pulling a rickety luggage cart behind her into the toilet stall. That girl had been dressed in elegant 60's fashion, bags and boxes crammed into her cart. The door wouldn't close, and when I'd watched, offering to help, she spoke in an angry tone, "Well, do you *always* watch people do their business?" Her fear had touched me as I felt her distrust –- expecting me to run her out, no doubt, or pass judgment. She had stood there motionless, staring after me until the outer door closed. I could only view her as one of my own out there: broke, hungry, scared and proud. So I dug into my wallet and pulled out a ten-dollar bill and ran back inside. Catching the girl's back to me, still struggling with the cart and the door, I quickly slipped the money into the pocket of her once-beautiful, frayed coat. She grabbed her pocket and was ready to scream, until she saw me through her matted beret she wore stylishly to one side and felt the bill. She pulled it out and looked at it before she gave me a questioning look. I turned and ran out quickly, fighting the tear in my eye. I had the same impulse again today as this young girl ran past me. I wanted to turn around and run after her and grab her and take her home where she would be safe and warm and loved. What had the senior George

Bush at one time called it? "A thousand points of light." This girl couldn't have been much more than twelve and my heart leapt into my stomach remembering myself at that age, and how close I had come to such dire circumstances. Only back then, the police would have locked us up. I guess that is what kept us off the streets — the fear of jail or the Funny Farm. Not now, not these days. But the young straggly looking girl was gone, and Hal would never allow it anyway. He was so afraid of being robbed as it was that he locked his cars inside his garage. So I let the thoughts and feelings slide off me like rain off a Mainlander's slicker. There was nothing I could do for her.

Before me were three empty toilet stalls. When presented by such a dilemma I usually chose the middle one, a moderator instinct born of years straddling fences. It was past the kiddies' dinner hour, the restaurant empty, so I sat down unhurriedly on my neatly arranged toilet paper appreciating its intrinsic value and the apt name of this room. As the urine splashed against the porcelain basin, I remembered the girl who just left and worried if I could get AIDS if a drop ricocheted. Imagining the Surgeon General at his next news conference reassuring us of such an impossibility made me chuckle, relieving my anxiety. "… ricocheting urine droplets…" I could just hear him say. What had the world come to?

A baby's whimper caught my ear. I pulled my buttocks in, surprised at the sound. I was sure I was alone. As I held my breath, I heard the muffled whimper again. I hung my head down under the door and saw no feet in any direction. I must be hearing things. Another muffled whimper. It must be coming through the transom. For goodness sake! Funny, they didn't come in.

At the messy sink, I was thankful I had my shoulder

bag. I turned the water on, stuck my hands under the running water, and rubbed my fingers together in the icy stream. The paper towels were stacked on the other end, so I quickly grabbed a couple rather than use the hand-dryer on my opal ring – a special gift from Hal, though beautiful, its delicacy was sometimes a nuisance. I hated wet hands, they were cold enough dry. I hastily shoved the used towels against the swinging trash can lid, and as I touched it, I heard the muffled sound again, a baby's whimper. I stopped, the lid freezing in mid air as I listened. Then a soft, pulsating cry came out of the darkness inside the can.

My heart was beating so fast I could hardly think as I lifted the lid off its hinges and set it on the floor. Newspaper encased the wiggly ball. A tiny white knuckled fist shot into the air. I moved the edge of the newspaper and saw a head full of black hair turn to one side. I pulled the paper down, away, and saw two big blue eyes, wide open, staring up at me from a pink wrinkled face. I was struck by such surprise and awe that my brain had stopped working; I only felt. I could see that the newspaper was all that covered the child as I peeked at the bloody navel that had been secured with a dirty, torn shoestring. A baby girl. "Awe, sweetheart. How did you get here?" I whispered, on the verge of tears. As I reached for the tiny bundle, somehow I knew the young girl I had surprised had been the mother. I would have to get someone to call the police, the baby looked so newly born. And if she was... My mind began racing. That umbilical cord would need alcohol and her eyes some silver nitrate, soon. I closed the newspaper blanket quickly to keep out a draft and picked up the baby.

Instinctively I wrapped my large coat around her for warmth allowing her tiny face to peek out through the folds of the cloth. She was wide awake and her eyes were fixed upon my face. I knew that she wasn't actually seeing me. She was obviously only hours old, or less. But the way her eyes were glued to my face made me wonder if all the research was correct. It was as though she not only could see me, but knew who I was, or at least was curious about me. "Sweetheart, how alert you are! Are you hungry? Did your mommy get scared and run off and leave you?" I asked her as though she would tell me. Her dark ringlets were matted to her head, still coated with white pasty stuff often present in newborns. Her mother must have had a yeast infection, I noted mentally, and I wondered *what else?* Her head was so beautifully formed, I thought, those big round eyes continuing to search my face. Her nose was mashed somewhat, still from her entrance into the world, I assumed. Her lips separated and she opened her mouth as though she would like to speak, or maybe cry. "What would you like to tell Grandma Molly?," I said, giving her a gentle squeeze. She kept surveying my funny hair but her dampness was beginning to come through the newspapers, reminding me that I must hurry before she caught cold. "Grandma Molly will get someone to find your mommy. She really loves you, you know. She was just scared. But we'll find her. You'll see. Everything will be alright," I said as I tucked her in close.

    The purse had slid off my shoulder. I grasped it with both hands, carried it under the bundle almost secluded from view which protruded from my middle, and used the bag as a support of sorts. My mind had jumped ahead, thinking about what the police would do with her. They'd probably take her right to a hospital, and then the Boston Welfare Department would have to find a foster home or some day-care place where she would be kept until they could find her mother, if they ever did. I was beginning to worry already —where would she end up? Who might abuse her? Another precious life lost through the cracks! I glanced into the mirror, and the thought suddenly struck me that I could walk right out and get into my car and no one would ever know I had a baby hidden beneath the thick cloth.

The temptation began rolling around inside as I walked out of the rest room, towards the register in search of help. When I found no one in sight, I started to call out, but the words stuck in my throat. I looked down at that bared face, so trusting in its innocence, and pulled the coat in tightly to my body. The urge to nurture pulsated in my breasts followed by a quick denial struggling against the need lying dormant since my hysterectomy years before. I was too old to consider such folly, I reminded myself. But as I continued to look down at her, seeing those big eyes searching me, *begging me for safety?* I found myself pulling my coat over her head, walking carefully past the quiet counter, through an empty restaurant, out the heavy door into a drab cold night that had suddenly turned warm and promising.

As I settled into my comfortable Fleetwood, carefully sliding back the seat to make more room, I opened my coat a bit to let in some fresh air and started the engine. Our own Boston Pops was playing *My Blue Heaven* and I hummed along... *and baby makes three...* I turned up the heater and hoped Baby would fall asleep from the music and the ride.

I was alone in the parking lot, save one other beat-up old jalopy parked way at the other end of the lot. As I turned the steering wheel, Baby moved, and a flash of rationality flitted through my confused brain. *What are you doing?* I heard it ask.

For an instant I thought of going back into the restaurant. But the incredulousness of the circumstances suddenly occurred to me. I could just hear the questions, the cross-examination. Where did you get her? You *found* her? In a *trash can?* Hearing so many stories about the way the law could misconstrue things, I suddenly got cold feet. *What if they thought I stole her?* Oh, dear. What *was* I doing? Fear struck at my chest. I must put her back. Then, as though my personal welfare had suddenly overshadowed the true dilemma, Baby let out a little cry, and I rocked gently and patted her, off, again, in my imagination.

Thinking about having her at home started the adrenalin pumping, confusing my brain. I had to think this through but my emotions had risen up to join forces with the powerful rationale beginning to lull me into submission. She needed me, and I needed her. She needed the love and protection I could give her to start this awful world, just a few hours might make the difference in her psyche down the road. And me. Thinking about how pointless life had become, I told myself I had a reason now, a reason to stay alive, to fight the depression — the empty nest syndrome — that lurked under all that laughter. My perkiness and enthusiasm for life would come back, Hal would see, the lights in my eyes that he missed. A tiny bundle in my lap, under the steering wheel, had just decreed it so.

Unconsciously I was still humming. The nesting instinct had me in its clutches, overwhelming me, propelling me to a safe place. Once there, I would figure out my next move. "I'm taking you home, Sweetie. Everything's gonna be all right," I told the little form in my lap. Everything.

It was a quiet night. I had turned onto the main road to find the streets deserted when I looked into the rearview mirror to see headlights turning after me out of McDonald's lot. The thumping of my heart reminded me of my age as I wondered if that could be Baby's mother following me home. That's alright, I thought. Maybe I could give her just the help she needs to get her on her feet. I speeded up. The lights remained fixed in my rear view mirror. Ahead of me, a traffic light had just turned red. I pulled over into the right lane and eased to a gentle stop, trying not to jar Baby.

What appeared to be the jalopy that had been parked in the lot pulled up alongside of me. A young couple was cuddled together, the radio blasting hard rock. I searched for their faces, hoping to make some attempt at contact. The girl was snuggled up in the boy's arms so I couldn't see what she looked like, or if, in fact, she was the same girl I had come upon in the restroom. The boy was young, with unkempt hair, and a cigarette dangling from his lips. He was looking my way. *Could he be Baby's father?* I wondered. I smiled and started to wave at him, but the light must've changed because all of a sudden the boy floored the gas pedal, taking off like a horse propelled out of its stall by the gun.

As the rusted out tin of junk raced away, I tried to read the license number. In the darkness all I could see through the foggy emission was that the first three digits were 508. I knew I'd at least remember that, it was our telephone area code. The peeling bumper sticker, *SHIT HAPPENS*, was still readable. Instinctively, I drew Baby in tightly, protectively, remembering that was a phrase I had heard first from Marty, my son. The thought of him tore at my heart, the way he wandered in and out of our lives.

I don't know how long I sat there, forgetting to drive,

wondering what could possibly be going through that poor girl's mind at this moment. My mind drifted back to our daughter, Janice, and her bout with drugs before we got her help, when she'd had an abortion. If I had only known, I told her. But Janice insisted it was for the best. Besides her own drug use, the father was a Head and she believed the baby could not have been anything but a "freak." Janice had cried when we learned of it, "I couldn't even take care of myself, Mom. How could you expect me to take care of a baby?"

A puff of smoke from the departing exhaust floated upwards towards the overhanging green light. Baby began twisting, beginning to fuss. I had to think about feeding her. I couldn't risk going into a store with her. What if she cried? I must get her home. *And then leave her alone? At least she would be safer than in the trash can,* I argued with myself. I would figure out something. Then I remembered the big blanket in the trunk. I also kept a cardboard box in there for groceries packed in plastic bags so they wouldn't roll all around. Hal had thrown it out several times. He hated junk of any kind. But I had managed to salvage it and finally get it through his head that I wanted it left in there. "After all, it is my car," I had teased him, and he had relented.

I pulled into the huge Target parking lot; its ample selection of infant needs would suffice, for now. I didn't recognize any of the few cars parked. I backed into a spot next to the fence that separated a wooded lot. It was away, in an isolated spot. In case Baby began to cry, no one would hear her.

Leaving the motor running with the heat on, I slipped the coat off of my shoulders and pulled it around so Baby would be covered. She was wide awake and looking towards the dim lights from the store window. "Grandma

Love 'N' Stuff

Molly is going to get you something to eat now. Just you wait." I wrapped her up nice and snugly, and laid her on the seat. The radio played softly as I went around to the trunk.

The blanket was a thick scratchy wool I'd gotten at a garage sale. I opened it and lined the long narrow box and folded the corners inside. I slammed the trunk quickly and got into the front seat with the box. Baby was rooting around, opening her mouth, looking for a nipple, it appeared. I slipped her out of my coat and into the blanket lined box, wrapping her up very tightly over the newspaper still intact. I slipped the box down onto the floor so she would get the most from the heat. I turned the lights off and left the motor running. I checked the gas making a mental note that I had less than a half tank of gas, so I had to hurry. As I slammed the locked door with the clicker in my hand, I would hear that newborn cry follow me across the large expanse of the parking lot.

Inside the store, my mind was jumping from one thing to another. *What am I going to tell Hal, such a stickler for law and order? But I have a whole week to figure it out,* I said to that side of my brain as I found myself picking up a package of disposable diapers and a complete set of baby bottles with life-like nipples. My steps grew quicker and my heart began to race as I reached for the set of shirts, gowns, and booties. The large pink blanket, so soft, brushed my cheek. The ready-made canned formula was just across the aisle...

Thankfully, there weren't any female clerks in the area to generate curious comments; a young man was at the register.

Literally running across the parking lot to my unresolved future awaiting, I opened the car door and reached for the kicking form inside the blanket. When the warmth and heaviness of that little body touched mine, in my reverie, my brain concocted its bit of solace: *Awe, Baby, a whole week holding you will be a vacation into heaven...*

~ ~

WHY?

Memoir

Do you ever wonder about things? About *why* things happened, or why they didn't? The day I went to school without my snow pants on makes me wonder. When the cold wind hit my legs I was shocked. It must have been 20 degrees below zero, at least. It was so cold my bare legs stung hot from the wind. But all I kept seeing in my mind was how good I looked in the mirror in my pretty thick socks, just like the big girls wore. I crept close to the house, so I would not be seen from indoors. We lived on a street that had two huge apartment buildings at the corner. To be sure Mrs. Simms didn't take a notion to happen by and catch me — it could happen — I was careful, ducking in behind the apartment buildings for an out-of-sight shortcut. It was scary back in there, with all the garbage cans, especially since I was where I "wasn't allowed." So I hurried, hoping to beat the cold.

School was not supposed to be farther than one mile from anyone's house, according to the school zones laid out by the city planners. And I believe I lived right on the line, as it was so many blocks to walk that my legs had gotten numb. So I ran. I'm sure it was the only thing that saved me from getting frost bite, it was that cold.

I couldn't wait to get to school. I was a dreamer then, dreaming always of being grown up so I could wear just what I pleased and not what Mrs. Simms or my daddy decided. Grown up girls walked by our house to their high school every day. I saw them, how they dressed. Their pretty bare legs shown so white above their thick, poofy, angora anklets folded down, what they called "bobby socks," If I could only have a pair instead of my long, ugly, cotton stockings. I wore brown ones everyday and white ones on Sunday only. One day I got this idea...

I tried on my white cotton stockings and folded them down. three inches at a time. By the time they got to my ankles the turned down cuffs were quite thick. From where I stood looking in the mirror, I looked almost like the big girls that walked to school in front of my house every day.

It was cold in the winter, the Midwestern freeze, and I had to wear snow pants every day. And I hated them because they were very baggy, like fat woolen bloomers, not fitted to the leg with a zipper like some of the better-off girls had. And the color was ugly too. A light brown. Just no color at all. If I was going to be someplace for a short while, Daddy let me wear them under my dress, with the suspenders hidden. That helped me feel a little better.

The day I decided to go without them and try out my new white look-like-angora bobby-socks, I put my snow pants on before breakfast so Mrs. Simms wouldn't notice.

She was very old, over 50, and hard of hearing, and not too keen on my doings most of the time anyway. I was able to get all the way down the back stairwell that led to the outside back door without her suspecting a thing. Past it, all the way down around the bend, was the basement. I got to the outside door, stopped, and listened. Mrs. Simms was busy doing something in the kitchen. So I quickly pulled off the ugly snow pants, suspenders and all, and tossed them down the steps into the basement onto the laundry room floor with the other piles of laundry and quietly snuck out of the house.

In the cloakroom, I hung back hanging up my coat just to see what the girls would say. Two of them snickered when they saw me. "What have you got *on*?" one of them said, her eyes big as saucers.

"Angora socks," I said, as light and uppity as I knew how.

"Oh no," one of them squealed right out loud. "Don't you look funny!" she said.

Oh my. Now what? I had to go all day with them laughing, and out to recess and freeze besides. But I did it.

All the way home, I ran, too, hurrying to look for my snow pants, but they were gone. Mrs. Simms had found them and hung them up in my clothes closet, but she never said a word about it. I was lucky. My daddy would've stung more than my legs. It was 1941, the year the war started and Daddy's mamaw died. I was five years old — to be six before Christmas so I was allowed to begin the first grade early. The memories are so clear, it's like yesterday. Why Mrs. Simms never mentioned the snow pants puzzled me... and I still wonder.

~ ~

THE SEVEN

FICTION

The slide bolt slipped into its hold with a sharp click breaking the silence of the select few gathered in the large back room. It was a flimsy latch installed to corral the children when the small church had been built and the room had been used as a nursery during Sunday services. The use of the lock had become more of an indicator the meeting could begin than an actual deterrent to trespassers. No one knew about these meetings save the significant other back home of the six seated in a circle waiting for Jimmy Orblocker, the assumed leader of the group, to take his seat. Jimmy was without a wife now, making it easy for him to arrange this secluded spot in his son-in-law's tiny church. The white-steepled chapel sat almost hidden from view on a densely wooded lot, facing a lonely country road a few miles outside of Charlotte, N. C.

The dip in the floor creaked as the large man stepped towards the empty chair. He settled himself into the hard, wooden frame, the cold from it giving him a slight chill as he hunched forward to set his briefcase down between his sprawled legs. He was visibly tired. The stress from the past month was beginning to take its toll. "Gentlemen," he said, looking around the group, giving eye contact to each and every one. "Miz Purdy. Evenin'," and gave a nod.

A rumble of voices responded in an assortment of tones.

The Reverend Corley Joe LeFevre just said, "Amen," his usual indication he was ready for business, having just spoken with the Almighty.

The ghost of Nadeen Orblocker hung over the room in a polite, gentle silence. The mystery of her death whispered its accusations, her unproven suspicions the torment of her husband's soul as he opened his briefcase and pulled out his Bible. He let it fall open to the word that God would give them. It was truly God's way of telling him things, and like a child he believed. His eyes fell on the highlighted passage. He put his finger on it and followed each word, reading aloud. *"Cast thy bread upon the waters: for thou shalt find it after many days. Give a portion to seven... for thou knowest not what evil shall be upon the earth,"* he read. Then he closed the book. "God has spoken," he said.

The TV Reverend whispered, *Amen.*

When Jimmy spoke, there was a strange undertone of deep humility in his voice. "I know you have all heard about my dear, Nadine... It has been a difficult time..."

He paused, letting his mind out run his words.

Martin Caravan and Ed Baron both leaned forward in their seats. A scoop unforeseen was manna from heaven. The elderly Martin quelled his racing energy out of respect. He felt his own ache anew, ten long years since he lost his Sarah. Even with converting from his Judaism to Jesus, new life, new friends, it never went away. Anyway, his newspapers had covered the confusing story. And one of his weekly's had gotten an exclusive. But Ed Baron was of the younger set. He got where he was by speaking out. *Talk* was his motto. And the world did – on his network, his radio stations, his talk shows, everywhere people were talking him into billionaire status. "Tell us," Ed was saying, breaking the quietness. "Tell us. This is the place to get it out, now, before campaigning starts."

"Yes, ex*act*ly. We need to understand the ramifications," said General Childer, the black, retired four-star. "So we can plan our strategy."

Chatter in whispers covered the room.

A streak of white, adorned with a solid gold cuff link, shot into the air, a tanned hand waved to quiet the buzz.

Arnault Dronkin cleared his throat as all eyes turned to him. His influence on Wall Street, especially in foreign markets, gained him international recognition, and he played par golf all over the world. His looks were a great asset, too, well built with a heavy head of dark curly hair he'd inherited from his German mother – who gave him his first share of stock. His Russian father had taught him to be daring, but kind. There was gentleness in his speech, clear, distinct, and thoughtful. "Gentlemen," he said, and then, remembering, he added, "and our distinguished lady, let me remind you that we are not here for our personal lives to be cross-examined," he said, glancing around the room. "We are here precisely because of who we are and how we have conducted ourselves in the public domain. We are here to contribute our support and to accomplish a goal, and that is to insure a policy of government that will keep the free markets of the world open and productive. And we happen to agree on what kind of people it takes to accomplish this, namely born again, dedicated, God-fearing Christians. And since it is not ours to make a judgment on the state of grace of our leader, I suggest that we give him a little trust and not press him for details," he said, then paused, and facing his host, added, "Unless, of course, Jimmy, there is something you feel compelled to share with us."

The questions Jimmy expected. The anger at himself and Nadine for forcing their necessity was not. His uncharacteristically subdued demeanor gave the impression that he was contrite. He spoke in his easy manner. "Yes, well, as you already know the coroner found… uh, somehow her medications got mixed," he said, crossing his arms in front of his chest. "… And… her little ol' heart just gave way, that's all." His voice broke, and he shoved his hands into his sagging coat pockets. His insides ached as he remembered her last words before she'd left his bed that night. *Don't worry, Jimmy. God will tend to you in His own way and in His own time.* She was crying hateful tears, moving her things into the "sick room," the extra bedroom they each used respectively when a nasty bug might hit in the stomach, or the mind. It was their retreat from each other through the years and easily explained to their mighty fine daughters Nadine had reared to be just like her. Yes, they were ladies every bit of the way, good Christian women respecting their husband's...

"What medications?" Ed Baron asked, his sharp intellect jolting from under his boyishly handsome appearance.

"I appreciate your concern," Jimmy said, and bent over to put his Bible back in the briefcase. He felt like the Captain of the Titanic heading down into a school of sharks. Dead in the water either way. At least he'd found the note intended for another. What Nadine had already divulged, he did not know. But he'd find a way to deal with whatever came out. He always did. Meanwhile, he'd have to be careful, maybe cool it some with the boy...

Jimmy sat back on his haunches and breathed a deep sigh. He looked down at his hands, picking at his fingernails. It was no use. Too many people knew what a fine woman Nadine was. Too fine for her own good, he thought, remembering. So he said, "As y'all know, Nadine suffered from terrible headaches from time to time; she went to many doctors." But Jimmy found he couldn't go on. His tears of grief, thus far hidden in fear, would not stay back, but ran blatantly down his cheeks.

It was clear the awkwardness of the moment could do with a woman's touch and Caroline Purdy never shirked her calling. The small woman looked around the room, took in each face, and added up the money they controlled. Her billionaire father had taught her well. She wasn't the wife of their country's vice president for nothing. She had a deep stage voice that resounded off the walls. It always shocked people into listening, expecting her voice to be as delicate as her frame.

She leaned forward and took in a big, deep breath to let out the tension that had mounted in her chest. She knew that when she spoke, her words not only carried the thrust of the Presidency, but when they were repeated, and inevitably they would be, they gained in stature. So she chose them carefully. "Dr. Orblocker, I think you've been through enough," she said kindly and with finality to her voice; her public speaking degree had not been wasted. "I think we're satisfied that you wouldn't risk the future of our nation and the world by withholding anything of consequence."

The hush in the room gave way to the sounds of bodies moving in creaking wood, a sniffing nose, a cough, as Mrs. Casper Purdy, plain and unpretentious though she be, relaxed her shoulders back into her chair.

"Thank you for that," Jimmy said looking at Mrs. Purdy through his tear studded smile. He knew God would take care of things. "Well, then," he said, "y'all know the arduous task at hand." His voice had a conciliatory tone. "We have four possible candidates to discuss here tonight." He reached into his briefcase and pulled out a sheaf of papers. "I have with me here some pertinent background information that I will share with you. I would like it all back before you leave you understand," he said distributing the papers as he spoke. "Four candidates," he repeated, "that, I believe, can pass muster."

While the extensive dossiers he'd prepared — for their selection of VP to run with Casper Purdy when he stepped up in just a few short months — were being read, Jimmy disappeared into the small kitchen smelling of fresh brewed coffee. He poured himself a cup and looked for the sugar. He felt lonely all of a sudden, more so than he'd felt for most of his life. There was no lite banter to lighten the air. His presence seemed to stop the natural flow of conversation these days. The solemnity of death is what weighed one down, he thought. The fear of trivializing one's loss cast its shadow. For the first time in his adult years he wished for anonymity instead of the spotlight he had so diligently sought. But he had maneuvered his way onto numerous boards and committees as the President's eyes and ears. He'd helped to oust the moderates in the Southern Baptist Convention and lobbied for the Thomas nomination while active on the Committee for Special Selection of Serviceable Candidates for Vacated Positions, known as the President's Triple S Board. The monthly breakfast with the President kept the lines of communication open and his weekly lunch with the Vice President helped solidify the tight support they had managed to develop since Watergate had nearly destroyed them. They had learned the need to be thorough and careful in searching out the perfect and pliable man, or woman should the case warrant it, to fill key positions. Gaining recognition in heading up the largest Christian college east of the Mississippi is what got him into the President's inner circle. Yes, Jimmy D. Orblocker had come a long way without ever knowing who his father was. And he wondered, as he stirred in the sugar, if *knowing* would have made any difference.

~ ~

GET OVER IT!

Essay

Do you suppose that the Religious Right, that boasts of their literal translation of the Bible, could really be Right? Wasn't it Jesus who said for us to *Love thy neighbor as thyself?* I mean, if we have to love our neighbor *that* much, we have to be pretty doggone careful *where* we live! You know the old real estate slogan, it's *Location! Location! Location!* Oh, dear... life has just gotten so complicated, worrying about who might move in next door, or god-forbid, a person of color now residing in the White House!

The above seems to be the insane reasoning that the scary Right must use in justifying their platform and political agenda, and which I hear coming from the mouths of the TV talkers and some congressional leaders. It is so disheartening to see such ignorance abounding in an era that is filled with so much technological sophistication. Living in this beautiful land, haven't we learned *yet* that loving is far easier on us — in body, mind, *and* spirit — than is hating?

~ ~

OLD SOLDIERS NEVER DIE...

ESSAY

March 2003

It hit me the day that it came over the news that the pentagon had ordered seventy-thousand body bags, that's 70,000, and I cried on and off for days. Up until then I think I really believed George W. was pulling the biggest bluff known to man-kind with all his war business, really trying to create a climate of "patriotism" so that to speak out against him became politically incorrect, or what is now being called "traitorousness," just so he could get reelected the second term — to make up for his father's defeat, I do believe.

After a few days of tears, watching the military hug their families goodbye as they got on ships and airplanes, and then the peace marchers came out in droves all over the world — that's what really did it, I think — that the pent up tears from that year in 1967, when the father of our four children was over in DaNang getting his ass shot off while they carried their signs and threw eggs on cars with military stickers, and I ended up in the hospital from not being able to sleep for nights on end, that the tears finally came pouring out these last days. *How could I have cried then? I had to keep my family going, food on the table and school clothes clean, and a stiff upper lip for those wives whose husbands* were *coming home* — in body bags.

We were called *Geographical Widows* then. We played bridge together after a dinner when we were caught up on whose hubby was missing, whose was found and being shipped, and some were in hospitals in Germany. Those were the lucky ones... a wife could fly over for a visit...

This past week I kept telling myself that I had nothing

to cry about. My husband *did* come home, and all in one piece, physically. The part that he left behind over there you can't see, the part that watched his buddies get blown up in front of him, his crashing in a helicopter over a burning field and carrying a dismembered Vietnamese child back to the base hospital; that part that he left over there which makes him jump clean out of bed if you touch him in his sleep, even a toe brushing against his leg could send him screaming across the bedroom, and still *can* — thirty-six years later. They called it startle syndrome — the first time I heard that term, now a recognized symptom of PTSD. He explained that it was because he got used to sleeping with a gun under his pillow, a knife at his side, a shotgun propped against his cot, all while his Vietnamese interpreter slept at the foot of the bed, who he was never too sure wasn't a VC waiting to cut his throat in his sleep. Getting to sleep in the first place was the hard part. It took lots of booze, 85-cents-a-quart gin, or vodka, or Crown Royal if, as an officer, he could afford a buck-and-a-quarter.

Now his VA psychiatrist tells him he shouldn't watch those war movies, so as not to start up those nightmares again. We found out he had PTSD during Desert Storm, when he had been retired and working in a civilian job for fifteen years already, and he sat in front of the 7:00 news in tears, while Dan Rather told us, in near tears himself, that the U.S. had led its first strike against Iraq. *Old soldiers never die, they just sit in front of the TV news and bawl...*

It's okay to cry now, finally, I tell myself. All those tears that I held back, first through Korea, then special training school before getting Orders for 'Nam. Some were going back the second time, the single ones, the ones who didn't know what to do with themselves after they got back and were spit upon. They went back to where *they* could do the spitting...

But those "chicken hawks" in this White House don't have any idea what I am talking about. None of them. They have these big theories based upon their religious beliefs that tells them somewhere in their Bibles that in the last days *He* is going to rule His chosen... and some kind of group psychosis has taken over this select few who have managed to arrange their own rise to power. And those peace activists in Hollywood who are speaking out the loudest are the very ones who backed Ralph Nader and took away the votes that would have not left any questions about who really won the 2000 election. When the republicans donated large sums of money to the Green party, shouldn't they have guessed that something was up? The ones who now are screaming for this administration to listen to them? Where were they when they could've stopped this band of brothers bent on power through destruction?

No, none of this is what all my tears are about. They are for all those many days and nights we lost to those wars, our family lost their father *and* their mother. For she was not there either. She was only there in body acting as the good mother robot, going through the right motions, but the tears had to stay locked inside. Those are the tears that keep coming. At the futile peace signs. And the flags waving -- they are the ones that are frightening, the ones who are too ignorant to understand what is happening. These Americans are acting like the frog in the pot of tepid water... slowly being boiled to death... Numbed to what is happening by the sweet-talking guy-next-door Texan, that the "blood will be to the horses bridle bits" by the time the water boils, and it will be too late.

~ ~

DOREEN

FICTION

She was waltzing with her darling... to the tune of the Tennessee Waltz... The Waltz... No, she was looking at the moon... and she was seeing a world of wonder, of magic, of happy faces filling the air. She saw laughter, she saw gladness, she saw herself in all those faces, yet she could not feel her own skin. Where was she? Where had she gone? What had happened to her, to her life?

She looked around her. There was nothing that seemed familiar. She felt for her head. It was there, hard, round, and covered with silky, slippery hair, the feel of not being clean. The way it felt as a girl, before they had an automatic water heater. She had hated to wash her hair. Having it lay, smoothly, in gentle waves that did not fly around with the wind was the object, to "control" it. *Control.* That was the motive that ran undercurrent in most everything one undertook then, it seemed. She felt the hair now, and wondered if that is what had happened to the world. There just wasn't any *control* anymore, anywhere. At least *she* had lost it somewhere, somehow...

She felt her skin. It was no longer soft to the touch. Her fingertips were so dry and shriveled, as though she had been soaking a hundred years, soaking in the tub of weariness. Her feet. How they hurt. And the dirt. How she hated it. She ran her shriveled fingers along her forearm, wondering what the fine grit was on her skin. Where had she been lying? Next to what forgettable lump? It had brought her warmth in the early morning hours when her bladder screamed for release. That physical reminder that she was still alive, that awful necessity that the human race had tried to blot out of recognition by enlarging the bath with elegant marble stepping stones, faucets that curved and hid their use with contorted swirls and turns, the toilet stuck away in a small dark hole that barely left room for the knees. And she hated the dirt. But it was the dirt that gave them their cover, their freedom. And freedom was what life was all about, wasn't it?

Doreen reached into her pocket, the one good one that she could count on to swallow up her revenues for the day so that they would not fall out on the street when she sat down, or was pushed down unexpectedly. She had found this long jacket with this hidden pocket that had been sewn so cleverly so that unless someone was specifically looking, would never find it. The noise of the change, though, is what had become her biggest problem. If anyone heard a rattle in her pocket, she knew she was dead meat. She had devised a careful method of wrapping each coin separately, in a tissue, if she could find one, or newspaper, or toilet paper, whatever. She remembered movers once telling her that paper provided more cushion than cloth. She would slide the wrapped coins down into the hidden pocket that was lost among the folds that hung from her pleated shoulders. As soon as she got enough coins, she would trade them in for bills. That was the hardest part. Trying to find a vendor on the street that would keep her secret. She had learned very quickly how to find out what someone's politics were by the way they treated her. Street people always brought out the worst in people. Especially in this town. Liberals were getting harder and harder to find these days...

Where have all the liberals gone...
Where are the hearts that blee-ee-eed?
Where has God departed to?

Love 'N' Stuff

> *To Somalia... to Ha—i—ti...*
> *to unknown lands not free-ee-ee...*

She could hear the tune in her head with words she made up to suit her frame of mind. The tune was getting old. She needed to think of a new one.

Her finger tips barely reached the bottom of the hidden pocket; her arms were short. And her fingers looked like they stopped growing where the knuckles should have normally been. Her small feet were her trademark. People from her generation all had big feet from the Going Barefoot craze. Her lame left foot from the fallen arch had saved her from the curse of The Big Footed Generation. She knew she was close to changing twenty singles into one bill. She couldn't find the wad of bills; the spot was empty. She reached again for the bills she had been saving for a better part of a week. She could feel her face get hot. It was the damndest thing lately. She felt like she was on fire and comments from the street didn't help, like... Blushing Bride, Sweet Sixteen, or Hot Stuff depending upon her heckler. *Old* didn't cut it here on Vine street. Maybe over on the Ave of the Stars she was held with a little more respect for her having lived a little longer on this earth, but not much. Mostly she was treated as the outcast she had always felt. It was that feeling that had driven her to the streets in the first place. She just got tired of fighting, pushing to be seen, heard, recognized. She could stand at a counter for an hour and the clerk would wait on a hundred people over her head. Was she invisible? She'd begun to feel this way and now she lived this way. But only as long as no one knew about the money, and then she knew it was only the money they wanted. She, the person, was still invisible. Maybe she could save up enough dollar bills to make herself a coat of them. Then maybe people would look at her really, see that there was really an alive person under there, under all the Presidents' faces. Doreen reached one last time and felt every inch of the hidden pocket for the wadded up ball that, when she touched it, made her heart pump a little extra loudly, a little faster, a little stronger. She was alive for another day... Her heart would react to the feeling of exhilaration that she always got for having outsmarted just a few more know-it-alls. The ones, if they had their way, she knew they'd be glad to cart all of them like herself, away to the desert, line them up, shoot them. Or worse, leave them out there to rot in the sun.

    Doreen tried to remember the last time she had touched the wad in her pocket. Was it this morning when she had to pee in Charlie's coffee can? Was it at midnight when she had found a whole doughnut wrapped up in a napkin tossed into the gutter, or was it yesterday afternoon when she had crawled under the plastic with Quick-but-Honest-John to catch a snooze while the sun was out for a change. She had felt warm for the first time in weeks. Sitting on the curb with her knees together, Doreen had both hands in her pockets, while she tried very hard to recall that last moment it had been at her fingertips. She couldn't remember. Her mind was a blank. She couldn't quite grasp the memory and hold on to it long enough to decipher what it was, color code it, and file it in duplicate into her lists upon lists of things she just had to remember to save her own life. This blankness in her mind had only happened a couple times that she could remember. But how the hell was she supposed to remember what she was forgetting? Oy! A car horn beeped. The low rumble of a purring engine sputtered into her face, inches from her bent knees. "Get the hell out of the street, ya dumb ass. Do ya think our taxes ain't high enough without having to pay to drag yer ass off to the morgue?"

She looked up at the light blue shiny metal as it slipped past her. At a more stalwart moment, she may have given the obnoxious driver the finger, or stuck out her tongue, or shouted the Indian War Hoop at him. She had become good at it, her You-Tarzan, Me-Jane yell.

Doreen suddenly felt very tired. Why couldn't she remember, whatever it was she was forgetting? She hoisted her skinny body forward onto the tiny Cherokee feet her famous mother had imparted to her. The flash in her memory of her wad of money shot crawly sensations over her scalp. She shook for a second. She had trouble stopping once she started shivering.

Into the bus station, is where she usually went to change her money into larger denominations. It was so early in the morning, the place was deserted; she had the rest room all to herself. Before the cleaning crew got there, she had taken advantage of the moment of privacy to strip and wash up. How she hated dirt. The dirt was the hardest part to take, besides the pain in her left foot. It got worse by the day. She had put the wadded up money behind the stack of paper towels on the narrow ledge in front of the mirror. Just in case some other homeless wandered in while she was washing and grabbed her coat. Never could be too careful. She had lathered up the pinkish hand soap with her hands, under her arms, behind her ears, all over her neck. Boy, did that feel good, even if it was cold. The shivers made her decide to leave the other parts to get washed next time. *I ain't going to no party. Not tonight.* The several layers of clothing, though soiled and smelly, gave her a feeling of warmth and security. She hugged herself while she studied the form in the mirror. This piece of humanity stared out at her from dark hollow eyes that had once dazzled the best and the brightest. Such intellect, she had been told, such ability for constructive thought, a searching mind. She could have gone on and on remembering all the things they used to say about her eyes, her mind. But she never really believed them. Never really believed them. And now she couldn't remember, since she had become part of that "throw away" society.

Once again, her mind took her out of the moment into a cloud of illusive wonderings: *When did disposable start? At birth, with the disposable diapers? It was in the mother's act of wrapping up her child's soil and putting it out with the take-away trash. What happened to looking at it, while dumping it into the toilet? There, it was washed away with the recycled water, into the reservoirs below, which carried all the other remnants humanity could not make disappear any other way. Seeing one's own human waste was the one remaining link to itself, to the beginning and the end, the alpha and omega of human existence. The "shit" of life, even its name was unmentionable. Where have we gone? Do we think we can really find a way to not acknowledge it? Pass it? The last of life still crying out to be recognized when it gives its last hurrah from the bowels of the dying. No. Now we need a bumper sticker to remind us.* **Shit Happens!** *Where, oh where have we gone?*

~ ~

OLLIE THE ELEPHANT

Allegory

Once upon a time there was a beautiful elephant named Ollie which was captured and kept by a Man of great stature in the town. Because the Man was very lonely and fearful he had a great golden pole erected in order to secure Ollie's leash. She had captivated the heart of the Man, you see, and he wanted her nearby so he could feast his eyes upon her, talk to her, pet her, ride her, whenever he felt like it rather than let her run free in the forest.

At first Ollie often tugged at her leash, to walk, to go back to the forest where her friends were. A bird, a flower, a butterfly would draw her attention, but always when she started to move, the leash would choke her and gag her, until she tugged no more. Ollie soon began to accept her station at the tall golden pole.

The people in the town grew accustomed to seeing Ollie and knew the Man's house by the elephant tied to the pole.

One day the Man who was now her master became very ill and died.

Days, weeks, went by before some young boys came by and cut Ollie's leash.

Years passed, grass grew, the house covered over, and still the elephant stood next to the tall golden pole.

~ ~

PRIMARY LOVE

Fiction

There was a yearning inside of her that she could not name. It was something that crept into her consciousness just before she awoke, before the guilt had a chance to settle in, distract her, be covered up. It was a slight shadow of a feeling, a feeling of wanting something she could not, should not have... This vague recurring recognition was quickly dispelled by the sun coming in strong and bright, the birds chirping, telling her it was time.

Again...

She reached for the silky thin robe that hung on the bed post. It was really not cool enough to need it, but it was there for covering should she awaken before dawn. Her newest neighbor she had seen bare at such a time, through the window left open over the kitchen sink, letting in the crisp night air. So fresh, stimulating, sensual, she wished she could capture the breeze to savor as she did the sight of his glistening skin.

The day before her loomed to fill all those empty cracks, those unfulfilled moments. It would be over soon, she told herself. Living through it, is how she managed, with the part of her that would rise up to resist. She had no say. No real part in the outcome. She only acquiesced in silence, and was despicably thankful.

The aroma of toast and steaming coffee warmed her thoughts, their taste comforting. She would relish a substantial meal, afterwards. Deliberately she dressed, grooming her face with meticulous care. A touch of rose, a blend of soft beige, a hint of blue that drew out the depth of her large, sad eyes. Once brilliant, glowing. Now dull and accepting. She sighed into the mirror, seeing only a ghost of the past. She used to hear whispers, softly in the night, *Alethea... Alethea...* but they, too, had gone.

In the streets, the unusually tired Saturday morning traffic, had an urgency, a thrust. She found herself hugging the brakes, slowing the flow. Only to have horns blasting, silent curses being mouthed behind closed windows, single fingers pointing angrily. She had forgotten the circus was setting up its tent, the yearly spectacle that stirred the town. Remembering, she relaxed her hold on the wheel.

As a small child, she had sat on her knees between them to see the clowns, the lions, the girls glittering in the darkness above them. Alethea Ann Sommerton was lucky, her mother often said. "You have a brother *and* a sister..." *They were right; mother would never, ever... Didn't they hover over her as though adoring? How could she be believed? No. She could not, would not, did not ever tell...*

The reserved parking space was left purposefully empty, her small foreign car lavishing in room. The dark, gray building standing high, foreboding, was only made alive by the sounds coming from open windows. She walked slowly, hesitatingly, as though being pulled by a giant magnet, a force strong, compelling against which she inwardly, fervently fought. *You have everything... Anything you could possibly want or need...* Voices taunt with fear, accusing, tying the knot tighter, the hold stronger. The huge, heavy fire door closed behind her, her footsteps moving noiselessly up the secluded stairwell. *Just a precaution...*

Inside and alone, she pulled her soft leather bag tightly to her, easing her sleek tailored skirt and paper-thin blouse into its opening. Soft sheer pink stood out from her, covering her slender, surrendering body. The French-rolled hem stitched to a darker version of itself — the flounces of a ballerina in flight. Voices muffled, the high giggle of a child of yesteryear, the course whisper of Zeus, Alethea slipped off her slim leather shoes and tiptoed into the heavily curtained darkness.

~ ~

THE CULTURAL DILEMMA

ESSAY

Although the practice of wife beating has a history centuries old, it has been brought into public view only in recent years as a result of the women's movement. "The work of Kempe and Helfer on the battered child syndrome, published in 1963, renewed overt public awareness of family violence.... [Also] the nation as a whole became more sensitive to issues of violence as a result of the civil strife of the latter 1960s and early 1970s, and perhaps... as a result of the war in Vietnam."[1] In 1984, the TV film, "Burning Bed," with Farrah Fawcett portraying the acquitted wife, Francine Hughes, for the murder of her abusive husband of fourteen years brought this issue before the public's attention as a serious social problem. Hotlines all over the country were swamped with callers following the showing of this film, many in similar straits needing help.

What constitutes battering?

In the 1985 edition of the Random House College Dictionary, the meaning of "batter" is given as follows: "beat persistently or hard; pound repeatedly; to damage by beating or subjecting to rough usage; to deal heavy, repeated blows; pound steadily."[2] Historically, the word was used to indicate the beating down of an inanimate object. An example of this usage is given in a description in the same dictionary, for a "battering ram:" an ancient military device with a heavy horizontal ram that was used

---

[1]Okun, Lewis, *Woman Abuse*, (New York: State University of New York Press., 1986) p. 07.
[2]Random House College Dictionary, Random House, Revised edition, 1984) p. 115.

for battering down *walls, gates, etc.*[3] In a later release of the same dictionary, 1991, the word "batter" has been revised to include, in the third meaning: to beat a "... person, *especially a child or wife.*"[4]

Although the subject of rape requires a separate investigation, for the purposes of this essay "the contemporary consensus on rape is that... [it] is a power trip, not a passion trip."[5] Rape is a violent act not a sexual act. Further, in battering, women are "... subjected to conjugal rape and/or other sexual abuses that amount to physically debilitating torture often committed against political prisoners intended to coercively control the institutional regimen."[6] The act of coercive procreation is often at the seat of rape, an act of forced disempowerment, not to be confused with the power trip taking place during the actual physical act itself.[7]

Emotional battering is just as detrimental as physical abuse, but it is often thought 'normal.' In Albee's play, *Who's Afraid Of Virginia Woolf,* the contest between the partners seems to lend "a certain *enjoyment* to the struggle... [implying that] those who stay together choose to do so, even if they seem to be bivouacking on a battlefield."[8]

Who batters who?

"One out of every seven American women is abused by her own husband but is too ashamed to say anything

---

[3] Ibid
[4] Random House College Dictionary, Revised edition, 1991).
[5] Okun, WA, p. 53.
[6] Ibid, p. 123.
[7] Ibid, p. 123
[8] Janeway, Elizabeth, *Man's World, Woman's World,* A Study of Social Mythology, (New York: Morrow & Co., 1971) p. 75.

about it."[9] Men of every class and race abuse women. In 1974, in Norwalk, Connecticut, a police study of the number of wife abuse complaints, per week, was made. It was found that in this affluent town, population 85,000, the same number of complaints was received as was in Harlem, a precinct of the same size.[10]

Women in the public eye have been recipients of abuse. In 1975, Doris Day went public with her story; her first husband beat her.[11] Oprah Winfrey, on her daily talk show, began self-disclosure of her childhood abuse as part of her interview technique and continued to speak out on a regular basis. Local and national talk show hosts such as Phil Donahue, Sally Raphael, Geraldo Rivera, covered this subject and received great telephone audience response from women disclosing brutality from all walks of life. "In 1974 the wife of Japan's former Prime Minister Sato accused him publicly of beating her. This caused somewhat of a stir in the press for he had been awarded the Nobel Peace Prize."[12] *Essence*, a magazine by and for black women, wrote a story in 1983 entitled: "Why Women Stay With Men Who Beat them, And Why They Finally Leave." Around the same time, George Levinger did a study of why people get divorced. "He found 23 percent of middle class couples and 45 percent of working class couples gave physical abuse as a major complaint."[13]

Why do men batter, and why do women allow them

---

[9]Russell, Diana, *McCall's*, (Apr 83)

[10]Kamisher, Michele, "Battered Women," *Women's Yellow Pages*, (New York: Martin's Press., 1978) p. 114.

[11]Day, Doris, *My Own Story*, (New York: Bantam Books, 1975), pp 61-63.

[12]Kamisher, WYP., p. 114.

[13]Levinger, George, *American Journal of Orthopsychiatry*, 1971, cited by Michele Kamisher, Battered Women," WYP, p. 114.

to?

Some psychologists believe that a woman learns to expect abuse from her familial upbringing. "Through the mechanism of physical punishment children come to associate love with violence. This occurs because a child learns that those who love him/her the most are also those who hit and have the right to hit. A significant though unintentional consequence of such experience is that the use of physical force becomes justified."[14] It is clear that women are emotionally conditioned, under the guise of "lady-like manners," to compromise rather than confront, to defer to their fathers and later to their husbands.

The traditional religious view of woman as the subordinate sex contributes to her abuse. Christian religions based on Biblical text explicitly instruct women to be submissive. "Wives, submit yourselves unto your husbands, as it is fit in the Lord. For the husband is the head of the wife even as Christ is the head of the church."[15]

In the famous story of Jesus and the woman at the well, the woman was being stoned for committing adultery, a common form of violent punishment engaged in by that society. This story is expounded from the pulpits across the nation, as well as it being TV evangelists' favorite tear-jerking sermon. Although the moral of the story is found in the words of Jesus — telling the crowd waiting to descend upon her, "Let him without sin cast the first stone" — the accepted violence in this mental picture gives a subliminal message of condonment. Jesus did not chastise the crowd for their violence, only for their misjudgment.[16]

How has this violence been allowed to continue?

---

[14] Kamisher, WYP, p. 117.
[15] Paul of Tarsus, *The Bible*, Col. 3:18-19.
[16] St. John the Divine, *The Bible*, John 8:7

Love 'N' Stuff

The stance of the law has been such so as to protect men through espousal immunity. In early Roman culture women had no legal roles other than to be mothers or wives. All women, then, were property of their fathers or husbands. Men were held responsible for their "property", thus their crimes. Therefore it was the duty of the men to keep their women under control. This was the logic behind the laws of chastisement, passed by Romulus, 753 BC, and "... best exemplified by the 'rule of thumb' of English common law, which stated that a man could beat his wife with a rod or switch, so long as its circumference was no greater than the girth of the base of the man's right thumb. No reciprocal right of chastisement was ever accorded to wives."[17] As late as nineteenth century, England "... husbands could murder their wives without punishment."[18] It is no wonder, with the archaic thinking that permeates our legal system that women are denied legal access to the courts to intercept the brutality she may receive at the hands of her husband.[19] This legal climate propagates the "... tacit assumption in the public mind... that a man's wife is [still] his property to do with as he pleases."[20] Despite the fact that the laws by which we are still being influenced and governed are centuries old, "cultural norms legalizing marital violence abound."[21] Our "male-oriented criminal justice system [makes] it difficult for a woman to secure protection from her husband."[22] In fact "there is no law on the books at present outlawing wife beating. [Instead] an

---

[17] Okun, *WA*, p. 02.
[18] Ibid, p. 3.
[19] Heymowitz and Weisman, *A History Of Women In America*, (New York: Bantam Books, 1978), p. 24.
[20] Leghor, Lisa, Transition House (Boston Shelter)
[21] Kamisher, *WYP*, p. 117.
[22] Ibid, p. 118.

assault and battery charge [must be] used."[23]

Some contend that women's new sexual assertiveness, at the core of the "sexual revolution," threatens men's masculinity. Women gaining their own sexual equality is what gave impetus to this "revolution" when Masters & Johnson went up against Freud's earlier belief clearly contradicting it, that women do not get as much enjoyment from sex as men do.[24] Violence by men towards women seems to be an "acting out" of the antagonism between the sexes brought about by the changing of roles and their beliefs about them.[25] When Farrah Fawcett was interviewed regarding her insight into the part she portrayed in "Burning Bed" she felt roles between men and women were greatly confused. "Men come home from a stressful day at work to find wives who demand equal say because they work too. Men traditionally have dominated and their masculinity is threatened."[26] Violence by men towards women illustrates very aptly the emotional neediness men seem to feel in their lack of superiority in personal resources for maintaining a power position in the family.[27] These feelings of power loss that men seem to feel, i.e., in the courts with custody battles, etc., is discussed at length in October's issue (91) of *Esquire*, a male magazine.[28] Erica Jong, author/poet, states that men are looking for male models of masculinity. She contends that since the industrial revolution — that took boys out from under the supervision of their fathers, i.e., the farm,

---

[23] Ibid.

[24] Rosi, Alice B., "Sex Equality: The Beginning of Ideology," *Voices of the New Feminism,* ed., Thompson, (Boston: Beacon Press, 1970), p. 34.

[25] Rosi, *Voices*, p. 35.

[26] Fawcett, Farrah, *People's Weekly*, (Oct. 8, 84.)

[27] Kamisher, *WYP*, p. 118.

[28] McDonell, Terry, ed., *Esquire*, (Oct 91)

the store, etc., and into a separate workplace, absent from their fathers — men have become confused and are looking for a father/son solidarity.[29]

Alcohol/drugs are often used to mask men's "acting out" anger. Ginny Foat, feminist tried for murder (and acquitted) because, as her attorney said, Ginny's husband "… was a vengeful alcoholic, suicidal man who beat and terrorized Foat — who later married him — while she cowered, too insecure to fight back or flee. She [was] on trial simply because [her husband] decided to carry out the threats he'd made when Foat finally left him…. On that day he beat her as he never had before. [Her husband] said, *I'll kill you…. If you ever leave me… I'll make you pay…. I'll see you behind bars rotting in jail.*"[30]

In a small New Hampshire town, Dr. Richard Gelles conducted a study of eighty families, interviewing them in depth regarding the amount of violence in their families. It showed that "54 percent of the couples had used physical force on each other at some time." This same study showed that alcohol played a big part in this violence. But it was Gelles' conclusion that "… rather than men beating their wives because they've been drinking, perhaps they drink because they want to beat their wives. In this way they can use alcohol as an excuse and claim they were not responsible for their actions while *under the influence.*"[31] Not only is alcohol/drugs often a mitigating factor in battering, but when it is present the number of assaults upon family members is higher and more violent.[32]

---

[29] Jong, Erica, *Good Morning America,* (ABC News, Sept. 19, 91)
[30] Warner, N. G. "Trying A Feminist For Murder," *Newsweek,* (Nov. 21, 83)
[31] Kamisher, *WYP,* p. 118.
[32] Okun, *WA,* p. 213.

What resources are available to counteract this problem?

Education is the first arm of defense. The switchboard of any hospital provides 24-hour hotline services for victims of abuse offering emergency direction. The National Coalition Against Domestic Violence in Washington, D.C. refers SAFE centers for women that are nearest to their homes. NOW (National Organization for Women) operates telephone hotlines, counseling and support groups.[33]

Reading material on the subject of violence against women is plentiful, much more than was available before 1970.[34] Women's magazines carry stories on abuse of every kind. Talk shows, network news and public broadcasting are becoming more responsive to the problem by running shows on the subject, sometimes with counselors to aid callers with immediate support by telephone, giving suggestions on how to get away from the abuser, listing hot line telephone numbers and the location of shelters.[35]

Shelters can provide a SAFE place to go in an emergency. They can also provide direction and assistance in the following areas: welfare (financial) help, job training, jobs, new homes, care of children, prenatal support, medical care, psychological counseling, legal information, and practical advice.[36]

Divorce is a possible escape route.

One way to alleviate an abusive situation is to leave, get out. However, women who are battered as children succumb to the "battered wife syndrome" so that they lose

---

[33] Kamisher, *WYP*, p. 118.
[34] Okun, *WA*, p. II.
[35] Ross & Barcher, *The Rights Of Women*, An American Civil Liberties Union Handbook, (New York: 1983) p. 237
[36] Okun, WYP, p. 143-144

Love 'N' Stuff

their will in the matter.[37] Studies show that many abused women come from homes where violence between their parents were present.[38] Rarely do these women have enough self-esteem to believe there is an alternative. There are many who still believe they love their husbands and refuse to entertain the thought of leaving them. However, often when these women receive support, counseling, and experience freedom from the fear and constant stress, they do consider this alternative. While in the process of making this decision, a legal protection order can be obtained requiring the abuser to stop the abuse, threats or harassment, whether or not a woman continues to live with her partner or not.[39] And often, even though these alternatives are exercised, the abuse continues, sometimes aggravated.[40]

Psychiatric counseling can teach a wife "to stand alone and capture the dignity and respect that comes with being an independent adult."[41] She can also be treated together with her abusive husband.[42]

The legal system is slowly changing towards women. Every time someone challenges it, it moves just a little. Several years ago in Connecticut, Tracy Thurmon sued her police department for $23 million and won after she had repeatedly begged for help but was ignored. She was beaten badly and injured so severely by her ex-husband that she is left with a permanent paralysis. Although she survived, she lived in constant fear of the time her ex-

---

[37] Ibid, p.60.
[38] Ibid, p.61.
[39] Ross & Barcher, *Rights OW*, p. 237.
[40] Okun, WYP, p. 43
[41] Russel, Diana, *McCall's*, (Ap 83.)
[42] Ibid.

husband would be released from prison.[43] As the result of abuse, another woman was reported to have killed her husband, but while in prison founded a group of similar females like herself. These women are finding healing in sharing their pain and fear they suffer as victims of a mutually experienced syndrome. The "battered wife syndrome" and how it pertains to a woman's mental state at the time she feels "pushed to the edge" is presently not recognized as a defense in most states with the exception of Michigan and Ohio. These two states have already changed their posture and reversed prison sentences when the history of abuse records, previously withheld from the court, have been brought to light.[44]

In other areas that effect women, discrimination against them in public places continues to be a major issue. But women are beginning to fight in the courts to obtain an equal voice and place. Midge Morton filed a law suit against Longmeadow Golf club (Massachusetts), winning for women the right to tee off on Saturday mornings along with the men. Women are now also allowed to eat in the formerly all-men's grill.[45] As long as women continue to fight legally for their rights, they will continue to win, one case at a time.

The abuse of women is an international problem. Britain seems to be leading the way in providing unlimited refuge with cooperative housing among its recipients a long term goal. Similar shelters operate around the globe: Sweden, Holland, Canada and other European countries.[46]

---

[43] Walters, Barbara and Downs, Hugh, *Pushed To The Edge*, 20/20, (ABC News, (Sept. 18, 91)
[44] Ibid.
[45] Jennings, Peter, *ABC Evening News*, (Sept. 18, 91)
[46] Kamisher, WYP, p.118.

Love 'N' Stuff

In continuing to examine the magnitude of this problem perhaps some insight as to how we have developed such a slanted view towards women in this 20th century society may be found among the ancient archeological ruins of civilizations past.

In a Canadian film *The Goddess Remembered*,[47] the unequal relationship universally accepted between men and women is suggested to have arisen out of the loss of the female as spiritual head of the very earliest ancient cultures when harmony, cooperation, and love were the prevailing influences, and both sexes worked hand in hand to preserve life. (The male phalanx was not to have been considered sacred as it was never found in the holy place where the artifacts of the goddesses were unearthed.)

As late as 3000 BC, in the Sumerian culture uncovered by Samuel Kramer in his dedicated research in Iraq,[48] the "priests, priestesses"[49] ministered side by side in the temples, the female revered and having influence. The goddess Inanna, of love and procreation, was believed to be the restorer of fertility to the land every growing season when she reunited with her husband, the god of vegetation. The Sumerian culture "had a moving vision of all mankind living in peace and security, united by a universal faith."[50] The Sumerians believed that it was the Goddess of Ninmah who brought forth life in the creation

---

[47] National Film Board of Canada, *The Goddess Remembered*, "Women in Spirituality" Series, Part I, (#C0189027).

[48] Kramer, Samuel Noah, "The Sumerians," Scientific American, Inc., (1957), cited by Schaefer, Resnick, & Netterville III, *The Shaping of Western Civilization*, (New York: Holt, Reinhart and Winston, Inc., 1970), p. 45.

[49] Ibid.
[50] Ibid

of man.[51] Looking back to an earlier time, a Sumerian poet seems to confirm that living under the female influence was, indeed, desirous:

> *Once upon a time there was no snake,*
> *There was no scorpion,*
> *There was no hyena, there was no lion,*
> *There was no wild dog, no wolf,*
> *There was no fear, no terror,*
> *Man had no rival.*
>
> *Once upon a time...*
> *The whole universe, the people in unison*
> *To Enlil* in one tongue gave praise.*[52]
> *(*the god of air)*

It is the thesis of the writer's of *The Goddess*, that it was the early Greeks (400 BC) that subjugated women in order to promote the superiority of male ego and power. This idea was corroborated by Taylor Caldwell in her enlightening historical perspective of Greece through her novel[53] about Aspasia, the wife of Pericles. Aspasia was a woman who dared to rise above her gender, to use her intelligence here-to-for only accorded to women of the brothel.[54] To sum up the "The Glory That Was Greece —"[55] Caldwell opens her novel with a chilling quote by Zeno of Elea, a great philosopher, mathematician, and personal

---

[51] Ibid, p.47
[52] Ibid.
[53] Caldwell, Taylor, *Glory and the Lightning*, (Fawcett Publications, Inc, 1974).
[54] Ibid, p. 271
[55] Ibid, p.7.

friend of Pericles:[56][57]

> "The genius of a nation strikes but once in its history. It is its glory and its immortality in the annals of men. It is aristocratic, discriminating, radiant and selective, and abjures all that is mediocre, plebeian and mundane. It is regnant. It is spiritual, It is the flame emanating from the core of the Universe, which is the generation of life. It is the lighting which sets fire to the small spirits of men, and raises them above the field and the plow, the house and the hayfield, in a sudden revelation of grandeur. It is, above all, masculine, for the aristocracy of the soul is purely masculine and never feminine, which is concerned only with petty matters and insistent trivialities.... If that nation which would survive in glory would cultivate only the masculine principle, its name in history will be written in gold and blaze through the centuries."

Words can condemn and destroy, or they can uplift and redeem. Having a voice that is heard and reckoned with is what women must fight to gain and preserve. The forces that drove the Greeks to glory in their masculinity are the same forces active today in still trying to squash femininity and render women powerless, apparently for the same prejudicial reasons. But with education, their weapon, and hope, their ally, the voice of women will continue to be heard. Active voices can insure freedom's choices. And

---

[56] *The New Encyclopedia Britannica,* Chicago:15th edition, (V. 9, p. 290)

[57] Ibid.

perhaps, indicative of their voices being heard will be Random House including in their list of pertinent, updated terms "battered-woman." But by then the frequency of its usage may well have bypassed the hyphenation stage allowing it to become a full-fledged word such as "chairwoman" or "wifebeating" — our language, society's mirror.

ENDNOTES

a. "Although Aspasia of Miletus is clouded by scandal and legend, it is easy to believe she possessed great charm and intelligence... [as she came from] a city with great intellectual traditions. It is clear that her own behavior and Pericles attitude toward her were surprising phenomena in Athens, where upper class women were kept secluded.... That Pericles was known to kiss her on leaving for and returning from work gave rise to speculation about her influence on him, and, thus, on Athenian politics." J. K. Davies, *Athenian Propertied Families*, pp. 455-460 (1971), *The New Encyclopedia Britannica*, Chicago: 15th Edition, (Vol. 9, p. 291). Perhaps this aspect of their relationship and the happiness he appeared to have attained with her gave rise to jealousies amongst the peers of Pericles, such as Zeno, a declared friend. "Zeno of Elea had often told Pericles that happiness was the dream of cattle, and not to be attained by thinking men..." a suggestion Caldwell played with in her novel. "Many [Athenians] insisted that they were secretly ruled, not by Pericles, but by a disgraceful woman. Others declared that Aspasia was only the weapon of Pericles against the people."

Caldwell, *Glory*, (pp. 399, 367).

b. Pericles (495 BC-429 BC. Athens, Greece) A statesman largely responsible for Athenian democracy and the construction of the Acropolis, begun in 447. From the society of Zeno, he was said to have learned "impassivity in the face of trouble and insult and skepticism about alleged divine phenomena." Under the reign of Pericles the Athenian's claimed "to have brought corn and civilization to mankind." His liberal views were often criticized in a day when military might and strategy very much decided a nation's fate. C. M. Bowra, *Periclean Athens* (1971), *Encyclopedia*, (Vol. 9, p. 289-291).

c. Zeno of Elea, (495 BC-440 BC) Greek philosopher, mathematician, and believed to be the father of metaphysics and who Aristotle called the inventor of dialectic, a form of logic arrived through questioning. He was especially known for his paradoxes that contributed to the development of logical and mathematical rigor. A friend and pupil of Parmenides, Zeno defended Parmenides' theory that was being questioned, that of the existence of "the one." From his hometown of Elea, in southern Italy, sprung the philosophic school of Pre-Socratic philosophy distinguished by its radical monism, a belief in the state of Being, and referred to as Eleaticism as opposed to the many Greek gods. He was thought to have had a great deal of influence on the thinking of Pericles. R. Meiggs, *The Athenian Empire* (1972), *Encyclopaedia,* (Vo. 9, p. 290, Vol. 12, p. 606, Vol. 25, p. 906).

~ ~

HEART SONGS

POETRY

Man Is A Dutiful Master

Nothing in the world is so distressing as
a man without a horse. He is lost.
Man is a dutiful master.
He makes his day with anything he can find.
He will hitch up to a tree and languor in the sun.
He is doomed to despair when he must walk
instead of ride.
Man is a dutiful master.
He needs someone to drive, to work,
to bed, to shoe, to feed.
Man is a dutiful master.
He wants to sleep, to loaf, to eat, to drink,
to laze in the sun,
yet he is miserable when he has nothing to do.
Having the goal out there waiting for him
is what keeps him striving toward it.
Man is a dutiful master.

I Wonder

I wonder what the time will be
when summer comes and I am free
I wonder what the night will be
when all is well and I can tell
the world what lies
in dead of night
the way one sleeps
and seeks his might
I wonder.
I wonder.
I wonder.
I wonder, is what I think
I think is what is well
Nothing is so fine as this
to write and speak of nothing yet
The night is dark and I am spent
the day is yet to be... till then
What is the way one has to go
to give to all a wealth of yore
Ahead, oh soul, await yourself
You are the one who drives the mole.

Wealth

Certain is he that makes his life
of fun and games and summer nights
He is the one who loves the most
He gives, and gets, and plays the host
He is the one that can and will
be first and last in proper wealth.

Why?

Night has gone and day is near
The kids are safe and I am here.
He is busy, the way to be
Yet why am I so lost?
The home is made of love and nest
Then why has it such cost?

Self

Lust and love and much to give
You are the one
You are the one that makes the day
You are the one that gives and gets
You are the one who makes the nest
You are the one who loves and cares
You are the one who wonders where
You are the one who learns and does
You are the one who makes the bed
You are the one
You are the one who tries and takes
You are the one who doesn't wait
You are the one who puts the foot
in certain spots and cries, yells
You are the one
You are the one who doesn't know
You are the one who lets things go
You are the one to cut the steel
You are the one to make the meal
You are the one to wind the clock
You are the one they call "the wife"
You are the one, the finest self,
the one real friend
You are the one;
You are the one.

Son

"Never will I wonder too far from home."
Yet out there somewhere lost is he
His eyes are searching for brighter suns
His ears hear music that silences guns
His feet are quick, his hands so gentle
He is the son who cradles never.

Daughter

She makes her way through troubled seas
And takes her children far
Over the hill and dale she goes
But always far from we.
Under the silence her heart does grieve
For love from others she does seek
The fever is high, the melody lost
as she makes herself scarce in search of we.
Where are you child?
What have we done to cut thyself off from we?
Your eyes so blue, they smile and scorn
the love we have given thee.
Come thither, please, and give us your charm
The world only waits for your grave
Others may say they accept you today
But none will care only for thee.
They want you should please
They want you should rise
They want you should suffer their dreams
But the father and mother who gave you such means
are stricken with empty arms.

Where?

What is the moment that makes love get lost?
Where is the time that is gone?
Where does one go in the heat of the day
Or the middle of winter, and frost
Nowhere, my friend.
Nowhere is best
Nowhere is nearer than hell.
As always, one finds that the end of the road
Is only a step, and a tell.

What I Am

I'm not what I want to be
I'm only what I have to be
What is the difference?
What I want to be is well
What I am is hell.

Nothing

Nothing I do seems to matter at all
Nothing at all seems to matter
Nothing takes time
Nothing makes time
Nothing is all in the chatter
Nothing can please
Nothing can do
Nothing can be what is pleasant
Nothing, my friend, is a moment to lose
Nothing. Nothing. Nothing.

He

He is the thorn that pricks the sweetest
He is the rose that smells the best
He is shit, man, shit...
Not in the least a quest.

Next Time

Next time be careful
Next time, be safe
Next time look before you jump
Next time stay all day, if you must.

Cradles, And Things

Cradles, and things, are blessings to lose
Much do they give and require
But nothing can make the heart sadder than these
or suffer the soul to expire.

Waiting

The earth is so cold
Waiting. Waiting
The love that is left
Waiting. Waiting.

Just As We

Where are you child, where have you gone?
What thing was done that makes you run wild?
You righteously cry: We need only "God"
But you have forsaken Him, too.
You speak of His love, His ways, His abode
Yet you leave us to die in the dust.
Come to us now, touch us, see us —-
You must
For no one will care when you frighten the air
Or save them to curse your mistrust.
Never, cry never, you say in your script
Never, like Always and Best
A child's whim is given; a child's wish is sought
A child's life, for naught — Look at you, listen.
Take heed to your God
What does he tell you to do?
Go to the ends of the earth, if you must
But give us a whisper, or two.
What you are doing, is fine for you now
Not seeing the end as we do
We've gone before sadly;
we'd trade with you gladly
If it would make giving worthwhile.
But oft in our dreams
There's a mystical theme
It is Never. Never. Not We.
Our days are numbered, it's said in the book
That you sing from the steeples you seek

One of these hours, days, in those towers
You'll see...
We, like thee, are as free
To make ourselves known, to get up and go
And leave you to be — just as We.

What Sadness Is This

What sadness is this that the heart cries, it rages
The pain lies in wait for the pen, and the pages
How does one go past the aching and sin
Or make for the day that the night does us in
How to. How to. Is what we are told.
Make it. Make it. That is the bold
The mean in us pounces
The hurt begs to plead
Come hither, come hither
Oh, my God, I am old.

Come Back

First it was mother, now it is child
How strange life makes sunshine
Makes everything wild
It turns hell to heaven in one little tweak
Or gladness to doom with only a peek.
Where is the humor, the writ, or the fire?
Where does one go mist the clanging, most dire?
You needn't see, you needn't be
Fairer than I
Only a lesson it was in the cry.
Make the mend slowly, be gone for awhile
But come back and try us
You might find a prize.

PRAY TELL

Pray tell, where is the nearest bar?
she asked of the first passerby.
Where is the end of the road?
Where is the moon in the heavens above?
Does it love you as no others can?

How can I know how to tell others how,
when nobody's wanting to hear?
How can I see where the road will come out
When twisting and turning is clear?

Life has its way of spiraling down
into darkness and doom, on a dime.
Hanging on to the edge like a cat on a rail
is living the reality tune.

You wander and search for the answers for much
But the questions are lost in the wind.
You make so much over the dirt on the floor
When crusting of muck sticks within.

You smooth out your silks and your baby skin talc
You color your hair on a whim.
But you miss the whole sermon that Jesus did teach
How to master the storm tides of sin.

You think if you relish the sun on your face
you will safely forestall any fall.
But Mister don't worry, you're missing the point —
the world is gone past you, and won.

You whisper your prayers to a make-believe god
in hopes by some magical means
you will somehow escape all the wicked rewards
that was promised before you were born.

One of these days you may find out the source
of that beautiful wondering star.
But don't wish upon it, it stays not for long,
so be gone with your mystical farce.
You might be so lucky to settle, and sweep
a whole lifetime under the rug.

I Like

I like toads, and stools, and everything weird
I like real, and what? and still.
I like shine and high, and over and all
I like up, and at, and here
I like blowing, whistling, singing, and straight
I like yellow, and pink and all in between
I like smiles and "hi"s and "y'all"s.
I like mountains, and skies and sunshine and clouds
I like over, under, all-the-way, and now!
I like Yes and "You're beautiful," all said real soft
I like feeling the touching of hands that are kind
I like knowing those eyes really see all of me, mine
I like reaching and pulling and pushing, and such
I like doing whatever makes music and lunch
I like to be open, loving, and warm
I love all the glitter of holidays, corn
I love having smiles that are sure
I love jumping jacks, clowns, and surreal
I love being loved, all the trappings, the effort
I love when the inside of me is "okay" and "all better"
I love when the words come out to the letter
I love sucking sounds in my ears or whatever
I love being loose, swinging free, up a ladder
as long as there's belts, handles, and railings
I love being sure, knowing when, learning why
I love all the things that are human and sigh
I love being me —
I have no idea why!

~ ~

A FUZZY TALE

FICTION

There was once an old lady who lived on a street in the old section of town. She had many cats. She loved the cats, fed the cats, and cleaned up after the cats. She was known as The Cat Lady to the kids. When she went to the store to buy her groceries, she bought cat food for her cats. When she went shopping for clothes for herself, she bought bows and sweaters for her cats. She liked adorning them like they were her children. But the cats didn't like all that fuss. They would tug and pull on their own sweaters, pull each other's bows off, and the old lady was forever fidgeting and fussing over them to keep them neat and proper looking. This was her occupation. She was The Cat Lady.

One day, The Cat Lady became ill. She woke up and couldn't move her left leg, and she had very little feeling in her left arm clear to her finger tips. But she was right handed, so she dragged the left foot behind her and used chairs, canes, banisters, whatever she could grab on to with her right hand to help her get around. She fought very hard not to take to her bed because if she gave up, she knew the first thing that would happen is that someone would come and take away her precious cats.

She had them named, you see. There was Minnie. She was a dull grey with no particular markings on her. She was the oldest cat and a baby of a litter born "in this very house." Then there was Theodore. He was dark, a silky black that shone in the sun. He had four white mittens that he kept immaculately clean. He was the youngest and the fastest. He is the one that kept them all stirred up and challenged their environment constantly. Then there was

Alicardo. He was a brownish color with one white tipped ear. He had two different colored eyes and he was a funny looking cat. But he was the smartest. He knew when the mailman came. He would come and crawl up on The Cat Lady's shoulder and nuzzle his nose into her neck behind her ear until she would go out to the mail box and get the mail. You see, one time when he was very little, the mail man had brought a sample package of Kittle Biddle that had the taste of fresh mouse in it. He never forgot. Every day he hoped that he would get another taste of delicious mouse. Then there was Pussywillow. She was the fuzziest, fluffiest cat you ever did see. And when she sat upright, with her feet in front of her, her shiny white chest shone like a mountain of snow. She was the color of the willows that grew at the end of The Cat Lady's big huge yard, next to the empty lot that the children used for a ball diamond — that is where she got her name, from the willows that grew so tall and fluffy. Then there was Charles. He was a proud cat. He never begged. Not for food, for attention, for anything. He would just prance around the house and wait until someone else got hungry or for someone else to get stroked. He would sit and watch, with his clear intelligent eyes, until The Cat Lady would take pity on him and pick him up and he became King of the Lap for a good five minutes. This sustained him. Because he was singled out and respected he was able to manage for the rest of the day on that quality attention. Yes that is what he got, quality respect. Then there was Sissy. She was a little cat. She must have been "the runt of the litter" The Cat Lady always said. Sissy was frail and she ate very little. Her favorite place was the rug in front of the fireplace, especially if there was a fire going. She would curl up right in the middle of the rug and never left much room for the other cats unless they overlapped her. And she didn't like to be overlapped anywhere on her body. She liked the whole rug to herself. She lay with her paws stretched out in front of her and her tail sprawled out so that she took up just about the whole rug. The Cat Lady called it "Sissy's Rug."

It was a spring-like day. The end of winter was at hand. The sun was shining and the birds were out in full force, picking and snatching whatever they could find after the winter's retreat. The Cat Lady had opened the door to let out her cats. She was holding onto the door-frame with her good hand, and she kept a chair by the door so she was able to hang on to it with her numb hand. She could use the hand a little, she just couldn't feel much with it. All the cats ran friskily out the door and were gone, quick as a flash, about their day.

It was so nice to be outdoors again. It had been a long, cold winter and the snow on the ground had been cold on their feet. The smell of the earth as the sun warmed it this particular morning, drove them all out, each to their individual secret place. Sissy loved the big pine tree that grew in front of the house. It had large branches that spread out in every direction. They were low enough so that she could disappear under there and no one ever saw her. There was just two glowing eyes peering out from under the lowest branch. There Sissy stayed for hours on end, just watching.

Alicardo and Theodore took off together and headed for the field. They liked to sneak up on the kids playing. The boys always had a game of some kind going, Tag, Scruff End, and Over The Tree if they could find a ball and bat. Alicardo and Theodore loved jumping all over the small set of broken down wooden slats that was put up for bleachers many years before. Old Man Iverstein loved baseball, and when he died he left a bequest in his will to purchase a set of bleachers for the empty field. The money ran out after the third row had been installed, and the rest of the rows never got finished, so three rows of bleachers got moved up and down the risers, at the whim of the players or spectators. Sometimes, just where the slats would finally rest became an object of dispute. Some of the little baby brothers and sisters liked to climb on the bleachers and the mother's were always afraid they would fall off, so the boys got tired of having to watch their younger siblings. But there were a couple boys who did not have younger siblings and loved looking up to the top of the tall bleachers to see their older brothers and sisters looking down at them like they were Babe Ruth or Casey Stengel. One day several boys had taken to fighting over whether the slats would be placed at the top of the risers, so it was easier to see their game, or at the bottom end, nearer the ground should a young child fall off.

The cats, Theodore and Alicardo, were romping on the bleachers this day, and, after much quibbling, the boys decided that they would allow the cats to decide where the slats would ultimately rest. The cats were romping, up and down, all over them, so the boys devised a system of counting how many times they landed on each slat. They deduced that if the cats played on the higher slats more than the lower ones, that would give credence to the high positioning of the slats. So they began to watch Theodore and Alicardo hop up and down the bleachers. Up and down they bounced, two times, three times on the lowest. Then on the upper slat. It seemed that the middle one got the most counts as the cats always managed to run down it, chasing each other's tails. But Theodore's tail always managed to hit the upper slat as he bounced, giving a slight edge to the vote for the upper positioning. When, after several minutes, the cats had finally tired of this rigorous play, they began to slow down. One of the boys jumped onto the bleachers with a hard bang trying to grab one of the happy cats, but he was not quick enough. Scat went the cats, off into the bushes that separated the lot from The Cat Lady's house. The matter of the positioning of the bleachers was thus decided: one slat at the top, one at the bottom, and one left in the middle with empty risers above and below it, as the cats had decreed —which became known as Cats Landing and the favorite place to sit on all of the bleachers.

Meanwhile, Minnie had found her way several blocks from home, browsing into a friendly neighbor's trash. She nosed around and found some left-over meat loaf that drew her attention. During the course of finding its way to the dump it had fallen on the ground, out of the trash can. Minnie had a hardy meal, and was sitting, licking her paws, when a little girl came around the corner of the house with her push-wheel toy. She spied Minnie and called, "Here, Kitty. Kitty. Here, Kitty." When Minnie just sat still and looked at the child, the child became very cross and stomped her feet and said, "Come here this instant, I say, Kitty. Did you *hear* me?"

Minnie, not being used to being spoken to in such irate tones, turned away from the child and continued to lick her paws. The child ran over to her, with the push toy whirring and bells clanging. Minnie stopped licking. The child came close to her, and was upon her, and suddenly let out a squeal. Minnie felt the strong fingers of a three-year old digging into her fur. The pulling Minnie felt, hurt, and she decided to get away. Just then the child let go. "Pretty Kitty.

Pretty Kitty. I *love* you, Kitty," the child said as she took her little fingers and wiggled them under Minnie's chin. Minnie liked that, though it was a little like tickling.

The child giggled. "Awe, pretty Kitty. I'm gonna take you and show you to my mommy," she said. Down dropped the push cart and the child put both arms around Minnie's neck.

Minnie felt herself being lifted off of the ground and being squeezed. The child was strong and held Minnie tightly by the head as she turned and rounded the corner, heading straight for the back door that stood ajar. Just as the child got to the door, she let go of one hand to push open the door so that Minnie found herself slipping out of the child's hands, onto the ground. The child started to cry dreadful tears. Minnie rubbed up against her legs, back and forth, until the crying stopped. Suddenly a voice from inside the house was heard calling in a very harsh tone, "Melissa, where are you? Come here this instant."

At these words, Minnie took her exit and darted back behind the house along her merry way.

Down the road, Pussywillow had a special rock that she had found in a backyard of a quiet house. She loved to sit in the sun. Nobody was ever home in that house. So she had the rock and backyard all to herself any time she chose to visit. Today, however, she was surprised as the door opened and a woman with a turban tied around her head, gypsy style, came out, with a dust mop in one hand and some small rugs in the other. She was heading straight for Pussywillow on her rock. But the cat had no inclination to move. The woman threw the rugs down in the grass and looked over at the cat. "Mighty lazy, you are, this fine day," she said, as she approached the rock with the mop in her hand. Then suddenly she struck the side of the rock with

Love 'N' Stuff

the mop head and dust flew every which way. Pussywillow closed her eyes and sniffed at the air. The dust had gotten into her nostrils. She sniffed and blew and wiped at her nose with her paw. The woman laughed. "Hey there, prissy one, see if I can't get you to move," as she shook the mop. Pussywillow saw the mop coming towards her, and she jumped through the air with a flying leap. The woman's laughter was heard half way down the block as Pussywillow tore through the yard lickety-split.

Charles, the epitome of elegance, was just dislodged from his viewing of the whole thing, when the door slammed behind the gypsy-looking woman. Charles had been sunning, sight unseen on the top of the timber shed, in the next yard. The empty swing set that was usually filled with neighborhood children, had left him a trifle lonesome, until he had overheard the laughter of the new cleaning lady shooing Pussywillow away. This day was not turning out like he was used to. But the sun was bright and the sidewalk had warmed so that his walking became easier and more collected. He was hungry and there were no children out to feed him. He headed for home. He stood on the step, waiting for his mistress to let him in. He would not meow like the other cats to be let in. He just sat with his back straight, and his paws in front of him waiting. Just waiting. It never was too long before the door would open and the voice of The Cat Lady was heard scolding. "Now, here, Charles. You were not out long enough today. What am I going to do with you? Staying indoors all the time is not good for a big, strong, healthy cat as my Charles. Here now, maybe you need a little energy. Come, my sweet. A special treat." She pulled out a crinkly, noisy bag from the cupboard and bit it open with her teeth. She pulled out several small pieces of something that looked like little fishes. They were made of chewy stuff that tasted like his favorite fish nip. They were chewed up and swallowed in a hurry. The Cat Lady said, "My Lord, Charles. You must have been hungry. Here, no sense filling up on treats. Come, let me fix you something sturdier for Your Highness."

Charles followed her as she pulled her weak leg behind her hanging on to an old cane. "Take your time, now Charles, dear. You don't want to get an upset tummy," she said, as Charles dug into the feast she had prepared for him. "Sometimes, I wonder if you don't just pull this on me to get special attention," she said over her shoulder, dragging her leg in a shuffle. "Yes, sometimes, I wonder," she said with a tone of satisfaction that she had finally figured something out that was very puzzling. Charles paid no mind but kept on eating until he could not hold another bite.

When he had finished cleaning his paws, he headed for the sunshine spot on the living room carpet. The Cat Lady had pulled her rocking chair right in the middle of it; it helped to ease the pain in her leg. She was sitting with her eyes closed, rocking, when he sat down in front of her. She opened her eyes and reached down and pulled Charles up, into her lap. She began to hum his favorite tune while she stroked his head and his back, and rocked. Then Charles stretched out his paws and rolled over so she could reach under his front legs. Oh, that feels so good, he thought. Sometimes one is so very lucky. And as The Cat Lady continued to rock and hum and stroke him, she was thinking the very same thing.

~ ~

A NICE WAY TO LOOK AT THINGS

Fiction

"Otto, Darling, I must run or I will be late for my hair appointment," said Harriet. "You're sure you will be alright?"

"Oh sure. Don't worry about me. Once I get through in here, I'm going over to the club and hit some balls."

Otto was just finishing his morning "dapper routine," he called it. (He thought this easier to say than SSS (shit, shower, and shave). Anyway, Harriet always got it confused with SOS (shit on a shingle), a name for the sick looking creamed beef on toast for which Army cooks were famous. Otto loved words; he had cute names for everything ever since he came home from the war. But he loved simplicity even more. When his illness started sapping his strength he became all the more energetic in finding ways to conserve it. The day that he would not be able to stand alone to swing a golf club would be the day he would have no more reason to be "dapper." But for now, his adrenalin spurred him on. He had a new putter to try out. His excitement made him have to pee again. What a nuisance. He was going to have to figure out a way around this newest inconvenience, the bladder muscles were slowly going to, she noticed.

Harriet closed the door behind her to the sound of the electric razor. She smiled to herself remembering their son's childhood pet name for it, The Buzzy Bear. Otto would put the razor on David's cheek as he stood on the toilet stool eyeing every turn and wrinkle the shaver took. "Do me, Daddy, Do me!" he'd squeal. "I want the Buzzy Bear on me." Now David had a full ruddy beard but he still used the Buzzy Bear to keep himself always neat. *Wonder where David is?* she thought, as she absent mindedly pushed the button to the garage door opener. David was a bee on a lake, on the go, moving from house to boat to live-in-jobs. She finally gave up trying to keep his whereabouts current in her address book. He needed a book of his own. Already he'd moved four times in five months of this year. *If he would only take his medication. He would settle down then.*

The sunshine poured into the dark smelly garage. Harriet looked around at the junk that had accumulated. *I just can't do it all. Maybe Larry will have some free time. With his help I could get rid of half this stuff, call the Goodwill, or something.* The Yellow Bird was still cranking up despite the looks of it. One of the fenders had been scraped and the dent was starting to rust. But the soft gold interior felt like the day they bought it. Was it already twelve years? Instinctively she looked at the mileage as she turned the ignition key. 89656 miles. She couldn't think about it. Time had become her enemy of late. She never had enough of it. *As long as he needs me...* was coming from the radio speaker. "Oh, dear God. And Otto does need me," she said aloud, the sound of her own voice shocking her. *Talking to myself again. But then who else is as interested in what I have to say?* She smiled and then thought of Larry. He was so sweet to her. Always making her feel like she was some special lady. Maybe she was and maybe it was Larry who was special. She wouldn't let her mind dwell on that possibility. *Just enjoy it, Harriet. Just enjoy it,* she kept telling herself. When the doors seem to be closing all around you, God always manages to open a window somewhere. And what a window Larry made! She pushed on the gas pedal a little harder at the thought. Larry didn't believe in accidents. "We were supposed to meet," he'd said, when she reluctantly sat down in his salon chair that first time.

Love 'N' Stuff

That was two years ago. Otto had just been diagnosed and she was frightened. Otto was so active, so healthy. She just couldn't believe it when he would drop his shoes before he got them into the closet. It was such a helpless feeling. She had always been able to "fix it." That's just one of the names they had called her, "Fix-it, Mom." But she couldn't fix this thing. She was lucky to keep *herself fixed*. Larry had offered an alternate view to things. "Be thankful," he always said, thankful for the knowledge, the scientific progress from all the research. And then they did have medical benefits, a lucky thing in these days, she thought. And friends. There were so many now. Some that she didn't really know before had came up to her in the grocery store, at the clubhouse after she'd drive Otto around for a few holes. People everywhere had given her courage and hope. Hope that a cure might stop the horrible sting of the disease from stealing any more life from them. Larry, though, was a godsend. So precious young and still naive in his simple faith. And he made her laugh. Laughter. It was an angel with a spear in hand that could pierce the saddest moments with a ray of hope. Yes, Larry was hope. He was youth. He was love personified. And he was a lousy beautician. But that made him human. She would never admit to anyone that she'd go home and trim the uneven ends that Larry had left. What had he said? "The scissors are only props. It's loving that takes center stage, you and I only the speakers." What about sex? she'd asked him once. "Oh, that just adds a little jazz, sound affects and colored lights," he said. "But we better not talk about that, Otto might sense it and feel left out."

Sound affects and colored lights? Her eyes were dancing when she stepped through the door and faced Larry behind the desk. She said good morning.

His face broke into a robust smile when he looked up and saw her. "You look smashing today. As always. Better than Jane Fonda," Larry said, as he took her by the hand and led her to his station.

It *is* such a nice way to look at things, she thought. So very nice.

~ ~

A HABIT SHE HAD

FICTION

She walked a short ways before it dawned on her that she had forgotten the most important thing. It was a habit she had, forgetting. She turned to return home, and within yards of her front door she spotted, parked upside the embankment of her driveway, a strange looking vehicle. It was at one time supposed to have been a small bus, she surmised, but it had rusted, and someone had cut into its metal frame so that it had a sort of rumble seat in the back. It reminded her of the one she rode in long ago. It belonged to her grandfather. It was a Model-T and the rumble seat was in the rear and open to the wind. It was a delight to a small child, but a fright to her mother who feared she may fall out on a turn. But she would cry and stomp her feet, and beg to be taken, until her grandfather would give in to his first and only grandchild. This strange looking seat, though, was upholstered with leopard skin and the paintings on what was left of the metal were bright colors splashed in stripes and circles over a background of bright yellow. It looked rather like something out of the circus. There were no windows, it seemed, either, and as she drew closer she noticed the keys were still in the ignition. On the front seat lay a large folder, a portfolio of sorts, she thought. An artist. The owner had to have some imagination. And some initiative also, to put so much work in such a project. She became intrigued now, wondering what this silly thing was doing on her property.

    She looked about, but saw no one. She had left the back door only closed, unlocked, in case the deliveryman were to come by with her order of books. She hated so to have to go after them, driving was not her favorite thing. She walked everywhere she could. She had more control that way, it seemed. Learning to drive late in life will do that to a person, she would often respond to comments by her friends about her aversion to the wheel. As she started towards the rear of the house, she had a thought, that maybe this was the delivery person bringing her books. One can never tell who is going to be hired to do anything anymore, dependable workers were hard to find. She picked up her gait at the mere thought of it. Of having the materials at hand finally for the research she was so anxious to pursue. As she reached the end of the house, she heard the squeak of the screen as it closed quietly behind what appeared to be someone inside her house. The inside door was still ajar. It was this unexpected sound that made her stop. Still. She could see some movement inside the small kitchen that opened directly into the back yard.

She had heard that one should never enter their house if they suspected unwanted guests. Go directly to the nearest phone and call the police, she was told. But the vehicle looked so inviting, so charming, surely whoever it was must have good reason to be in her house. So she took another step closer. And listened. There was water running now. Perhaps the person was thirsty? Then she heard a scuffle, a scratching noise, and the sound on the hard surface of her kitchen floor. Then the sound of metal, perhaps a chain striking the hard floor.

Sara began to question her first intuition. Should she go inside and face the intruder? Or should she turn and run? Her curiosity was about to overcome her when a white furry head appeared in the doorway. It was a small man with very curly hair which seemed to grow from every spot visible to the human eye. He was pushing the screen open to exit, when he looked up to catch her observing him, about four feet away. He stopped abruptly, and shoving his hands deep into his pockets, he lifted his face and looked at her dead on. Into his eyes a gentle smile began to flow, and he said, "Might you be the lady of this here house?" As he spoke, a small dog slipped past his legs and out into the grass.

The fright that had stopped her minutes before was forgotten, as Sara reached down to pet the small shaggy ball. Anyone who loves dogs couldn't be bad, she had always believed. She looked up at him as he watched her petting the animal and said, "Yes, matter of fact, I am. What can I do for you?" she said, in her well worn way of getting straight to the point. It was a habit she had.

"Well, ma'am, I was told in town you were looking to rent a room, and I was told you liked animals, and wouldn't mind a whole lot for my little Bum here to root around some in your place. And I don't need a place for too long. I'm a roaming sort. Don't need to rest too long. But I knew if Bum here liked your kitchen, we was in the right place. So I just went ahead and let myself in. They told me in town you was the friendly type, so I took it upon myself to give Bum here some water. He was a might thirsty. I used the Cool Whip plastic you'd put into the trash, so's you wouldn't mind."

By now, little Bum was licking at her toes that were protruding from her sandals. It tickled and she pulled her foot away with a hushed giggle. It distracted her attention momentarily, and she felt suddenly shy. She had been alone for so long, it had taken a great deal of thought before she decided to try to rent to someone. But she hadn't really done anything concrete about it, just mentioned it at the library, that she was thinking about it. But Cornwall was a small town, and strangers were treated as folks. An unusual place one might suspect if one paid attention to the TV news, which not many natives did. They were a staid lot, them who grew up here, and especially those who never left. Sara pulled her large soft embroidered bag around to her front, as a protection, a shield, as she spoke. "I must say, Mr.... ah..."

"Name is Sam," he said, pulling his hand from his pocket and shoving it towards her. "Sam Freely. Born and raised in Kansas, and come to these parts to paint some pictures for my laddie back home."

She took his hand and gave it a quick shake. "Nice to meet you, Mr. Freely," she said. And then added, "I *think* anyway."

"Well, we's easy to get to know, Bum and me. Just a bite here and there and a place to powder our toes," he said laughing right out loud.

The sound of the man's belly-laugh forced Sara into an acquiescent smile — to spite herself.

~ ~

KISSIN' COUSINS

FICTION

He had felt her watching him for two weeks. He always shied away from her, though, when he'd notice her looking with those big round, soft eyes of hers, fixed unmovable-like on him. It was the softness in her gaze that got to him. Yes. That was it. The gentleness that seemed to part his scalp right down the middle. It seemed to penetrate through to the innermost part of him, the part hid away from even his closest kin. Maybe it was her being *nearly* kin, a cousin twice removed on his mama's side, that gave her some special fix on him. *Kissin' Cousins* is what his mama called them when they were little. But that was so long ago. Way before the whole world got turned topsy turvy and hell let loose with a mighty vengeance — before the fire.

He could still hear his mama's voice singing through the trees that night, "Angel... Angel... Honey, please answer your mama, now," her whine stuck to him like sorghum in winter. "Don't you be hidin' from your mama like this." And then the crackling sound of the light, dry timber catching fire, pierced the heavy night air. "Angel," came the weak, whiny voice again, through the darkness. "Angel, you know better'n to do this to your old mama, stuck away in this here sick bed like this." Then the crackling sound turned into a blazing inferno.

The feeble whine got softer, softer...

First one piece of decaying wall collapsed, and then another, until the whole place lit into high flames, reaching straight up, licking the sky, with no wind to pull them to one side or the other. He'd let his breath slide out real quiet like, so no one would know he was anywhere near.

Had to do it. Don't you understand? Surely you must,

he told his heart. *I had good reason... all she had... Good reason... The lookin' after. That's what tore into me. And her whinin'. That beggin', pitiful whine. Her angel. All she had. Ain't no one ever to know what done it. Nobody...*

And still those big, round soft eyes watched him, penetrating clean through. His *Kissin' Cousin.*

Melanie liked the boy-man, his hair beginning to thicken like Brillo in front of his ears. There was a mystery about him that mushroomed, when he slid his eyes quickly away from her gaze. As he threw the large barrel over his ever broadening shoulders, she wondered what he wondered -- and if he cared any. He came everyday to load and unload, and they exchanged a friendly, "Hey." She would watch the back of his muscular arms, exposed by the torn shirt-sleeves and tanned by the hot Georgia sun, as he slipped past her and out the back door. A shame about his mama, Cousin Adelle. A poor soul. A lot to care for, but *still* it was somebody.

The inventory of Hampton's Feed and Grain - a dull sort of job, matching the stillness in the heavy summer air — couldn't keep her attention from drifting back to the boy-man... and the banana puddin' she was hankering to make. *Wonder, had he heard about her?* It had been so long since they were kids, playing on that old rubber tire swing down in the hollow, jumping into the swamp when the rains were up. *Wonder, would he care?* Then it struck her that she had no call to speak his name in a month of Sundays. Angel was all, before the fire. *Wonder... if I can save me back some extra egg whites... banana puddin's got to have it high.*

~ ~

OTHER PATHWAYS

MEMOIR

It was strange how I ended up in the beauty shop that day, sitting next to her husband while he waited patiently for her last curler to be rolled — the lady with the overly bright smile and disjointed speech. But it really began earlier that morning, the first day of our weekend jaunt to Bar Harbor celebrating the return home of our youngest son.

Visiting Bar Harbor is one of the rewards of living now in New England. Just one of the small seaside towns that dot the rugged, watery coast of Maine, Bar Harbor is breathtakingly grand on its worst day. But this aside, the spectacle of spring bursting before us this Memorial Day weekend couldn't help but trigger the memories of the home of my youth: Milwaukee — a town, similarly wrapped around the shores of that mammoth Lake Michigan and, like Maine, suffered the same bitter winds and icy waters that cruelly reminded us daily of the treachery beneath its splendid beauty. I especially shared in the Mainlander's gratitude for the warm sunshine as it softened the famous northeasterly whipping through my ill-barbered hair. As we walked back to the hotel from breakfast, Sean, then twenty-one, and always fastidious about his own hair, commented, "Mom, you've got a hair out of place."

Sean's notice of me had always given me pleasure, but it especially did so now, being unaccustomed to hearing it. Having him back in our lives again, after the long three-year separation, had me flying high on my adrenalin.

Born on his Irish father's 30th birthday, Sean was the youngest of four. His birth had been welcomed by an excited family — especially his older brother Kelly — and friends toasting our final addition. It was then that his father discovered Dr. Spock and even shared in Sean's feeding and diapering. A first! Sean continued to receive this initial love and attention from all of us despite his flunking kindergarten. His inability to sit still, unless the teacher held his hand as she read to the class, was upsetting but not devastating, until the new school psychologist, just retired from the federal penal system, made the grand diagnosis. The baby of our family had a "criminal personality." You can imagine the anger this young mother felt at such a label. But I quickly dismissed it, believing this doctor surely had been in the prison system too long. Further, I determined that I would *never* let that come true. Hyperactive? Yes. Brain damaged? Maybe. But sociopathic? Definitely not!

By the third grade, when we became aware that Sean was having great difficulty learning his alphabet, in spite of the strong medication he was taking, I decided to tackle his learning problem head-on. All of this concerted effort, I was later able to see, made me extremely receptive to the predicament of my, soon to be, new friends.

In Sean's case, his medication, theoretically, was supposed to energize his "lazy brain" and at the same time slow his body so that the two — body and mind — would be in harmony. This would enable him to settle down and, hopefully, learn. Unfortunately, it also took his appetite away. And he already was very small for his age. In the hope that he might eat more, we tried to stretch out Sean's mealtimes by entertaining him.

He and I cut out letters and pictures and pasted them on a large cardboard. While he studied this collage, we managed to get at least one hearty meal into him before the medication took effect. Besides this, the collage became an important learning tool as he chose pictures ature represented to him the sound of the letters he was having the most difficulty remembering. His memory, or lack of it, was the most disconcerting part. One day he would know a "k", the next day the sight of it drew a blank. This would be the story of Sean's life: a memory bank full of random unpredictable forgetfulness that would create immense frustration for him.

It is no wonder his alcohol and drug addiction, that erupted at puberty, was almost unavoidable. Even though his doctors had warned us of a tumultuous adolescence ahead, we did not really understand then, even slightly, what he was having to cope with. Strangely, through all of this, his musical abilities seemed to flourish. When it was explained to us that music utilized a different part of the brain than English or math, we provided piano, organ, and trumpet lessons in the hope of providing an alternative path. Unfortunately, his learning almost stopped as the result of his substance abuse. This problem came to monopolize our attention and that of the doctors, forgetting the war of words we had waged together to get him through elementary school. As many parents in the '70's did, we had to learn "tough love" the hard way. After nearly losing him through two failed suicide attempts in his 17th year (which kept him hospitalized for nine months) we were told by the doctors that Sean *would* recover, if we "let him go." Learning on his own was the only way. Knowing that it is our memory that teaches us to not repeat painful behavior — what learning is all about — didn't help us as parents as we watched him having to learn his lessons, like the collage, over and over again. But to continue running interference for him would only prolong his pain.

We gradually refused the frantic pleas for help, tearing us apart inside, until one day when he called — sober, begging for another chance to come home and "get straight" with the help of AA — we said yes.

All my lessons of the painful past were replaced with the highest kind of optimism that only a mother knows, a belief that "now my son would be all right." I was confident that the decision we had made, to allow Sean his freedom to learn on the street as opposed to long-term residential treatment, would now be vindicated.

We were ecstatic. How many parents, like us, didn't get a second chance, I was thinking, as I watched him and his father drive off together that morning, golf clubs in tow. I was remembering the first time I'd seen Sean get up on water skis at the age of four, he and his father out there on that great body of water. I had cried happy tears of pride that day also, just as I fought back the tears now.

Slowly through the town I walked, past the specialty shops just being set up for the season. Looking into the windows I felt absolutely buoyant thinking about Sean's determination to find an AA meeting not more than thirty minutes after arriving the night before. Now I breathed in the glorious fresh air, and I fought the wind in my hair as it reminded me of his subtle hint that it needed attention. I headed for the hairdresser.

The angular path went through the small one-block square park that was the mark of the center of most New England towns. A *common* it was called, an old English term somewhat unfamiliar in the rest of the country. I finally found the beauty shop hidden away in one corner of an old house that I was sure had been built well before my time. The large shop, equipped with several work areas and hair dryers, was surprisingly empty, with only one customer and one beautician. She looked over at me as she was finishing, and said, "Are you the one that called wanting a

Love 'N' Stuff

permanent?"

"Yes, but I'll settle for an even trim — since you said you haven't time."

The customer in the chair, a very thin, strawberry blonde woman, was looking at me and smiling brightly — just a little too brightly, I thought. But I smiled back, thinking her to be the age of my mother, had she lived, and then glanced over at the man who sat near me — her husband, I assumed. He was looking at me, too, but he smiled only a little as we caught each other's eye. Embarrassed, we both looked away. The woman still had that very bright smile, and then she stretched out her hand, pointed to me, and spoke to him, "I know. I know. I know. I know," she said.

The beautician continued to talk, ignoring the woman as though no one had spoken, saying to me, "No. I don't have time for a permanent today, but there is a shop on the hill, just as you come into town, where you can probably get one."

"Oh, thank you for telling me, but I'm *walking* today, and that would just be too far for me. My husband is golfing and he took the car."

At the sound of the word "golf" the man's head turned my way. He spoke very quietly in a distinctly familiar Bostonian accent, "Is your husband a member of the club?"

"No," I answered. "We're here just for the weekend, but we've been here before, and he loves that beautiful golf course. The view is spectacular isn't it, with those rolling hills and grassy dunes? Sometimes I enjoy just riding around in the cart simply soaking in the sight."

"Yes, It *is* beautiful. I'm a member there," he said proudly.

"Oh, you *live* here, do you? My husband would love to

retire here, during the summers. We're living in the Boston area now.

The woman with the bright shining eyes was speaking and pointing to me again. "I know. I know. I know," she said with emphasis as though saying something of far more importance than the words themselves conveyed. Her husband looked over at her kindly and nodded, but he answered me instead.

"Oh, yeah? Where, exactly? I'm from The North End myself. Name a few towns around where you live, he said.

"Westwood. Dover. Norwood," I answered. I looked over at the woman again and saw the overly bright smile in her eyes and thought of the nursing home and the many stroke victims I had seen recently staring with that same brightness in their eyes. "Norwood is where I work in a nursing home."

"You a nurse?" he asked immediately.

"No. No. I just volunteer there once a week." Then impulsively I asked him, "Did your wife have a stroke?"

"Yes," he said quickly, seeming thankful for my rapid assessment. "She has been this way for three years now."

"I know. I know. I know. My darling, I know. I know." The woman was pointing at me again and speaking very excitedly.

The man got up and walked over to his wife and helped her up and over to the hair dryer.

The beautician directed me into the vacated chair while I continued to listen to the gentleman describing his wife's illness. The girl managed to glean, amidst the flowing conversation, cutting instructions for my hair.

In answer to the gentleman's last question, I projected my voice across the room as we were the only ones in the shop. "Yes, I do play golf, but I hurt my back recently, and I can't play right now, so our son came along to keep his dad company. Do you get to play very much?"

"Oh, I try to get out there once a week, but it's hard. She just had another seizure six weeks ago. She's a world famous writer, you know, my wife is," he added. "She's written over twenty books."

"No kidding. What kind of books?" I asked with enthusiasm. Writing was what I enjoyed doing more than anything else.

"Astrology. Harper & Row published several of them, then I published the rest."

"You're a publisher?"

"Yes, I have the business in my basement, but it's not so good anymore. Too many people writing books."

I giggled at the disdain in his voice. "Yes. I know. *I'm* even writing one, a novel," I said, as though writing a book was as easy as breathing.

He'd put his wife under the hair dryer as we talked. I paid the beautician and walked over to them, the woman still smiling that bright smile. I sat down next to her and asked him, "Mind if I talk to your wife? My name is Sam, for Samantha."

"No. No. Go ahead, Sam. Her name is Frances. They call me Sark. It's short for Sakoian."

Then to Frances, he said, "Sam is writing a novel."

At this, the woman grew very excited. She threw back the hair dryer and spoke rapidly. "I know. I know. My darling, I know. My darling, I know. I know."

Her enthusiasm was contagious. So I responded immediately by leaning closer to her and took her hand and stroked it gently as I had been accustomed to doing in the nursing home, where touching was a scarce commodity and badly needed. I looked into her bright eyes trying desperately to understand her feelings. Unconsciously, my hand came to rest upon her wool-covered knee. Softly I said, "My, what torture it must be for you to have all those words, that a writer must have, locked up in your head bursting to come out."

While I was speaking, I felt a hand come up under mine and ever so quickly bring my hand to rest back upon my own knee. This was done so quickly and caught me so by surprise that my laughter bubbled forth. I was, after all, in Maine. And the response was as if, like Geraldine, Flip Wilson's comic character used to say, *Don't you touch me. You don't know me that well.*

My interest then, had been truly kindled. Here was a woman who appeared outwardly to be incoherent, irrational, and simply "out of it," judging by her speech, but yet lost no time intercepting, which was apparently to her, an inappropriate gesture. The movie of Patricia Neal's life immediately flashed through my mind. I remembered Neal's struggle portrayed on the screen, to come back after a severe stroke and learn to speak all over again. All the things about stroke victims I had heard and read came pouring into my head, reminding me how the brain still continues to function, but the pathways from the brain to the speech center are left impaired, requiring tortuous exercises to regain their use, often with little success.

"Is she getting any therapy?" I asked.

"Yes. A lady comes in once a week. But according to her astrological charts, she is supposed to have a big change for the better... in October, her birthday month, if it's all true. I hope it is. But I don't know," he said, rather softly, allowing his skepticism to show through and still trying to retain faith on his wife's behalf.

"I'd like to work with her, if I could, with pictures," I

volunteered.

"Sure. Come over to the house. We just live up the street. We're going to lunch after this, though. " Then added, "Say, why don't you join us?"

I hesitated, trying desperately to control my impulsiveness, answering, "I'm not used to all this walking…"

"Oh, I can come by in my car and pick you up when we are finished here, if you like."

I thought for a moment, and then decided to follow my instincts and accept his invitation.

At the hotel, a while later, Sark and Frances arrived. She was sitting in the front seat of the car looking straight ahead with a blank stare on her face. I knocked on her window as I got into the back. Her face lit up with her bright smile as she said, "I know. I know. I know. My darling, I know. I know, my darling."

I rubbed her on the shoulder, acknowledging the communication.

Sark drove us to a small café.

Frances slid into the booth, aided by her husband. He stood, waiting for me to sit down. On the spur of the moment, I decided to slide in next to Frances, but looked to Sark for approval.

"It's okay, if you want to," he said, and Frances indicated with the satisfied expression on her face as she smiled at me that she seemed to approve.

Her hand was still quite stiff from her illness, but Frances managed to push the menu towards her husband in an agitated manner. "Do you want a hamburger with mushrooms?" he asked her.

"She was shaking her head "no" but saying, "Yes. Yes.

Yes," emphatically.

Sark ordered her a hamburger.

This exchange between them fascinated me and filled me with questions. So as was my nature, I began asking them. "How long have you been married?"

"Twenty years," he said.

I turned to Frances. "Do you have children?" I asked her.

But Sark answered for her. "Yes, from her first marriage. They're in their forties. Several grandchildren. But they don't come up here much. Been a year and a half," he said. And then in sadness and slight irritation, he added, "They could, too. They fly to Mexico, and the Islands, and all over the place."

At these words her excitement overcame her again, and she said, "I know. I know. I know. One. Two, Three. Four and five." In her counting she was speaking in a conversational tone, using her hand in gestures as though explaining something in great detail. "... six... seven... eight... nine..." Her voice rose as in irritation and excitement and then lowered as in resignation as she finished, "... ten... eleven... twelve... prayer, prayer." When she finished speaking, she looked at me, as though waiting for me to answer.

Compassion welled up inside of me as I felt this woman's plight. A writer, with thousands of words roaming around in her head and no way to get them out. So I answered her as though I understood every word she would have spoken had she been able to speak. "That must make you feel very sad, that your children stay away from you, doesn't it?"

I thought she would cry then, her voice grew high and wispy. "I know. I know. I know. I know. I know." Her brow wrinkled as if to speak again, but I continued.

"But you *do* understand that it is not that your children do not *love* you, that they stay away. It is precisely that they *do* love you, but that they do not know what to do for you in your condition — they feel so helpless, and that hurts — so they just stay away."

Her voice broke into sobs. "I know. I know. My darling, I know."

I had almost forgotten Sark sitting across from us. I looked over at him and saw that tears stood in his eyes. Then he said, "That must be why our friends don't come around anymore, much. Like they used to, huh?"

Frances burst out into sobs then, saying, "My darling. I know. I know. I know. My darling, I know. I know."

And at that moment, under the table, I felt her small frail hand grasp mine and place it upon her knee.

I returned the communication with a soft pat, saying, "But today you've a friend. *I'm* with you today."

Sark looked at me and began to smile. "You must be a Sagittarian," he said. "They're very outgoing and friendly, you know. They also have the unique ability of saying it like it is."

My eyes widened, embarrassed, amazed at his deduction. I said, "I *am* a Sagittarian." I looked away rather sheepishly, realizing that my husband and Sean were also Sagittarians and how little I knew about astrology, but I definitely would investigate it now.

Frances squeezed my hand again. This time the words were, "I love you. I love you, my darling. I love you. My darling, I love you."

All I could think of at that moment was how fascinating were the recuperative powers of the whole human condition; and how fortunate for Sark, a remarkably devoted life partner, assuredly lonely and frustrated, that words he most needed to hear were words that still found their pathway.

Since that day, we have visited Frances* and Sark whenever we could. My husband and I were able to walk with Frances through her beautiful home, sharing the picture of her with President Kennedy, feeling the beautiful leather bound copy of her best seller presented to her by her publisher, looking through the many foreign language copies and the other books she'd written. We viewed the video of her on a talk show filmed just before her illness. What vibrance, what insight into human behavior. We were told that she foresaw many things in the future through her clairvoyant powers; that she was one of the first ones to speak out publicly against the abuse of drugs in the 60's and personally to Timothy O'Leary when she taught at U.S.C. in Berkeley. It was then that she foresaw the drastic swing in the world towards peace, which has come to pass in 1990.

The miracle of our chance (?) meeting still leaves me in awe. It taught me that when the customary means of communication — that most of us depend upon to get acquainted with someone, such as language — is blocked or distorted, somehow we can manage to find a way to know them. Sometimes it starts though, with not being afraid — *like the child Jesus spoke of?* — to let ourselves be known. Perhaps the unusually excited response that Frances gave to my presence was her acute sensitivity to others' needs that she had demonstrated by reaching out to them throughout her whole life. Losing my mother at an early age had left me very needy, leaving me strangely vulnerable, but at the same time exceptionally attuned to the sufferings of children such as Sean. I sensed that his first psychologist had mis-diagnosed him, and it was confirmed years later at Tuft's New England Medical Center. The neuro-psychologist explained the confusion Sean grew up with one side of his brain having the I. Q. bordering genius and the other side bordering retardation. His "charming" sociopathic-like behavior resulted as a way he had learned to cope with himself and his environment, an easy out to get him by, when in fact he was trying desperately and feeling severely hurt at his failure to understand. He was much like the elderly I saw at the nursing home in their struggles to cope with the changes in their lives. The futility in their situation, as with Frances, really gripped my heart. Sark suggested that in Frances' clairvoyance and her ability to read auras, she must have sensed something about me, possibly a future for me through my writing. This encouraged me to work even harder, with the hope that I would someday be able to share the unique experience of our meeting and my observation of this man's dedication and care for his wife. How poignantly his feeling shown as a shining light amidst a dark sea of pain and loneliness they both suffered — an unmistakable pathway of love.

---

*Note: Frances Sakoian was born October 08, 1912. At the age of five she began to be aware of her unusual clairvoyant powers. She became interested in astrology when her young son, who had been given a chart at birth, became ill, and she realized she had been forewarned of his illness through this chart. Through this interest she began teaching, helping to legitimize the subject of astrology for credit, for the first time at JFK University in California. She began writing daily, as many as eight hours. Her first book, *The Astrologer's Handbook,* co-authored with Louis S. Acker, was submitted to Harper & Row, Publishers, Inc. In 1973, after charting some of the decision makers at Harper & Row, the astrological readings she did were so accurate, Frances won their respect and was published. *The Astrologer's Handbook* sold over 150,000 copies. *Astrologer's Handbook, Predictive*

Astrology, and Astrology of Human Relations, all co-authored with Louis S. Acker, have been re-released in paperback by Harper & Row.

Frances had her first stroke on May 20, 1980 while at a book autographing at Fanuil Hall, in Boston. She died March 03, 1989 in Bar Harbor, Maine. Sark Sakoian died in 1991 after a long battle with cancer.

Sean and Samantha are synonyms.

~ ~

THERE COMES A TIME

Fiction

She saw him before he saw her. His appearance was striking. Of light complexion, so were the colors of his clothes softly muted. The green in his trousers blended into the garden behind him and the soft rose and white of his shirt gave her a feeling of warmth and clarity. She felt as though she knew him immediately even though she had only yesterday heard that he would be there to meet her at the airport. She would know him, she was told, by the sign he held. It would have a name on it. His. To protect her privacy. She liked that. The sign read: Manuel Petersen, with an e. A Swede. But it was more than this that struck her as she stepped out of the aircraft into the warm sunshine covering the tiny Palm Springs airport – the gateway to the Coachella Valley. It was the freshness of the air and the beauty of the surrounding mountains that rose up as walls, walls that would envelope her, protect her from the world for a much needed rest. Manuel was to be at her disposal to take her wherever she wished, for whatever she desired.

She knew Manuel would be someone with whom she would be able to converse. Her friends were thoughtful in that way. They recognized her intense need to communicate, to be heard and understood. And she knew that no human being ever had wasted her time. There was always some tidbit of learning that she acquired from the least amount of interaction. She was at once receptive to people. It was an openness she had acquired from her father. The measure of skepticism she had learned from her mother was her savior, or she would have been gobbled up with empathy for her fellows.

The man holding the sign turned and when he saw her, it was as though he had been an old friend out of her childhood. Peering through thick, unruly eyebrows, his face opened up into a smile that cast lights into his eyes. He immediately took a step in her direction. As he came nearer, she was reaching out already, to shake his hand. There was something in his countenance that told her she was in for a splendid time.

"Dr. Fairbright?" he said, as he reciprocated in the solid handshake.

"Yes. Just call me Lynn," she said immediately. She hated all that doctor stuff.

"So. Lynn," he said, smiling through teeth that had avoided orthodontics. "How was your flight? A bit bumpy, I would guess, from the winds about."

"It was rather exciting really," she said. "I didn't honestly believe Helen's warnings about that small plane. But at one point the turbulence was so sudden and sharp that my arm rests lifted straight up as I held them. The child in the seat in front of me screamed. Fortunately, I was more concerned about her fears than my own. So I got through it all right. Did you say it has been very windy here?"

"Yes. The desert valley is known for it, you know. That's what makes it so pleasant, even in very hot weather. But of course, you are missing the penetrating heat, coming at this time of year, and in the mountains it's always a bit cooler. You shouldn't have it to either extreme. Which do you prefer, hot or cold?" he asked, as he unobtrusively slipped his hand under hers and took her bag.

She instinctively wanted to resist. She had managed her own affairs quite well, thank you, without the coddling many women took for granted. But she at once remembered how tired she was. And the lightened load reminded her of her mission. So she quickly thanked him without adieu and answered, "Oh, warm, of course. And the older I get the warmer I prefer it. It must be in the bones," she said with a chuckle.

"I know what you mean," he said. "I share your appreciation of bones."

They laughed together then, understanding one another already. As she got into step with him, she let the breeze lift her hair and fill out her soft cotton skirt as it caressed the bare skin of her sweaty legs. She had wisely changed to barefooted sandals in LAX. A suggestion she had taken to allow herself the informality of the desert that had a way of bringing with it a new intimacy that one loses amidst suits, briefcases, and computer printouts. The looseness of her garb made her feel like a girl again, remembering the spring when the birds led the way, and the animals on the farm followed while the young Lynn had looked on in awe at the ordinary earthiness of the biological processes.

Lynn Fairbright had a reputation for unending devotion to the career she insisted chose her, rather than her decision to choose it. She had been the youngest of a large country family headed up by two strong and independent parents. Her father had worked hard on the land and his business acumen and love for his fellow man had turned a squalid fifty acres into a thriving pecan grove. Because the harvest was so tedious, the fruit of the yield so small, it took many farm hands in the beginning, before they could afford the huge combine to produce any real profit. Her father had been a man of sturdy beliefs in the equality of a man's soul and the integrity of his intelligence underneath the color of his skin. She had seen his fairness yield dedicated laborers that would do "anything for the Mister," as compared to McGlaughlin's farm down the road where whips hung on the barn wall in plain view. The Mister stood up to his beliefs, dedicated to the preservation of human dignity at all costs. His wife, The Missus, was equally solicitous of even handedness, although she never closed an eye to a slippery hand taking more than its share. She had a way of knowing, of seeing through a false smile or an empty promise.

Lynn, the baby, had learned well from them both, as well as her sisters and brothers. They had all married sooner or later. The girls had completed the required two years college their father deemed appropriate for their sexual calling. She had been the only one to go on to compete with her brothers in the academic arena. She had seen the gene pool at work through her nieces and nephews, and the more she studied that complex world of spin and get, the more afraid she became of parenting a deficit-challenged child. Her fear had become the impetus for her study. And she had gradually become a leading genetic specialist of her time.

Manuel was pointing now to the small white van in the first space of the adjacent parking lot. They stepped into the street to cross just as a long white limousine eased past them. Its windows were darkened and she turned her head to catch a glimpse of the rear. Manuel noticed her interest. "That's Frank's driver. Sinatra. He lives here, you know."

"No. I didn't know. I'm not up on show business, I'm afraid. I'm only here at the generosity of a dear friend who happens to be married to a man who loves golf."

"No other place in the world offers as many opportunities for that as it does right here. I think the count is up over a hundred courses now."

"For goodness sake. Whatever use could there be for so many?" she asked. "Do *that* many people play?"

"It's the occupation of the retired male. And many females taking it up, too. Can't beat it for taking your mind off of what ails you. Ever been out on the course for a round?"

"No. I never had any interest in it. It seems like such a waste of time. What is there about it that draws people, I wonder."

"Well, besides the sheer beauty of it, I think it has something to do with challenge. And most of the challenges are right up here," he said, pointing to his head. "It's a funny thing. You hit the ball a country mile, and you think, *Ah. Now I have a chance to score well. This time I figured out how to keep my head down, how to bend my knees just right, how to connect with the ball.* Then you go to where your ball is and it is sitting right down in a darn hole. And you can't move it, you know. So the club that you think will put it on the green, is put back into the bag and you settle for an iron, for a shorter distance because you can't get to it very well with the longer wood down in that hole. So there you are. It's never as you expect it to be. Just one challenge after another to test you, to teach you sacrifice."

"So it is not really a game between contenders but with oneself?"

"Yup. It's the way you handle all the little unforeseen things. Adjust to new situations. Some guys get so mad, they break their clubs. Others just give up in despair. And some persevere, of course. It shows your metal, that's for sure."

"I just can't imagine spending a whole day chasing that little white ball all over the place. But then again, I guess my work could be considered strange too."

"I know you do research under a microscope. What are you looking for, exactly?"

How could she tell him of the joy she felt when a solution to a long studied dilemma was evident one day that was not present the day before. It is what kept her going back again and again. Never giving up in her search for new ways to detect the existence of malformed genes and how to interrupt their transmission to offspring. Ways to eliminate the suffering she had witnessed of the son of an older sister, a victim of Down's Syndrome who had one surgery after another just to keep him alive. And then a brother's child never really grew up. In her teens, she met with a frightening onslaught of mental and motor activity that overwhelmed her ability to concentrate, leaving her, in essence, a permanent child emotionally. It was genetic research that was getting closer to finding the origin of that traumatic brain disease. But this didn't seem the appropriate moment to disclose all of that, so instead she said, "Just trying to make one small contribution to eliminating human suffering. There is so much..."

His look was one of complete understanding. Somehow she knew she didn't have to say more. The silence that followed was a peaceful quietness.

When they reached the vehicle that would take them to the hide-a-way set in the mountains, he turned to her. "I have much time for you," he said. "I would consider it an honor to be of service."

She was moved by his directness. And instinctively she reached out and touched the top of his hand. It was warm, human. She gave it a little pat. "Thank you. Thank you. Helen told me you would be pleasant."

He turned away quickly so she could not see his face. Had she embarrassed him? Already? Then he reached for the back door of the van. "You can sit here, where there is more room, if you like," he said politely.

"If you don't mind, I'd like to sit up front where I can see better. I'm such a nosey one, you know. I never could stand the back seat as a child," she said with a tone of apology. "It always made me feel, well, second best. The youngest one always gets stuck, you know."

"I wouldn't know," he said, laughing. "I was the oldest of seven, all sisters. But my age didn't matter much. They decided for me most of the time anyway. So I guess we were in the same boat, so to speak," he said as he opened the front door for her.

"That's interesting," she said. "I would've thought the oldest brother would have deference in every situation."

"Not in my country," he said. "It is not the skirts that count, but what sits on the shoulders. Skirts. Pants. Not important. The only thing that matters is the grey matter. And I think you would have fared very well," he said with a smile. "Swedish women would love you!"

They turned off the main business thoroughfare onto a wide double-lane road that went straight up into the mountains. It was a sight to behold. The sun was behind them so the mountains that spread out before them held points of gleaming light here and there. As they reached the first sharp curve, the unpracticed woman grasped the arm of the van door. At one spot she looked straight down into the side of a grassy hill filled with sage brush and mountain bushes. "Don't look down," he said. "It might make you dizzy."

"I can see what you mean. What a sight though. I'll bet this is a treacherous drive in the winter months, huh?"

"Oh, yeah. This road gets closed sometimes. Too slippery."

"Then how do you shop?"

"We don't. We stock up and live carefully, just like everyone should anyhow. Only if we don't, we could get mighty hungry. So you learn."

It was the simpleness about him that allowed her to relax and enjoy his company. His tales of his family reminded her of her own, of the days of her youth that seemed only yesterday. *Where had the time gone?* It was the first time in years she had really thought about the loneliness of the single life she had inadvertently chosen. It had come to be. And she had accepted it. Rarely did anyone comment upon it anymore. Life had changed and single women had come to be admired, respected in their independence. But she had not counted on the "clock" that ticked away in her groins. It had been years since she had allowed herself to think about such things. She had managed to keep herself so busy she didn't have time for misgivings. If she felt deprived, she had only to go home for a weekend. And there it was. Her reasons. All magnificently wrapped and tied securely in human suffering. But she was a long way from home just now and the melodious sound of a man's laughter had engaged her ear. Her impulse was to turn around and run, as she'd always done, but there comes a time when old maxims fail and noble causes no longer bury the fears. As she looked up at the tall mountain that reached straight up before them, she realized she was coming to the end of a particular road. That it lay at the top of a mountain was only symbolic of the unchartered week rising as a challenge before her. Looking forward to a vacation, away from her work, was something she definitely had not encountered before. But in every life there comes a time...

~ ~

FAREWELL TO MAKE-BELIEVE

MEMOIR

The passengers were deplaning, and I scanned them for a curly white-headed female. Sheena said she may have to use a wheelchair, if the distance from the aircraft was too far. But there she was, upright and walking, on the arm of a young Airlines' steward. She was talking in his ear and he was laughing. I waited for her at the gate until she saw me. "There you are," she squealed in delight.

As she reached the gate, I said, "I am so happy you decided to come. You just look terrific." My smiles of happy anticipation had overcome the fleeting moments of apprehension I'd had wondering how I would fair against her occasionally sharp tongue. I put my arms around her frail body. Holding her reminded me of what my oldest daughter said when she hugged me, "You are so *little*, Mom. I'm always afraid I will hurt you. Like when you pick up a bird?" I had the same feeling now. I believed this elderly woman was the closest thing I would ever experience to having my own mother. If anyone could give me guidance in my mothering role, with which I struggled daily in my relationships with all four of my adult children, I believed Sheena could. My biggest problem stemmed from not being able to say *no* to anyone, much less my kids. Although Sheena had remained childless herself through a life-long marriage, I was sure her growing up with a sibling, enjoying a close relationship with her own mother for several decades, might offer me a new perspective. I had recited these things in my mind for days, awaiting her arrival.

"My dah-ling, you are too-oo thin," she responded instantly. "It doesn't look good, you know." She pulled at her own tight-skinned neck for emphasis.

At age 76, no one should have a neck that smooth! Covering mine completely with my clutch bag (a new survival technique I was just learning) I said, "I hate my neck. But I feel so much better with less weight. I'm back to my old size eight now, you know. I like that." Swallowing back, literally, my unattractive neck, I thought: So *this* is how mothers get to you! I never knew. She was right though, my ugly neck *was* more noticeable lately. *Where was all that confidence I had been feeling — before the plane landed and I got stabbed in the wrinkles?* Right then I wish I could've said, *Would you like to get right back on that plane and fly straight back home again?* But of course I couldn't, and didn't.

I had invited Sheena to meet me at our California desert house set into the beautiful Santa Rosa mountains. The very recent death of her husband, Grady, whom she had nursed through a five-year illness, had left her alone and physically exhausted. A proverbial godmother. (Didn't God give us to each other for us to *learn something*?) A diabetic on heavy insulin, Sheena was now the same age my own mother would have been had she lived.

We had not seen each other in months. Originally we had met as next-door-neighbors when she moved to Florida from Jamaica. She still lives just a mile from our youngest daughter, so we see Sheena almost yearly. She plays great-grandma to my little granddaughters occasionally. To them she is Grandma She. Her beautiful lyrical accent, so perfectly British or Britishly perfect, seems to exaggerate what she says to me whether it be complementary or critical.

But I had not expected the "critical" so soon in the visit. I breathed deeply, and took her by the arm, relieving the young man she seemed intent on taking with her.

In the car, Sheena looked around at the beauty of the mountains. Awed, she said, "Oh, how lovely, dah-ling. What a beautiful place. It is so nice of you to invite me. You have no idea what I have lived through these last months. It is only God's grace that has given me the strength. Grady was so ill, you know, and he just didn't try." She broke down then, as she would intermittently, through the stories, showing her anger at his "giving up."

Unpacking was typical of every day I had ever visited her. Sheena loved clothes. She had the same unhampered figure of her youth, no childbearing to leave extra poundage (although I heard often of the one child she miscarried). Her closets were filled with unworn cottons, woolens, silks, and furs. Her prime of life had been filled with a plethora of social engagements all over the world. Her husband had been a world-wide financier. For this trip, Sheena had bought several beautiful gowns, for evening wear. I had told her that the desert was extremely casual, that such dressy attire was really passé, or at least reserved for "celebrity" functions, to which we were hardly invited. She still longed for the days of her youth, when she moved in Royal circles in London's elite. So much she had experienced, and her stories were fascinating compared to my palish life.

Listening was no sacrifice; rather, I soaked in the international flavor of it. I, too, had lived abroad, and understood loneliness for a mother country. Unless one has experienced such, it is hard to realize the melancholia from the bombardment of foreign words, foods, customs, songs, that tiny touches of home can dispel; a refrain in the night from a national anthem, the smell of a favored food cooking, a child speaking in your native tongue.

And she was so loving. Her expression of affection so warm and genuine, I marveled at how I was blessed to have met her. As we walked in the evenings, she took me by the arm, wrapping herself up in it as we enjoyed the gorgeous sunset slipping over the mountains. *"I will lift up mine eyes unto the hills..."* she said, as tears gathered in her eyes, recalling some moment of a day gone by. "He was very well liked, very respected."

Then there was the girl, the bitter blemish in their fifty-year marriage. "I gave him a choice, you know," she said through angry tears, "and he chose me." Grady's eventual depression, like a plague, cast a shadow over their lives. Sheena was still trying to solve the mystery of what caused "the death of the spirit," she called it. "How does one know?" she asked of the wind as we walked. "How does one know if forcing that choice is what did it?" It was clear, the pain of it loomed as a ghost between them to the end.

Her memory came to her rescue as she recalled happy times, moments of pride she had felt in Grady before the illness overtook him, his business acumen, his dependability, his marvelous, racy, sense of humor. She agonized now over the decision of where to put the ashes—in Jamaica, his beloved native home, or in Florida, near her? For hours that turned into days, she debated this, as well as the difference of opinion awaiting her at home over his family portraits. We walked, arms entwined. She pulled me closer, calling me her daughter, and told me how much she loved me. Often it was dusk turning into night, when we'd peek at the sleeping houses and giggle at our uninhibited affection on parade. "Obviously mother and daughter," she said to my wondering aloud just what people were thinking about us two.

Sheena learned how to play honeymoon bridge very quickly. I was amazed how intent she was about winning. I couldn't say a word while she was playing, either. "Pst. Stick a pin," she'd say, shushing me as she'd slam down an ace on my king.

Perhaps it was her overzealous competitiveness that started her on the mean path, for when I dealt the cards, she was already complaining. I'd practiced for years to be able to slide them over the table very low and smooth so no one could catch a peek. But they slid too far and were "messy," she said. At one point, she picked them up and dealt them very crisply in a neat, straight pile. "Now *that*," she said with pursed lips, "is how you deal cards!"

I had to laugh to hide my irritation. And she said she'd never played a game of cards in her life!

Her ideas about how I should look, especially my hair, seemed to trigger an unusually harsh reaction. "Oh dear! What have you done to it?" she complained, standing at the bathroom door, watching, as I fought with the stubbornness of the Cherokee straightness I had recently cut a little too short. "You look just like your father, with that butch," shaking her head in disgust. Finally, one day I kept the bathroom door closed until every hair was in place. But the closed door only irritated her. "Whatever is taking you so long?" she said loudly while knocking impatiently. When I opened it, she shoved one of her bright lipsticks at me. "Here. Try this color; you look so dull."

Her scrutiny was beginning to make me feel like a wretched teenager, making me behave secretively, sneakily, about the most insignificant details of my life. And I had thought having a mother at long last would be such fun! Dinner became difficult, too. She cheated regularly on her diabetic diet. And the sweeter the treats, the better.

Her birthday happened while she was visiting, and she picked out a rum-raisin cake just loaded with sugar. When I frowned, she said, "Well, for goodness sake, you only turn seventy-six once!"

But it was I who took the brunt of her sugar-lows. Sweets made her so tired, she wanted to do nothing but sleep. And, of course, when she couldn't, her irritability grew more pronounced. I would suggest lunch in town and maybe a movie, to at least get her going in the mornings. But I'd find her in the recliner chair, dressed, and fast asleep by the time I was ready to leave. "Come now, Sheena. We can't let you sleep away the day, or you will keep us up all night," I'd say, teasingly.

"Dah-ling. You know I'm just exhausted. Taking care of a sick hubby wears you out," she'd say, and promptly go right back to sleep.

One day, I became especially concerned about her extended sleepiness, a possible pre-coma warning in diabetics. So I suggested lunch at a pricy little mall, the Palm Springs version of Rodeo Drive of Beverly Hills. I knew she needed to get out and walk, and shopping anywhere was her regular delight.

I did manage to get her into the car. But when I tried to talk to her on the way, suggesting she try to stay awake "to burn up your sugar," she became very cross and said, "Oh for goodness sake, can't a body catch a nap now and then?" and promptly fell off into a snooze.

When we found the restaurant full, we signed in. While waiting, I suggested a walk through the adjoining shops, an opportunity she would have never turned down in former days. She would try on every shoe for fit, feel through every handbag for hidden pockets, while I wearily trudged along. But this day, instead of my usual tugging at

Love 'N' Stuff

her to leave a store, I held her by the arm and steered her inside. "Look here, Sheena," I said, "aren't these silver sandals just your size?"

Every attempt at physical activity would ultimately be good for her, I knew. But my too-obvious tactics failed to elicit anything but a testy, "Really, Dah-ling," as she plunked herself down into a lone chair. From the look of the elderly proprietor, I surmised the chair was either hers, or meant for a bored but "paying" husband.

It was several days into our visit before I finally found a moment not filled up with Sheena's grief, to broach the subject on my mind. As we took our nightly stroll, I spoke of my children. Each of them had their own set of problems, alcohol, drugs, and, from time to time, they each exhibited some form of affective disorder. Raising them was a moment by moment challenge that Sheena had learned about through the years. After I had brought her up to date on all four of them, I told her, "Now that they are grown, I both wish and fear for the phone to ring. I know you think having children would leave you less lonely, but... I get so lonesome and depressed sometimes... If it weren't for my writing and my supportive writer's group... I..."

Then came Sheena's agitated response, interrupting my spinning tales and shocking me into stunned silence, "I. I. I. Really. You're too preoccupied with yourself. Do you realize every sentence begins with *I*? It gets tiring, boring..."

It was as though I had been slapped; my tears would not stay back.

"Oh, stop being a crybaby," she said. "It is nothing more than a mother would have told you."

In shock, I said, "But I'm fifty-three years old..."

Hush, child, hush! That old injunction of early

childhood seemed to reach out past all the years of therapy and assertiveness training to silence me, the *I* which had succumbed to the authoritative parenting, reawakening it a life-long task. And now, finally thinking I had found that special someone who would be different...

That night, after a pillow-soaking sob, I went over the exchanges between us and all the hours spent listening to her grief as she relived all fifty years – one day at a time it seemed. *Didn't I now get a turn? Why was I supposed to listen, but she wasn't?* I just didn't understand. In trying to regain some semblance of self-esteem, an angry thought rescued me: *"She isn't really my mother or I her daughter!* Then my own mothering, its stumbling, groping for direction, reminded me that in my need to communicate with my children: to protect, to parent, hadn't I been, at some time or other, equally guilty?

And I really *was* their mother!

Sheena and I managed our remaining days together with polite friendliness, but that special intimacy, no longer kindled, seemed to shrivel and die.

Seeing her to the plane that final day, the ache from the chasm dividing us reminded me how desperately I had wanted *us* to work. In the past, I had withstood the sting of her biting words in exchange for those precious moments of female affection. As I watched her being wheeled out across the open flight deck, I realized the trade-off was no longer palatable.

Although we both seemed resigned to the obvious shift in our relationship, it was a touching farewell, each of us blowing loving kisses and waving sad goodbyes to the people we never were.

~ ~ ~

THE IMAGE

MEMOIR

The sky was a dull grey behind the soft blue-green of the house tops. The rain came down like dancing fairies, sprinkling its magic in the narrow gutters below the cobblestone walk. It was a clean rain, a sparse rain, one that cleared the air like a fresh shot of brandy cleared the mind of cobweb worries. Winter had given up its hold on the earth and spring was gently pressuring itself into the air. The grass, through the brown, had begun to turn greenish.

Could you just tell me a little? she thought, directing her inner spirit to the knowing prophet of her soul. Surely a taste of it, a speck of forewarning would help her to prepare.

Her body sat at attention as she watched the droplets grow pluckier and more determined and the gutter grow wider in their path. Ah, it is too much for comfort, she thought. Too much for comfort to dodge them as she would if she were to get her limbs moving lithely through the morning drool. When did comfort begin to exact its penance? she wondered. At what point in the predetermined saga called life did she give up the ghost of beautiful for the ease of loose and airy and simple? She did not know. She always dreaded that turn she foresaw as a young woman. She had made a note to herself in her twenties that Ms Hutch, her neighbor of sixty, wore shorts and a halter and won jubilantly at cards. When she saw in Ms Hutch the signs of aging, the veins and bumps in her solid legs, she had told herself to remember how little they mattered. It was *the image*, the image one saw walking down the street. It was the image one remembered being badly beaten in Gin. It was the image of the shorts and halter that she saw through the rain as the guttered water widened into the street. Image was master of her domain, but comfort had stolen the key.

A lonely leaf suddenly appeared in the wash, rolled over, and flopped helplessly in the wind. She watched it slowly give up the fight as the sprinkles had turned to an even splatter of water, pulling it flat against the pavement. She sighed. It was just one little leaf. *Where had all the others gone?* She turned away from its stark reminder and looked to the young limbs that stretched past her window. Buds covered their bark, to the tips. Upwards they reached as droplets hung to them, under their bowed arms.

Suddenly the whole of it lightened, a soft illuminating, gathering of tempting sun. The wind had settled its movement. The drops were slower, fewer, the gutter narrow again. The leaf had disappeared. Ah, the image, so quick, yet subtle, as it comes 'round again.

Then the leaf reappeared, sitting pert and daring above its receding bed. Its fight to the end gave her spunk and assurance. She pulled up her coat about her, wrapping it tightly to her breast. As she stepped lightly to the door, she slung the scarf a twist about her bare throat, now a monument to earlier, smoother, more sensuous days. She passed the mirror on her way, *the image,* and another day.

~ ~

The End

BIOGRAPHY

L. L. Morton was born in Obion County, Tennessee, but grew up in Milwaukee, Wisconsin. Although she dropped out of high school in the 50's, in 1971 she and her first child received their diplomas together in Carlisle, Pennsylvania – where she went on to Shippensburg State College. Finally a graduate of Lesley College, Cambridge, Massachusetts (now Lesley University) Morton received her BAL degree in writing at the age of fifty-seven. As a career Army Officer's wife, she traveled extensively and lived in both Japan and Thailand. While in Bangkok, she taught English as a second language to the Thais. Her first major literary work, *A Make-Believe Face*, a fictionalized autobiography, was published by *Independent-House Press* in 1992. *Love N Stuff*, a collection of short pieces of mixed genre, is Morton's second literary work. The mother of four children, the grandmother of six and the great-grandmother of three, Morton presently lives with her husband of over fifty-five years in Southern Oregon.

~ ~ ~ ~